GILD THE

MORNING SKY

Will Hannah Stoddart's Dream of Worldly Riches Be the Fulfillment She Yearns For, as She Flees From Woeful Darkness Into the Unknown

Molly Glass

Copyright © 2000 by Molly Glass.

ISBN #:   Softcover   0-7388-5642-8

This is a work of fiction. Names, characters, places and incidents either are the
product of the author's imagination or are used fictitiously, and any resemblance
to any actual persons, living or dead, events, or locales is entirely coincidental.

This book was printed in the United States of America.

To order additional copies of this book, contact:
Xlibris Corporation
1-888-7-XLIBRIS
www.Xlibris.com
Orders@Xlibris.com

I dedicate this novel to Carolyn and Bob Ellis, my youngest daughter and her husband, along with certain members of the staff at Evangel Church who, between them, made it possible for this manuscript to be in the proper format for publishing.

Thank you all from my heart . . . MG

"Black clouds, heavy with the soot from a thousand chimneys, hung dripping in the air above the uncovered heads of the two young girls, as they hurried through the empty streets. Plans for improving Glasgow's slums with any such thing as street paving had not yet reached this section of the Cowcaddens in the year of our Lord, nineteen hundred and ten. The Stoddart sisters, un-heeding of sodden hair and clothes, still knew well how to avoid the heaps of stinking waste floating in the gutters. Both had their minds set on what might await them at home. Another hard work-day at the weaving sheds might be over but they still had to face their Pa. This being Friday he would be at the door, his hand out for their pay packets.

His shouts penetrated the thin tenement walls as the girls reached the opening. By this time Ellie, the younger girl, could barely drag one weary ill-clad foot after the other. She shuddered in terror as the words came clear, leaving no further doubt that their father was the shouter.

You're nothing but a leech, an ill-gotten useless creature, how you could be a son o' mine I'll never know. Get out of my sight before I sin my soul by braining you!" The girls stared at each other through the gloom and Hannah grasped her sister's arm.

"We'll wait a wee minute Ellie, when he's done strapping Lachie we'll go in, but we'll give him time to go in the room and lie down."

"Aye Hannah, but what if he's watching the clock again? He's never too drunk that he forgets it's Friday and pay day." Hannah Stoddart chewed her lower lip in deep perplexity, Ellie's words were only too true. What would be the worst, risking her Pa still being in the kitchen waiting for them, or. . . Before she could consider further, the door at the far end of the corridor crashed open and a lad, Lachlan Stoddart was sixteen but being of short stature, he seemed no more than a lad, shot through the opening and rushed past the girls, to leave the door swinging on its rusty hinges. He spotted his sisters and paused for a moment then ran on again, shouting over his shoulder.

"He's mortal drunk Hanny! Mam's cowered in the closet but he'll bash the door down to get at her. I'm away. . . I'll not stay here another minute, and I'll not be back this time!" Fear lent Hannah a fresh spurt of energy and she ran after her brother.

"Wait Lachie! Och, will you stop a minute and tell us what—?" They had reached the street and Lachie gazed at his sister for a moment before gasping.

"He found some of the money Mam was savin' for the school. He made me go for a pot of whiskey, and. . . Och Hannah, you know fine what else would happen. I'm leavin' now before he. . . Hannah, make sure you get to the school somehow before it's too late. I'm for the docks at Greenock, and a boat goin' as far away as I can get. Hush now Ellie, I'll come back and see you some day. Watch each other!" With that he vanished into the dark and the rain, just as a harsh bellow echoed along the streaming walls, and a man stood in the doorway facing out. For the space of a few minutes Gavin Stoddart could see nothing, but then he caught a glimpse of his daughters where they cowered and shivered against the wall. He began at once to rail them.

"Come here the pair of you, and let me see how much money you got this week. I warned you if you didn't do better this time it would be a belt for every penny you're short!" Hannah stepped forward then.

"Can we not go in the house, Pa? Folk'll hear you and anyway, we have done better at the piece work this week." His reply was a grunt, and as the girls approached the door, he could not resist a slap on the side of Ellie's head as she cringed past him. Then Gavin Stoddart, a man who at one time had been the envy of every lad in his village for his handsome face and grand muscles, followed his daughters into the miserable hovel that was their dwelling, and pulled the door closed behind him. Hannah breathed a sigh of relief. By the time her father counted the money, and raged some more, Lachie would be too far away for him to pursue.

Less than half an hour later the Stoddart home had resumed a semblance of normalcy, if that word could be used to describe such a place. The so-called head of the house had partaken of the poor meal, his own share plus the small portions intended for the working girls after their long hard day at the mill, before he left for his usual Friday night of drinking at the corner pub. Nothing more had been said about Lachie and as each moment passed, Hannah's breathing became that much easier. Surely her brother had escaped at last. She watched Ellie as she limped toward the box bed where their mother now lay on the straw mattress. Ellie knelt down and began to pat her mother's head, as if soothing a baby, while Hannah brought a dish of water to bathe the poor woman's battered face. Their father must have managed to pull his wife from the closet, and proceeded to make her suffer, for whatever poor Lachie had done.

Bella Stoddart accepted her daughter's ministrations without demur. What could be said anyway? Scenes like this happened at least once a week and she and her children bore many scars to prove it. Long ago she had ceased her weak struggles against it. Tonight held one difference though, her son, her Lachlan, named after her own saintly father, had at last flown the coop. Bella might have smiled if she could have moved her poor swollen lips without pain. Hannah had a question.

"What did Lachie get it for this time, Mam?" Bella groaned, but gazing at the two girls as they waited to hear, she decided to suffer the pain of speech to try and explain.

"'Twas the five shillings your father found in the tin where we had it hidden on the top shelf. He was desperate for the drink tonight. I would never have told him but when he threatened to smash my face in, Lachan owned up to it." Tears erupted as Bella remembered the scene, and that her face had been smashed in anyway, but she rallied quickly to go on with the all-too-familiar story.

Long before her own family had been hit by hard times, and before she had made the foolish mistake of marrying Gavin Stoddart, Bella had cherished a dream that her children, or at least her son if she should have one, could receive an education as close to her own at the grammar school as it could be. Recalling those shattered hopes now her voice trembled even more. "There'll be no mill school for Lachlan now, wherever he ends up." Suddenly the stoicism, garnered through the awful years of her marriage, deserted Bella. The possibility that she may never see her son again, along with the realization of her own wasted life, opened the floodgates. The scalding tears, flowing over her rapidly swelling cheeks, were not the healing kind. She turned toward the wall whispering more words to herself but Hannah caught them. "I'll not be moving out of this bed again, let him kill me if he wants. Maybe he'll hang then, and my lassies will be free from him as well!"

Ellie did not hear the last part of this speech. The exhausted child had laid her head on the edge of the bed and was sound asleep. Trying not to wake her for the moment, Hannah turned to begin a hunt for food. The man would not return for hours, and if no food was in the cupboard above the stone sink, then she would just have to spend the sixpence she had hidden in the pocket of her knickers. She would slip out to the corner shop and buy a half loaf and a slice of bacon.

By the Sunday morning their mother had still eaten nothing, and if she had moved from the bed it must have been while the girls slept. They had heard their father raging for what seemed a long time, but finding his many words had no effect on his wife he had given up at last. Although still shouting and cursing, he had lain sprawled on the room's only chair, until he ran out of breath, and the place had gone quiet. The girls had slipped out to go to work in the cold but dry Saturday morning. On Saturdays they only worked a half shift, and when they got home their father had disappeared again, much to Hannah's relief. Ellie had kept trying to get her mother to take some tea, or a bite of the bread, but Bella had meant every word about not taking any food.

Sunday was the strangest day in this already strange household. Gavin never missed the chapel services. When the children had been smaller, the whole family had turned out as best they could, but when things got to where they had no money for shoes or clothes, gradually only Gavin, quiet for once despite his obvious suffering from Saturday night's indulgence, accompanied by one or other of his daughters, would make his way, regardless of the weather to the chapel on Gordon Street. The girls had to take turns wearing the only frock and shawl they owned. Today was Ellie's turn.

No sooner had father and daughter left the house when Bella roused herself enough to speak to Hannah, her voice hoarse and cracked.

"I'm so sorry for you lassies, especially you Hannah, Ellie's too fragile to survive but you can, and you will, but you'll have a hard row to hoe for a while." Hannah moved to protest for Ellie, but her mother held up a weak hand. "Tis the truth Hannah, but I still have something for you. My plush cushion!" Hannah sighed. Her mother thought the ragged old cushion had some value. The thing was a sorry sight, its velveteen plush long since worn off. Working in a textile mill's weaving shed, Hannah knew enough about cloth to be sure the cushion was ready for the rag bag. Once she had come upon her mother darning the thing, explaining how a mouse had chewed a hole in it, and the cushion never left Bella's sight. She held it up to Hannah now.

"Here you are Lass. 'Tis for you. Don't let him touch it or even see it, or he'll know."

"Know what Mam?" But the long speech had exhausted Bella, and the girl turned away resigned. No harm in pretending to hide the cushion. She came back and began to poke up the meagre fire. When they returned he would be raging for food again, and she only had three potatoes to boil and serve for their Sunday dinner.

Hearing footsteps she tensed in readiness, but only Ellie appeared as the door opened.

"He's not coming home yet Hanny. We had a new minister this mornin', he's awful nice but Pa doesn't like him." This proved the last straw for Hannah's worn out patience.

"Nice! Nice you say? Easy enough to be nice when you've a full belly and nothing to do all day but talk, I'd like to—" She stopped as she saw her sister's stricken face. "Och never mind Ellie, do you think Pa'll be home for—" But Ellie had walked toward the wall bed. Placing her hand on the slight mound that was their mother, she whispered.

"Mam, will you not rise and eat some dinner? He'll not be home for a while." But the mound did not stir, and Ellie came back to stand beside Hannah, who was pouring the water from the potatoes into a soot blackened stock pot swinging from a hook above the pitiful fire. It would do fine for the morrow's soup with a turnip and some split peas or lentils. Ashamed of her earlier outburst she called to Ellie.

"I didn't mean to rage at you Ellie. Tell me more about the new minister." The other girl brightened at once.

"His name is Mr. Cardross. He talks nice, like Mam you know, kind of fancy and genteel, and he never said a word about us being content to be poor, or suffering being the Lord's will, or anything." Interested in spite of herself Hannah responded.

"What did he talk about then, the demon drink?" A bitter laugh escaped her but clearly Ellie did not understand.

"Och no! He talked about Jesus. He said the song is true and Jesus loves us all." Hannah turned away. Time to change the subject.

"Oh, I see. Will you have yours with the skin on, or will I peel it for you, Madam?" Again her sarcasm was lost on the simpler girl.

"Leave the skin on Hanny, that's the best bit, have we no gravy then?" Hannah's answer to that only baffled her further.

"Gravy? For gravy we need fat drippings. Aye, we've got drippings, the roof in the corner above the bed is dripping! You'll not want that on your plate though. Och Ellie, don't look at me like that, it's just in fun. Here, I got some milk from the milkman this morning, you know how it's always old Geordie on Sundays, Farmer Strang being a hypocrite just like Pa, but never mind that, Geordie filled our wee jug for a halfpenny!" The sisters slowly savoured the simple meal, chewing each tiny bite and supping a mouthful of sweet milk to wash it down. All too soon it had disappeared, and Ellie licked the crumbs from her plate before saying.

"Aye, Mr. Cardross said one of the worst sins against God is when we don't love each other." But Hannah could not allow that to pass.

"He's touched in the head! Imagine anybody lovin' our Pa? Och, I'll just let you go again next Sunday, I don't want to hear muck like that." Ellie began to sniffle.

"I only thought you'd be happy to hear that Hanny. I'm still awful hungry. Could we not share Pa's dinner? He'll be out for a while yet." Hannah considered this for a moment.

"Better not. The pub shuts at two on a Sunday. Never mind, there's some flour left, I'll mix it with the rest of the milk and some water and salt. We'll make some scones." Ellie had more to say about Mr. Cardross.

"Hanny, he says if we pray hard and believe hard, we can have whatever we pray for. My prayer is that Pa'll not be here to eat his dinner. Is that a sin?" Hannah's lips quivered as she stared at her sister, not sure whether to laugh or weep, she clasped the young girl tightly.

"It can't be a sin Ellie. You don't say it to hurt anybody. But if we're going to pray for a bit of dinner. why can we not pray for some money? Or a better house, or a pair of boots or a new frock or—" Her voice rose hysterically with each exclamation, as she poured out her heart in simple wishes. The girls clung together for a moment but the woman on the bed had heard and she roused herself for a word.

"My own prayer is a sin lassies! I'm praying that your father will drink himself to death, even this very day, and that he'll never walk through that door again." Her daughters gasped in unison as she continued. "Aye now, there's a sin for you!" Hannah rushed to the bed but the woman under the covers had subsided again. The girl closed her eyes as the words of her mother's prayer still echoed through the dismal room. . .could this truly be their gentle Mam? Praying their father will drink himself to death this very day, never to come through the door again. . .she added her own thoughts. Never to hear his mad screeching, or feel his cruel hands strike her head, in a fury for nothing. Pulling her thoughts back she scolded, but her tone denied the words.

"Och Mam, that is indeed a wicked prayer, and if he ever heard you! Don't say it again now. I think I hear him." Ellie cowered in the chimney corner as Hannah quickly cleared a place on the board set on an old box that served as their table. The plate with the one potato did seem pathetic but she could not feel sorry for Pa at all, if he put drink first then. . .Her thoughts stopped there as she heard the footsteps halt at the door. The watchers waited with tightly held breath for the latch to lift, and the bellowing to begin, but instead, the sound of a fist pounding on the wood was all they heard. Ellie shrank even further down as Hannah moved slowly toward the door. The person who stood in the opening was a complete stranger to Hannah.

"Mistress Stoddart?" No premonition stirred as Hannah answered. truthfully.

"She's sleeping, she's not very well. She's my Mam." The man appeared shaken.

"What age are you, Lass?" The lie slipped glibly off her tongue without thought of sin.

"Sixteen, what's up? Did something happen to Lachie?" For a moment his doubt showed then he shrugged.

"Is your name Hannah Stoddart, then?"

"Aye, I'm Hannah Stoddart." Alarm sprung up then as her thoughts were still on her brother. What could have happened? The man still hesitated.

"Gavin Stoddart would be your father then?"

"Aye!"

"I'm awful sorry to tell you this lass, but a wee while ago Gavin ran out the pub as if Auld Nick was after him. He fell right under the wheels of one of they new fangled motor cars. It had no chance to stop, and—" At these words suddenly the cold silent room behind Hannah became filled with sound. The sound of laughter, unholy laughter. It came from the heap of ragged covers in the box bed. Ellie leaped from her hiding place and ran to her mother, but the laughter kept on. Perplexed the kindly stranger replaced his cap and stepped backward. His voice came haltingly.

"I'll away then. I just came myself because I was the only one there who knew Gavin Stoddart's house. I mean. . .Anyway, they'll be here any minute. They're bringing Gavin." Slowly Hannah closed the door, and standing with her back to it, she stared at the scene by the bed. Bella's laughter had changed to a pathetic whimper.

"Sin or not! My prayer has been answered. My last will and testament to my children, even if it's too late for my lad. As for me, soon I'm going to go to sleep and I'll not waken again, but Hannah, there is money in the cushion, enough to bury me decently in the kirkyard for I've made my peace with God, but not near your father, he can lie in a pauper's grave for all I care. Watch each other my lassies, be respectful and learn at school, and may it do you more good than all my learning ever did for me. Get away from all this, that's what I'm going to do. Farewell then!" Both girls bent down, ready to argue, but before they could, a second hammering began at the door. Again Hannah went to answer it, but this time her heart held only curiosity, and a strange lightness. The awful fear had vanished.

* * * * *

"THE LAMBERTS"

According to her mother, Maggie Lambert was a dreamer, spoiled by an indulgent father and tolerated by her two big brothers. Sophia pretended to be annoyed about this, and there were times like today when Sophia wished the lass would be a bit more practical, when instead of gazing out the window watching the sky, she would help her mother to get ready for the morrow's trip to the seaside. The red sky only meant the next day's weather would be fine and not an excuse for the dreamy lass to stand for hours admiring.

"Come away from the window then Maggie, help me to pack the picnic baskets with the blankets and things." No answer. Sophia knew well it was not disrespect that kept her daughter silent but the fact that she had not heard her mother at all. "Did you hear me Maggie or are you in a dwam again? I said—"

"Och leave her be Mother, I'm sure you'll pack the baskets just fine." But Maggie swung around as her father's voice penetrated her thoughts. She saw his smile and walked toward him.

"Do you know what makes the sky so red at night Daddy?"

"I do not my dear, you're the scholar in this family, and you'll need to tell me." The young girl started to answer but before she could the kitchen door flew open and Willie appeared with a delirious Lizzie clutching his neck.

"I've got a horsey Daddy, Willie's my horsey." Her daddy grasped her as she threw herself from the 'horsey' and the scientific discussion had to end there for the moment as the rest of the family joined them.

Robert Junior, the terror of Eastkirk school playground until he had left last year to join the Terrys, the local nick-name for the Territorial Army—in his case the Glasgow Highland Division, walked more slowly into the front room of the Lambert's modest railway cottage. He had discarded his uniform for an old pair of trousers and one of his father's pullovers as neither his own or Willie's would fit any more. Robert knew the family had planned this trip during his leave for his benefit and so he tried to appear as excited as the rest but Robert had heavier things on his mind. He wanted to pick the right moment to tell his father and mother that he had been accepted for officers' school and would be away to the training grounds in Aldershot in a day or two. Another thing he didn't want to mention was the talk of war that filled the barrack rooms these days. Knowing his father was a true pacifist who objected to killing of any kind, and who had kept quiet about his son going in for a soldier even if his heart broke every time he saw the uniform, Robert junior, would not be telling the family that bit. Here and now though he would join in the family fun.

"Come on Lizzie, I've some pictures and scraps of real horses to show you, not just show you either, some you can keep for your scrap book." Lizzie squealed and their mother tried to hide her pleasure behind a mild frown.

"Don't get her to excited now Robert, she's to get to bed early for the morrow's trip." But the tone belied the words, if her man spoiled Maggie, then she, Sophia must confess even if only to herself, that she did the same with Robert, and of course everybody spoiled Lizzie, the eternal child.

Willie walked to the window to join Maggie who had returned to her sky gazing. She turned to smile at him but said no words. These two were in one accord. Far quieter than Robert, but every bit as determined to jelly the nose of anyone who dared say a word wrong about either of his sisters, Willie struggled with the strange feeling that this special day coming on the morrow would mark the end of something very precious. He could not put it into words except to think that it would be last of its kind.

The next morning dawned bright and clear and Sophia, unaware of undercurrents, or choosing deliberately to ignore any kind of strain, sat in her corner of the carriage, apparently well content.

The train had crossed the Firth of Clyde and soon they would be pulling in the station at Dunoon. As usual when they came on one of their day trips to Dunoon the big picnic basket, packed with everybody's favourite food, had been loaded into Granpa Cowan's delivery cart, and Old Jock, the driver, had volunteered to drive them to the railway station.

Preparation for such excursions seldom varied. No soggy tomato sandwiches for Sophia! Time spent in Granpa's shop the day before had yielded up a harvest of good things. A pile of wafer-thin slices of boiled gammon and another one of jellied veal rested in a bed of lettuce all wrapped in shiny waxed paper with the Cowan name stamped on it. Thick wedges of cheese, the kind that made your eyes water that Father liked, wrapped up in thick pads of newspaper lay on the bottom. Fruit salad with big chunks of pear to melt in your mouth, and Mother's baked scones, as light as a feather, smothered in farm butter, then a wee bit of shortbread to finish.

One of the best parts, for Maggie and the boys, always came when the giant bottle of Barr's Iron Brew was opened, but Maggie wondered if Robert would not think himself above that now. Maybe not, he had gone with Willie to buy the delicious fizzy stuff at the sweetie shop on the corner, another one of the rituals performed each time the Lamberts took this jaunt from Eastkirk to Dunoon. Rented deck chairs would be set up just so, following a serious discussion between Father and the old man who rented the chairs, about politics or the weather, subjects normally of no concern whatever to three young folks straining to reach the sea-shore. On this day, after all the rituals had been taken care of and the delectable feast only a memory, Father with his red hair slicked back into place and his moustache tidied up, had settled back with a contented sigh for a nap. Mother on the other deck chair, already had set her knitting needles flying and the boys paddled about noisily looking for such awful things as crabs and whelks in the shallows. Wee Lizzie was sound asleep on one of the blankets beside Father's chair. Tired of building sand-castles, Maggie wandered up on to the esplanade. She had a poem to memorize for Miss Paton tomorrow.

If she got it perfect she would have another chance at the "Mystery Box" and maybe Friday she would win a diary! How did the poem go again? Glancing round quickly to make sure no one would hear if she said it out loud, she began to recite.

"Winter's Gone. . . by Thomas Carew."

Now that winter's gone, the earth hath lost,

Her snow white robes and now, no more the frost. . ." Oh my what came next? Suddenly the poem was truly forgotten as she glimpsed a procession coming toward her. A funeral! Even thinking the word caused Maggie to gasp in horror and she turned to run back to the beach but found she could not move. A hand touched her shoulder and she tore her fascinated gaze away from the magnificent team of high-stepping black Clydesdales with their glossy coats and dancing plumes as she sensed, rather than saw, her father at her side. Grasping his arm they stood there together for a time not speaking and soon her mother joined them. The three watched enthralled until the majestic parade disappeared. Her father broke the silence:

"You can put me away in style like that Sophia when my time comes! Eastkirk will turn out in full force to see the sight on that day!"

"Don't talk foolish Robert, with you still so young and strong. Tempting the devil you are!" Maggie shuddered again and just at that moment the sky, threatening for the past half-hour, erupted in a downpour. Scrambling to pick up belongings and return the deck chairs, before dashing for the railway station, she soon forgot the picture of a big black box draped and decorated with silken tassels.

While the rest of the family settled down for the journey Maggie's mind returned to the poem she had to memorize but that was crowded out as Lizzie, who had slept enough for one day, began to leap up and down with excitement.

"The boats, Maggie, see the big boats and the sailor men are watching us on the train!" Wondering how this sister of hers could work all that out from this distance Maggie smiled and nodded

her agreement. Lizzie jumped off the seat and began to pull at the
strap to open the window and before anyone could stop her she
had leaned out dangerously far to wave to the sailors lined up at
the rail of the merchant ship. One young fellow waved back and
shouted something that no one on the train could hear. Maggie
pulled her sister to safety while Robert secured the window. As
Sophie scolded her errant child Maggie sat back in her corner and
found herself softly reciting, not the poem for Miss Paton but
something else altogether.

"Ships that pass in the night, and speak each other in passing.
. ." Robert joined her.

"'Tales of a wayside inn'! Longfellow, I think, but hardly appropriate as we are not a ship and that old tramp steamer is hardly
one either, did you catch the name? Something like ". . . Brigand",
and the speaking, except for our Lizzie, was rather one-sided what!"

"Smarty knows it all as usual."

Neither Lambert knew, or ever would know, just how appropriate the quotation might have been as one sailor lad, newly signed
on in the merchant steamer 'The Atlantic Brigand', turned sadly
away from this brief encounter. For a moment Lachlan Stoddart
had thought he was waving and shouting to his own two sisters,
Hannah and Wee Ellie, as he wondered would he ever see them
again.

* * * * * *

Through her mother's hysterical laughter Hannah's thoughts had
repeated the foolish phrase.

"We could have et his dinner." Over and over again, not realizing she spoke it aloud even as she pulled the door open. A well-
dressed gentleman stood there now, a baffled expression on his
face. He must think he had landed in a houseful of dafties. Hannah
shook herself.

"We're that shocked Mister. I don't know what to do?" The
man held out his hand.

"I'm Dr. Avery, I'm sorry about your father but he ran out in front of me and I had no chance to stop. The onlookers told me where your father goes, I mean went to kirk, and I took the liberty of sending the bearers there with the body. What can I do to help? The man who just left told me your mother is ill." Hannah recovered her senses to say.

"She's not well right enough, just tell me what to do, we've no money for a doctor." The man waved his hand at her.

"Don't worry about money, although the accident was not my fault I do feel responsible in a way. I'll be taking care of all expenses." More noises erupted from the close and adding to the din, Archie Carmichael's whippet began to howl, just as another knock sounded on the still open door and Mrs. MacPhail from the upstairs stood there, looking defiant. Keeping her eye on the tall stranger she called out.

"I heard that Gavin's been killed! Is it true Hannah lass?"

"It seems to be true Mistress MacPhail." Hannah's answer was civil enough but the woman kept her gaze fixed on the doctor, waiting for him to speak.

"It was an accident Madam, and yes, the man Gavin Stoddart is deceased I'm afraid." He drew a gold watch from his waistcoat pocket as he spoke. "I've already told the young lady I'll take care of all the expenses of burial etcetera." At that a shriek came for the box bed.

"Expenses! Expenses of burial. Throw it in the lime pit, that's what he deserves! As for you MacPhail, you can just get out. You wouldn't help my lassies when they needed you, they don't need you now." With a snort the large woman stamped off muttering about good Christian burial. She had to press through a gaggle of other onlookers crowding round the door. Arguments sprang up and suddenly Hannah had enough.

"Shut your faces and get away, the lot of you. Like Mam says you weren't here to help when we needed it." Shocked surprise made the crowd obey and within minutes the room and doorway cleared of all except the doctor and the Stoddart women. Hat in hand he waited as Hannah quieted down. Bravely she faced him.

"If you are a doctor then, and you'll not be chargin', could you take a look at our Mam. She hasn't et for three days and she—" The man moved to the bed. He touched the ragged blanket but it was snatched away at once. Bella's voice too had quieted and her tone refined as she said.

"Thank you sir, I'll not be needing your services as I've decided to go. It's too late for me, but if you'll help my daughters get away from all this I'd be much obliged." She closed her eyes at that, and this time as the doctor leaned over to take her pulse, he met with no resistance. Quickly he whipped out a stethoscope from his cape pocket and moments later he straightened, crashing his head on the low canopy as he did so. His face and his words full of wonder.

"Dear Lord, she meant it, she's gone, never in my life have I seen the likes of this." Anthony Avery nodded sadly. He could not deny the possibility of the woman having willed her own death. He had seen it only once before but that time it had taken a week or more. Recalling the girl's words that the woman here had not eaten for three days, and likely not much before that, he saw how it must have been. Already he felt too much respect for the young girl standing before him asking the obvious question to try to deny this, and his thoughts raced to what came next. Doubtless a double funeral and then what. He glanced about for a place to sit down but finding none he remarked.

"Your mother is dead I'm afraid. I know it's too early to decide what you girls will do now, I assume you are all alone for the moment but you must have relatives somewhere." Blank stares made him explain. "You know, aunts or cousins, or even grandparents." Ellie started crying again and Hannah, dry-eyed through it all, smiled wanly.

"Aunty Mary Carmichael, but she bides in Kilbride and never goes ootside her door. She's Pa's aunty anyway."

"If we take you there could you stay with her?"

"Och no Doctor, she's only got the one room and a lot of cats, she doesn't like bairns. Can we not just bide here and wait for

Lachie to come home?" The man's face had resumed its puzzled concern. He shook his head.

"Lachie, who's Lachie?"

"He's our brother. He was goin' on a boat but when he knows about this he'll come back and—" The doctor kept shaking his head.

"But that could be a long while, no I cannot allow that, you're both far too young and besides, with the breadwinner gone, how—" Ellie stopped whining to gape at her sister, then they amazed him further as both burst out laughing. They knew the term breadwinner very well from the kirk sermons. He waited politely for the near hysteria to abate and Hannah wiped her streaming eyes.

"Breadwinner Doctor? That's us, Ellie and me and Lachie, we've been winnin' all the bread here for the past two years. Could we not just carry on?" Another bustle outside ended with a thunderous pounding on the door.

"Open up in the name of the law!" Hannah stepped forward again.

"Thank you Mister, I mean Doctor, but we'll have to manage. With him not here drinking up our wages we'll be well enough off." The door burst open, and a policeman pushed his way in, bending his head for the low lintel. Purple faced with exertion he gasped out.

"What's all this I'm hearing then? What's this? Somebody better tell me quick-like or—" Catching sight of the doctor he checked his outburst. "Beggin' your pardon sir, but I have my duty, with two folk that were hale enough this mornin' now corpses. . . I'll have to take these lassies in for questionin'" Wondering how the man knew about the dead woman so quickly, Avery held up his hand as the policeman hesitated.

"Just what do you mean Constable?" The bobby spluttered.

"What I mean is, these two are minors and cannot be left here. I'll need to take them in. They have no means of payin' for the burials so—"

"Constable, I fail to understand how you, by arresting these children, will help the situation or change the state of their finances. I venture to inquire how you know all that in any case." He did not wait for the man to answer but continued. "No, I have a better suggestion. I have already stated that I will accept responsibility for the burial expenses, for both the man and his wife here. Although it was Stoddart's own fault it was still my vehicle that killed him, and as I fear the widow died of the shock, I will take care of that as well." Stunned, Hannah and Ellie said no more as matters moved swiftly out of their hands. Within a few hours all was settled to the apparent satisfaction of the policeman and the doctor, and soon they were being helped up into the strange carriage, clutching tightly to the hastily wrapped, pathetic little bundles.

* * * * *

Some inner sense kept Hannah from protesting further. She could think of no more reasons to stay in the empty house with no food or coal for the fire and no money until pay day on Friday. She had overheard the doctor tell the bobby he would be providing all they needed. By the time the carriage stopped she had recovered a bit and as someone reached up to help them down she managed to whisper to Ellie.

"We'll be fine now Ellie, don't worry." If her voice wavered slightly on the last word Ellie neither noticed or cared as she was lifted gently and carried into what to her seemed a wonderland.

"Hannah?" Ellie's whisper reached her sister where she lay beside her in the enormous bed. Hannah had not been asleep but was gazing up into the blackness of the curtained canopy seeing nothing. Earlier the doctor's maid had grudgingly put out the lamps but before that Hannah had noticed the ornate decorations that formed the top of the four poster, although she did not know the term. The bed itself was bigger than the room in the but and ben. Never having known that such luxury existed the girls had been too awestruck to make any remarks so they had allowed the kind doctor's servants to prepare them for this sumptuous bed. A fire still glowed in the grate, and on the floor in front of the fireplace, a thick fur rug lay. Another rug decked the floor beside their bed and Hannah's toes had curled in appreciation of the softness even as it tickled them.

"What's wrong Ellie?"

"Nuthin', I just wanted to be sure I wasn't dreamin'. This is real isn't it Hanny?"

"Aye, 'tis real enough, and 'tis real that our mother's dead and buried and our dad as well. Och Ellie, stop your whimpering. Mam wanted to go and well, we can't be sorry about our Dad. Anyway I'm still wonderin' what the cost of all this is goin' to be."

"Maybe we'll find out in the mornin'."

But in the morning if they had anything to find out nothing showed up. Used to early rising the sisters wakened while it was still dark, and hearing no sounds except their own breathing, Hannah whispered.

"I think we can go back to sleep Ellie." The next thing they knew was when the drapes were being swished back and an angry face appeared in the opening. Hannah leaped up and clutched the covers round her sparse frame. A different maid stood there holding a giant tray full of food. More food than the Stoddart girls had seen at any one time before. The maid placed the tray on a small table by the bedside. Turning back she riled the girls as they still gazed in wonder at the food. Her words struck a note of discord.

"If your ladyships would be so kind as to finish your breakfast quick like, Mistress MacQuarry will see you in the morning room at nine o'clock!" She moved toward the open door as she continued. "Don't expect breakfast to be served in your room every day mind and don't expect—" Hannah moved swiftly to place herself between this person and the door.

"We expect nuthin' Miss. We never asked to come here. We don't want your breakfast nor your charity. If you've a bone to pick, pick it with the doctor who brought us here, and don't be so cheeky!" A completely intimidated Ellie gasped, first in fear and then in admiration as the belligerent maid seemed to shrink at the mention of her employer, but her voice held no apology as she retorted.

"Well, excuse me I'm sure. Will you move out my road, I've work to do if you haven't."

"I'll move when I'm ready. If you can have a civil tongue you could tell my sister and me what we're here for. Maybe it's to work. We're not feared of work if somebody tells us what to do." Ellie echoed her sister's words.

"Aye, tell us what to do." Amazingly this idea brought a look of real fear into the maid's eyes.

"We can manage our jobs fine without your help thank you. The very idea of you ragamuffins from the slums touching . . . Will you move or will I have to make you?" Hannah moved then and the maid left quickly enough. My would she have a story to tell cook and the other staff. Meanwhile Ellie began to tuck into the succulent sausages and eggs and other good things revealed as she removed the silver covers from the platters. Hannah hesitated for only a minute before joining her. Filling a plate she muttered.

"I still think we'll be payin' for this someway."

"But Tony, what do you want me to do with them? We don't need more staff." Rachel Avery's voice was more of a wail as she gazed at her husband.

"No my dear, these children are far too young to be working, give me a day or two to make arrangements. I think I can get them into a boarding school, I'm not sure yet but—" He stopped as he felt her eyes drill him.

"Do we need to go to all that trouble dear, after all they are only—" Once she saw her mistake she quickly changed tack. "Would it not be sufficient if we placed them in an orphan home. There's the one where we give a donation every Christmas and—" But he ignored that.

"I feel partly responsible for their orphan state. Rachel, I must make restitution." She turned away to hide her impatience.

"But Tony, you are not to blame. The man was drunk."

"No more 'but Tony', my love. Give me three days and if no relatives turn up in response to my inquiries then. . . goodness look at the time, I'm due in surgery in five minutes. I'll be home for dinner." He rushed from the room as his wife continued to wail.

"But what will I do with them for three days?"

The doctor had warned his wife that the elder Stoddart sister was very sensitive but she had not bothered to tell this to Biddy. Biddy had duly reported the cheek she had taken from Hannah, so when she came to pick up the dishes from the breakfast and to order the sisters to bathe and dress, she opened the door to find Ellie licking her plate. Biddy exploded.

"You dirty wee guttersnipe, had you not enough to eat without licking the plate, why I—" She got no further as a raging virago, still attired in one of Biddy's own nightgowns, erupted from the chair by the window and placed herself solidly in front of the maid.

"Don't you dare call my wee sister names, you stuck up thing. Call her that again and see what you get." Forgetting the tray of dishes Biddy turned to run but felt her arm being caught in a firm grasp. "'Tis just the wee lassies you insult then is it? Well, let me see if there's more in you than the spoon put in you!" Hannah snatched the mob cap from the maid's head, freeing a tumble of black hair that had quite obviously been pushed hurriedly inside the cap without benefit of comb or brush. Ellie dropped the plate and set up a whimper. Hannah was going to get them thrown out of this nice place. It never took much to get her into a fight. She had watched many a scrap in the weaving sheds so she knew what her sister would do next. Grabbing a handful of the abundant hair Hannah pulled with all her might at the same time letting go with her foot on the maid's shin. Biddy screamed and screamed. The door flew open again and the housekeeper stood there with her arms filled with clothes.

"What in the name of Heaven is happening here? Biddy stop your screeching and go to the kitchen. You, missy, leave go her hair at once." This proved more difficult than at first supposed as Hannah's fingers were tightly entangled in the ungroomed mass of curls. It took a few minutes to extricate her and by then the hallway outside had filled with people. Ellie had slipped back into the bed with the covers pulled up to her chin. The voice of authority came from outside.

"What is this terrible commotion?" Before anyone could enlighten Mistress Avery another commotion brought everyone's attention to Ellie. Hannah ran to her sister.

"Ellie! Ellie! what's up with you? Oh my, she's chokin' to death. what is it Pet? what's in your mouth?" Her only reply came in the form of painful gasps as Ellie struggled for breath. Suddenly she went rigid. The doctor's wife took charge.

"Out! Out! Everyone out and back to your work. Mistress MacQuarry, telephone the doctor!" She hurried across to the rug where Hannah knelt beside a still gasping Ellie. Pushing the hysterical girl aside she began to fish about in the distressed child's mouth, finding no foreign objects she picked the frail form up and placed her on top of the bedcovers. A frantic Hannah pulled at her sleeve.

"She's not to die, I've lost my Mam and my brither, even my Pa as well but not Ellie. Don't die Ellie, I need you. We need each other." Mrs. Avery halted the flow of self pity with a sharp command.

"Be quiet, I'm trying to listen to her chest. If you keep chattering I cannot hear anything else." Rachel Avery could hear nothing anyway and for a dreadful moment she thought the child had indeed died here in her guest bedroom. She felt the neck for a pulse the way Tony had showed her. At last she found a faint thready beat, and again remembering her husband's instructions for emergency, she began to administer breath to the child from her own lips. What had he said again. Never stop until you're sure they can breathe fully on their own.

On hearing the barked order to be quiet Hannah subsided. She sat back on her heels with her hands tightly clenched against her mouth. Sheer amazement held her spellbound and silent now as she watched the lady kissing Ellie. The doctor's wife at last looked up.

"She'll do. Put a pillow under her head while I pull her up." Hannah obeyed and a moment later Mistress Avery stepped back from the bed. "She's breathing again, thank God! But I don't know what the matter could have been, does she do this often?" Too stunned to answer Hannah just stood and stared. Rachel turned away. "Never mind, Doctor Avery will be here soon, he'll know what was wrong and what you should do now." But the doctor was as baffled as the others.

"It sounds like a possible asthma attack yet she's breathing normally now with no other signs of that." He repeated his wife's question to Hannah. "Has this happened before?" Finding her tongue Hannah piped up.

"She's never done that before but she fell asleep under the looms plenty times. Maggie Oates and me always hid her from the foreman." Avery raged.

"Children at the looms! Dear Lord help me to wipe out this kind of exploitation. I'll not rest until—" His wife held up a restraining hand.

"Yes dear, we know, but is this the time and place? Our concern is for those here and now. I repeat, what are we to do with them." He glanced at her sharply before placing his attention once more on the sisters.

"They seem healthy enough otherwise, except for malnutrition. A month or two of good food and rest will take care of that. Then we shall see about boarding school." His wife nodded sweetly. Her mind fastened on the phrase 'a month or two.' Oh no, not if she could help it. Those two ragamuffins were trouble and would not remain under her roof a moment longer than she could help. Glancing up she caught a mirrored image of her expression on Mistress MacQuarry's face. A secret smile passed between them, and without a word being spoken each knew that somehow they would rid the house of these pests. The doctor, being too kind for his own good, need not be bothered with the where, when or how.

Rachel Avery did not have long to wait. After making sure the young girl breathed normally once more, and her husband had gone back to his surgery. the household seemed to settle into its everyday routine. Rachel curled up on the sofa for her meditation hour in the morning room and fished out her current romance novel from under a cushion. A discreet knock sounded on the door and she quickly tucked the book inside her bible before calling out peevishly for the disturber to enter.

"What is it MacQuarry?"

"Sorry to disturb you Madam, but it's the young. . . the young—" Unwilling to describe the unwelcome visitors as ladies, or even guests, the normally calm housekeeper struggled for a word to fit the Stoddart girls.

"I know of whom you speak MacQuarry, what now?"

"'Tis just that Biddy and Annie are refusing to wait on them or even go near the room. In fact Biddy is packing her bag at this very minute and I must say I don't blame—"

"What nonsense! But, you're right, I don't blame the maids either in a way. However the doctor insists on helping these strays and so we must put up with it for the present." She looked directly into the other woman's eyes as she said this and the servant was the first to glance away. She did not leave the room though but hesitated at the door.

"Well, get on with it, surely if Biddy wishes to leave then you can take care of the matter, she'll be no great loss."

"With your permission Madam. I have a solution that would end the whole matter." Her mistress raised expressive eyebrows but she spoke only two words.

"Go on!"

"The strays are not happy either, if they ran away no one would be too surprised." Impatient with this foolish idea and anxious to get back to her reading Rachel almost shouted.

"Run away! My husband would find them quickly enough and who do you think he would blame? Yes not only me, but you MacQuarry, for not watching them more carefully. Don't be a fool."

"If you would allow me to finish Madam." Rachel groaned. She had insulted the woman and the huffs could last for days. Besides the house ran like clockwork with MacQuarry in charge. She softened her tone.

"Finish then and please make your point." Only slightly mollified the housekeeper continued.

"If the doctor is told they've gone away with a relative, who came for them, he would be content with that, would he not?" Rachel's eyes narrowed.

"He might, but what relative? They have none, wait though, he did mention an elderly aunt but he also said she was out of the picture."

"We've only got their word for that Madam." Hoping she need say no more the servant waited. At last Rachel began to understand.

"Oh, I see, we bring the aunt here to take them. Give her some money for their keep and. . .I'm not sure I want any part of this MacQuarry." With a resigned sigh the housekeeper reassured her mistress.

"You need know nothing about it Madam. You are going out this afternoon, and as this is the doctor's day at the hospital. . . By dinnertime tonight the strays will be far away with their aunty." Rachel still looked doubtful.

"What if he decides to visit them at their aunt's to make sure?—"

"I would presume to mention Madam that the aunt will leave a nice letter telling him she is taking her nieces to live with her. No address will be given." Rachel turned her head to hide the self satisfied smile.

"You have thought it out well MacQuarry. However I still wonder about the doctor's reaction." The housekeeper smirked.

"I have it too Madam, from a well-informed source, that those suffragists are planning another of their marches in Bath Street today. We all know how the doctor's surgery is always overcrowded when that happens." Rachel had heard all she needed to hear.

"How much money will we give to this kindly aunt?"

"Twenty pounds should see it right Madam. Believe me it will be worth it and the strays—" She had found a word. "They have turned the place into near Bedlam. One with the devil's own temper and the other having fits." Rachel shuddered as she rose to fetch the money from her desk. Yes it would be worth it to have her household return fully to its peaceful normalcy. She didn't need this disruptive element.

"I wish nothing more to do with it."

"I understand Madam. There'll be no more trouble." But Rachel had stopped listening and had already returned to her reading as the door closed behind the servant. Her sigh as she reached for a chocolate was one of contentment.

"They feed us awfy' good here Hanny. I wish Mam could have some as well. Do you think Heaven has cream cake like this?" Hannah nodded absently as she picked at the rich cake. It tasted too sweet for her and they were not used to such fare.

"Och no, I don't think they have cream cake in Heaven, and don't eat so greedy Ellie, mind you were sick before." Ellie hung her head.

"I forgot Hanny and it just slipped down, do you not want yours?" Again Hannah just nodded as she swallowed a few more spoonfuls. Suddenly she jumped from the chair.

"I don't like it here one wee bit Ellie. It's just like a prison." Bewildered Ellie did what she always did in any kind of crisis. She began to cry. Absently the elder patted her shoulder.

"Hush now, somebody's coming." Ellie hiccupped out her answer.

"Will it not be yon maid for the trays?" It was not the maid but the housekeeper who entered with a swish and a rattle of the string of keys at her belt. She wore a sickly smile but Hannah was more intent on the figure behind the woman. This tall strange person dressed all in black and wearing a hat with the veil completely covering the face said nothing as it waited. Mistress MacQuarry spoke in a soft voice.

"Your Aunty has come to take you to her house." Hannah backed away until she felt the chair on her knees. She didn't recall much about her Aunty Mary but she had thought the woman to be small and rather stout. Her mind didn't seem to be working right though.

"Aunty Mary? You're our Aunty Mary, but I thought—" Ellie ran toward the two figures still in the doorway.

"Are you truly our aunty?" But it was Mistress MacQuarry who answered.

"That's correct my dear. Get your bundles. The cabbie is waiting." Ellie ran back to where the bundles still lay on the floor on the other side of the bed. Hannah put a hand to her head which had started to throb. The room swayed about her.

"But, but!"

"Come along now, don't keep everybody waiting." In a true daze now the girls obeyed, and if Hannah wondered why they were being hustled down the back stairs and bundled into a closed cart she said no more, as by this time a lethargy was taking over her mind. She slumped down on the bare wooden seat opposite Ellie who was already fast asleep. Before darkness overcame her completely Hannah forced her eyes open once more to take another look at 'aunty'. The veiled hat had been replaced by a workman's cap and Hannah was still alert enough to know this could be no Aunt Mary, but a strange man who leered at her from the corner of the swiftly moving vehicle. She managed to blurt out her thought.

"You're not our Aunty Mary!." The leering face came closer.

"'Tis a clever wee lass we have here as well as bonny. It'll fetch a good price although the other's not worth much. Have a wee forty winks then, nobody's goin' to hurt you if you behave yourselves." With that Hannah sank into oblivion.

As the cart made its progress along Bath Street, a sudden movement at the other end of the long street caused the driver to emit a curse or two, but only his horse could hear as he muttered.

"Not another march for the vote!" It soon became evident that indeed some kind of a procession was in progress and within minutes the horse was surrounded by a crush of humanity, mostly female. The driver, knowing that he must deliver his passengers safely to their destination within the hour if he was to collect his sovereign, cracked his whip high in the air. The animal refused to budge, planting its huge feathered hoofs firmly on the cobbles. Instead it twisted round to glare at the driver. Tam Fleming continued to hurl abuse to no avail. The big Clydesdale had been trained by himself not to trample on folks, so the looks the driver was receiving from Jezebel could only be his own fault altogether. That did not solve his problem of making the delivery within the hour as his agreement promised. He did so need to earn the sovereign to be paid when the job was done. He yelled one more curse at the horse but the proud head just kept swaying up and down with the occasional glance at him. The feet did not budge. Tam glanced quickly up at the small window opening high in the front of his van. A furious face glared at him and Tam could see the lips moving although he could hear nothing above the uproar in the street. Guessing the question he tried to answer but the face had disappeared again. He brought his attention back to the crowd pressing in on all sides. One woman stared inquisitively at him and he shouted at her.

"What are you lookin' at Wummen?" He could not hear the answer but then he knew that women after the vote, could be very inquisitive. He could not afford to have too many inquiries about his business. They had nothing better to do then try to keep a man from making a living? Tam never asked questions of the clients who hired him and his van. He never allowed any surprise to show and during the loading and unloading he conveniently paid no attention whatever to any noise he might hear. His vehicle had once been used as a Black Maria but he had painted it brown and changed the inside a bit to suit his clients. A movement beside him brought him to the present moment again and he was startled to see the nosy woman he had spoken to a minute ago swing her way up to the seat beside him.

"Here! Here! you can't sit there, this is a private vee-hicle Missus, not a public bus."

"I know it is but my feet are so sore I beg you to allow me to rest at least while you are at a standstill."

"Even although, I must ask you to get down! I'm on hire and shouldn't have another passenger."

"You'll not push me off I know. Please allow me to sit for a while, I've been on my feet all day and—"

"That's not my fault Missus, if you will do daft things like join in they processions, I've no sympathy at all—" Tam glanced over his shoulder to see if his client watched. The man glared at him murderously and signaled with a cutting motion across his throat. Suddenly Tam balked. Who did the big fella think he was anyway? The van belonged to him, Tam Fleming, and he would allow whoever he liked to sit on the front bench. His uninvited passenger still talked. She had followed his glance but quickly looked away to hide her aroused suspicions.

"I should introduce myself. I'm Florence Crawford, what's your name?"

"Tam. Tam Fleming!" He had said it without thinking, amazing himself as he was usually more cautious. The woman held out her hand.

"How do you do Tam. This is surely a big van you're driving." But Tam would not be caught so easily again.

"Aye." She talked on.

"A nice horse too. I'm very fond of horses especially Clydesdales. This one is well cared for I can see, and is champion material. I'm surprised though she doesn't get hysterical in such a crowd." Jezebel being Tam's pride and joy, and his biggest boast that she had a mind of her own, he forgot once again to be cautious.

"Och Jezebel's above hysterics. See, she's looking down her nose at all the silly women. They're the ones with the hysterics." Flora smiled.

"A very smart horse, she knows a good master who would never load her down with too heavy a cargo." Talking of cargo reminded Tam. He would brag about the horse any time but not about the cargo. He never discussed that or his passengers. As long as he got his pay, whatever or whoever occupied his closed cart was none of his business. "Business is good these days then?" He grunted into his muffler. How could he get rid of this nosy parker. He glanced about at the crowd.

"When will they start moving? If I don't get away soon, there'll be no feed for Jezebel, nor me ." She shrugged.

"Oh them. They're here for the night I'm afraid. That house belongs to Mr. Mason Angely and until he comes out to talk to them they'll not be leaving."

"You think he'll not be comin' out then?"

"If he doesn't they'll be doing some more damage. Oh, why do I say they when I am one of them. We are determined to be heard. I don't approve of damaging property but the cause is worthy." She faced him again and her clear eyes sparked fire at him. "We are going to stamp out exploitation as well you know, 'tis not just the vote. Oh, I know we have the Criminal Prevention Act of the late eighteen hundreds but it is not being enforced when it runs up against vested interest, especially here in Glasgow so far from the seat of government. Tam, I'm sure somebody like yourself would be horrified to know how many young girls, and boys too I might add, are still being abducted and sold as playthings to rich old men, and. . .Why Tam, whatever is the matter?" Tam wasn't sure what could be the matter. Deliberately he kept his eyes from the window of the van. The back doors could only be opened from the outside by somebody removing the bar. Cautiously he leaned to look behind his cart. Other vehicles, cabs and horse buses and some motor traffic as well, lined up behind him. Nothing moved along Bath Street today. Some of the other horses stamped and tried to rear, whinnying with impatience and fear at the press of humans. Yes, movement of any wheeled contrivance was impossible. Flora Crawford saw her advantage. He had hardly been listening to her for the past five minutes.

"I don't suppose a law-abiding citizen like yourself has ever been in one, eh Tam?" But Tam's attention had wandered to the cart's occupants once more.

"Beggin' your pardon, Missus?"

"Prison, Barlinnie, have you?" His hands shook on the reins.

"Not me Missus, as you say I'm a respectable carter trying to earn a decent livin`.."

"I'm sure you are Tam and should be too. I used to be a re-spectable member of society, going to charity teas and such, but I must confess to having spent quite a few weeks in gaol this past while, the women's quarters in Barlinnie to be exact. They say it's worse than the men`s." His face registered shock and he could not speak for a minute. She leaned closer.

"Tam, tell me truly what's in your cart. If it's what I suspect then you could go to jail yourself." He started to protest but she kept on. "Oh yes you could, even if you don't know. Ignorance of the law is no excuse. Now, there's quite a few bobbies hereabouts. None of them will pay any heed to my movements over here, so if you want to get out of this predicament, and let me tell you Tam Fleming it is a predicament to be transporting minors in the white slave traffic, help me to rescue whoever is in there." Flora was guess-ing, following her instincts and his extremely guilty eye move-ments. "You won't lose by it as I will reimburse you for your loss of the fare. In all this crush no one else needs to know." She had the rights of it, and he had taken a strong dislike to that big fellow anyway, his answer was blunt when it came.

"'Twas a sovereign, but I'm not that sure—!" She clapped her hands. "I knew it. . .Oh Tam, you'll get two sovereigns for this. Come on while the bobbies are here and before it gets any darker. You'll never be sorry."

* * * * *

At first glance the Right Honorable Flora Farquarson Crawford
had indeed viewed the wide bench on Tam Fleming's van as a
refuge for her weary body. Since her most recent bout in prison,
when she had refused to eat and had been force-fed for a week, her
strength had evaporated. When her brother, Sir Frederick had finally insisted on paying her bail money and having her carried
home, she had been too weak to resist further. But that had been a
month ago and for the past few days she had been back at the
agitating again, although being more discreet until today. So sure
she could handle a full day's campaigning, and that this would be
peaceful demonstration, she had taken a more active part. An hour
ago she had spotted Sheila, her old nanny, who though retired,
still claimed responsibility for her beloved bairns, the two adult
Crawfords. Sheila had squeezed her way through to Flora's side.

"I brought you some soup Miss Flora. But do you not think
you should come away home with me now, the demonstration is
nearly over."

"Yes Sheel, I know I should, but I don't want to miss the
finale. The honorable member should be here any minute." Sheila
shrugged and poured the soup from the silver flask, holding the
bowl out and exchanging it for the banner and the bag of pamphlets.
Flora drank the soup then wiped her mouth.

"Good soup! Cook's beef barley broth is still my favorite bever-
age." A nod from Sheila was the only response to that. The faithful
retainer would not be sidetracked from her purpose.

"The motor's only two streets away and Denny's waitin' to
drive us. Will you not come Miss Flora? We could wait a long time
yet." Flora extricated the fob watch, which she kept pinned inside
her satchel for safe keeping.

"Give me another half hour Sheel, then I promise, even if he
still has not appeared, I'll come home. Which direction is the
motor car?" Instructions had been given and Flora knew that the
chauffeur Denny would wait, along with Sheila, for the minute

she was ready. Nanny disappeared into the crush just as Flora remembered her banner. "Oh dear Sheila could be a bother trying to get that thing past the bobbys at every street corner." She had searched the sea of placards but hers looked exactly the same as all the others so she could hardly expect to pick out her old nurse. That was when she had noticed the high van. Recognizing from past painful experiences, the shape of the Black Maria, Flora shuddered. The authorities had promised no arrests would be made today unless some serious damage took place, like smashing windows or pelting someone with rotten fruit, but still Flora's knees began to sag before she realized the color was wrong for an official police van. At the same moment she thought" I better not fall down or I will be trampled!" She gazed again at the van. The driver looked decent enough, not rough and mean like some she had encountered. He obviously cared for his horse too, that told you much about a person's character. She had squeezed her way to the side of the van and clutched the shafts, and while the driver seemed diverted toward a face in the van's window, she had summoned just enough energy to pull herself up. Thankfully she had sank on to the bench beside the driver and her questions had begun.

Their plan worked without a hitch. Describing it all later to Sheila, and a loudly protesting Freddie, she marvelled at how easy it had been.

"Sheel, you must have been praying, maybe not for those two poor girls so much as for me. When the kind man got to the back of his van and removed the bar I spotted Sheel, still in the crowd but then with Sara and Martha in tow." She turned to her brother. "Oh stop whining Freddie, don't you see providence at work here? Somehow the ladies got to me just as the driver began to open the van door. The man inside vanished so fast I only had time to notice he wore a long black cape. Anyway, nobody stopped us as we carried the poor children through the crush and round to where Denny waited in the motor." She stopped for breath and to flash her brother one of her brilliant smiles. He responded with a wave of his hand.

"Carry on Flo, you will in any case."

"Thank you Freddie my dear I didn't mean to shout at you but. . .Oh it's the idea of children being abducted like this that makes me furious, and all the more anxious to get the attention of the public. We've managed to save these two but the Lord only knows how many more are not. . .Elias Angely is going to hear every detail about this if I have to. . .he'll need to listen this time. Yes Freddie I realize he's a good apple in a barrel of rotters but he's so slow, and in the interval children are being—" Suddenly the excited voice faltered and to the amazement of those present, the Hon Flora Crawford, that strong advocate of women's rights and equalities, began to weep. Before Sheila could go to her, Freddie moved. He caught her to him and the nurse stepped back. Such a show of emotions being unheard of in this household she knew better than try to interfere. Instead she did what she had been doing all the days while the impulsive Miss had been in that terrible gaol and every day since, Sheila prayed.

"Oh thank you Dear God, sweet Jesus for hearing and answering prayer. Make Yourself known to these two dear people as You are known to me, and Lord, as for the two waifs! Show us what we are to do about them and for them, Amen!"

Although Hannah Stoddart had lived all her short life within a few miles of the ocean, the only glimpse she'd ever had of it was when a woman in the weaving sheds had brought in a picture postcard to show them. A place by the seashore called Prestwick. So nothing in Hannah's own experience could account for the feelings she now had. The floating sensation for one thing with no weight on her body as the soft water held her up. She liked the feeling and didn't want it to stop. Once through the dream the water had changed to a sea of faces, and for a short time she floated above the crowd of people wearing hats and waving banners. That had gone and she had returned to the delightful water. Suddenly through it all a noise began to bother her. Not loud at first but it soon gathered strength. At the same time the water under her began to break over her head and she, who knew nothing about swimming, started to thrash about madly with her arms in a swimming motion. She raised her head above the water and began to search for Ellie as she screamed her sister's name.

"Ellie! Ellie! Where are you? We've not to be separate. Where are you Ellie? I'll save you!" Strong hands caught her wildly thrashing arms and the dream changed again. "No Mam, you've not to take Ellie, we've to stay together!" Then. . ."Stay beside me Ellie that's not our Aunty Mary at all." The scream ended in a wail and Hannah at last began to drag herself out of the drugged sleep. Two strange women stood beside the bed she lay on. One clutched her hands while the other held a soaked sponge with which she had been dabbing Hannah's forehead. Hannah struggled to sit up as the person holding her hands spoke.

"It's alright now. It's alright. You're safe and so is Ellie." Hannah collapsed back on to the soft pillows. Could they be back at the doctor's house she wondered or could the whole thing be just a dream, or?. . .

"Am I dead and in heaven then?" Hearing a soft chuckle she tried again to focus her eyes as a different person spoke.

"No, you're not dead, and this is not heaven. Just lie still and give yourself time to recover a bit before asking questions." But Hannah had been quiet too long as it was and her biggest question came now.

"My wee sister Ellie?" The words came out in a croak and without speaking the woman who still held the wet cloth turned Hannah's head round to face an alcove window. The sight there amazed her further. Inside the alcove, large as life, sat Ellie. Beside her a table loaded with food had Ellie absorbed as she tried to decide between the nice sandwiches and the cream buns. She reached for the buns as Hannah watched. That was when Hannah began to laugh. Weakly at first but with a note of near hysteria that gathered momentum as the two women glanced at each other. Letting her hands go completely the older woman spoke one word.

"Now?" The answer came at once.

"Now!" With no more ceremony the bowl of cold water descended on Hannah. The laughter stopped abruptly as she shook herself, finally she spoke, and for the first time her words made sense.

"You're not Aunty Mary either, are you?"

The last of the autumn leaves lay thick on the ground outside Craigiehaugh, the Crawford mansion. A rosy sunset gleamed through the trees making Sheila decide to take the dogs for their evening walk. Flora had gone off again on one of her secret ploys and Sheila had some communing to do. One of the Labradors gamboled about in a pile of leaves left by the gardener and soon the others ran to join the game, all except old Excaliber who was too proud for such nonsense. He crouched at Sheila's feet as she seated herself on a stone bench. Forcing her thoughts away from Flora she concentrated her attention on the many statues, and the beautiful marble fountain, located within a few feet of where she sat. Not even the Roman style bench, interesting enough to make a fit object for a history lesson of which Sheila was inordinately fond, distracted her for long. From the corner of the house leading to the kitchen garden the sound of voices caused Sheila to frown slightly. She closed her prayer as Hannah and Ellie Stoddart, residents in the mansion for the last five months since their dramatic rescue, came into view. Excaliber raised his head and moved his tail in the mild wag that displayed the fullest extent of his enthusiasm for anything. Hannah had some questions.

"Will Miss Flora not be home soon, and where did she go anyway, last week she was awful sick again. Is she in a hospital or what?"

"One thing at a time Hannah, remember your lessons on good manners. Well it is decidedly not good manners to ask so many questions about your hostess. Certainly she has not been well and she wears herself out for girls such as you and Ellie!" Seeing Hannah's stricken expression she immediately felt remorse. "Och my dear, Miss Flora has aye been like that but I cannot tell you more, you must ask her yourself when she is home and recovered from this last. . . er . . . bout. Could you wait for your answers 'till then?" Giving both girls lessons Sheila had quickly gathered that not only was Hannah much further advanced in learning capability than her sister Ellie, the girl far exceeded any child her age that Sheila had ever encountered, including her charges, the Crawfords. The thought brought her mind back to the question.

"How old are you Hannah?"

"I'll be fourteen on my birthday Miss! High time I went to work for our living again." Sheila ignored the last part as she asked.

"When is your birthday then Hannah?" For a moment Hannah hung back. She wasn't sure if it was right to say. The woman mistook the hesitation.

"Maybe you don't know?" Hannah tossed her head. Any reflection on her mother's ability to try and give her children a good upbringing brought this defiant reaction.

"Och I know right enough." Sheila once more congratulated herself on the improved diction as she replied.

"You don't have to say if you don't want to."

"'Tis on New Year's day. Mam always said—" She stopped again and Sheila finished the sentence.

"That you were extra special because of that!"

"Well, not exactly. . .Lachie was aye the special one to Mam, but she said it would make me sig. . .signi. . ." Again Sheila finished the phrase.

"Significant, and I believe it too Hannah." Absorbing this Hannah neither confirmed nor denied it as Sheila addressed her again, her voice low. "You know how you wanted to learn more about the day be brought you here Hannah?"

"Aye!"

"Well, I'm going to tell you what I know of that story myself. I believe it was the hand of the Lord who led Miss Crawford to rescue you and Ellie!" Sheila related the details of that grim day in Bath Street. Showing no reaction except when the speaker mentioned the spells in prison, Hannah's interest stayed polite, and at last Sheila's spate of many words began to run out. Hannah chased a lady bug on the seat beside her with a long index finger as Sheila finished up her long discourse.

"Although I help Miss Crawford a lot with her work for equality, it is not truly a cause after my own heart." Hannah raised her eyebrows slightly. Encouraged Sheila plunged on. "Yes, I have another cause Hannah, far more important than the vote, in fact more important to me than any other cause I've ever heard of . . ." Still Hannah said nothing. "My cause has results that go much further than the vote or equal rights, it can go even further than anything in this life we live the now." This brought a different reaction as Hannah had not been completely ignorant of the undercurrents in the Crawford mansion. She and Ellie were cared for in the servants' quarters, and had a most comfortable room there on the second floor. At meal times they joined the servants and sometimes the nurse. Sheila would allow no criticism of her mistress, either from the maids or from Denny the chauffeur, but all the same Hannah had soon picked up that Sheila did not altogether agree with the movement or the 'cause', but she had pointedly ignored the 'sermonizing' until now when she suspected she was about to hear more.

Ellie still played with the dogs but they soon tired of it and she ran to her sister and pulled at Hannah's sleeve. Sheila called to the younger girl.

"Is it not time for you to go and help cook with the tea Ellie?" Obediently and gladly Ellie disappeared in the direction of the kitchen.

"Excuse me Miss Sheila, I want none of your sermonizing! I'll not listen to that religion stuff. I had enough of that when. . .Och never mind. But I'll not stay here to listen to it from yourself or anybody else." Quite taken aback the older woman stood up.

"I would never give you a sermon Hannah, but there is something I want you to know, and it has nothing to do with religion. Jesus loves you as He loves me and Ellie. I overheard you say to Ellie to stop singing that wee song. I think you should not interfere with your sister's simple faith."

"That's just it, simple is the right word for Ellie's faith, but I'll not be cheeky Miss Sheila, and I'll not argue so I'll say no more. Could we go in now, after tea I want to try that new crochet stitch you showed me yesterday."

Shocked but undaunted Sheila nodded and followed the stubborn young girl. Then she began to smile. Her plan of telling Hannah of the fate she and Ellie had been rescued from had seemed to have little effect on the girl, maybe that was a blessing as Hannah seemed to have no idea of the danger they had been under. The birthday on New Year's Day though, Sheila knew exactly what she would give Hannah for a birthday gift. Not only that, she would ask Miss Flora if they could make a surprise party. It would not be easy as the staff liked to go home early on that big day on the Scottish colander, but she would manage it somehow.

From the corner of her eye Hannah noticed Cook waiting on the step for Ellie, but as often happened her sister had forgotten her instructions to go in and help with the tea. They reached the door leading into the hall and Sheila called the dogs. Girl and dogs came running. Ellie never wished to be late for mealtimes and she knew their tea would be ready.

Leaving mittens, scarves and tams, along with the warm woolens coats that had been produced from somewhere for the Stoddart sisters, in the huge cupboard in the servants' hall, they proceeded to the kitchen where Nessie the cook had tea and crumpets waiting, and they had settled to the feast with Ellie chattering happily to Cook between mouthfuls.

After tea, crochet was the last thing on Hannah's mind, but as she dutifully struggled with the hook and strands of cotton she was recalling words her father had used to threaten his children many times.

"I'll take you all to the Cowgate and put you up for farm service. They auld farmers are not particular when they come there to get cheap workers. They take you away to their farms and make men and women out of weaklings such as the Good Lord has seen fit to curse me with." The Cowgate! That was her answer. Hannah had traced the directions out from a large framed map of Glasgow she had found on the wall of the library where she went every day for her lessons with Miss Sheila.

But before Hannah could set her plan in motion, a plan that had been brought to a head by today's talk on religion, to escape from this grand place and find work, or before Sheila's idea for a birthday party could be followed through, something else happened to drive every thought from the minds of the residents of Craigiehaugh. The wild story to reach the servants' hall was that Miss Flora, while patrolling with her placard outside the meeting hall being picketed, had received a cruel blow on the side of her head with a bobby's truncheon and had been rushed to the Western Infirmary. She was not expected to last through the night.

Cook's tears flowed down her plump cheeks unheeded as she sat, idle for once, awaiting news. A thoroughly frightened Ellie crept up on her lap and began to wipe the tears away with a small work-scarred hand.

"It's alright Cookie, Jesus will make Miss Flora all better." She whispered into her dear friend's ear. Just then Sheila entered the kitchen followed closely by Hannah and the scullery maid who was also drenched in tears. Cook bellowed out a reply to Ellie.

"Aye Ellie lass, if Jesus is going to make Miss Flora better, why did He not stop her from getting hurt in the first place? Will somebody answer me that now?" Cook's strong brogue surfaced under stress and showed through her hysteria. She made no apology even when she became aware of Sheila and Hannah's presence but she began to deride the nurse. "You and your Jesus, Could He not have kept her safe. She wouldn't hurt a fly. Maybe she is silly enough to do things that get her put in prison but still, it's not fair, she's all talk without a bite." As a fresh paroxysm gripped the loyal servant Sheila stepped forward to take command.

"Stop that Nessie! You're burying Miss Flora and she's far from dead, surely she has had a bad knock on the head, and has concussion, but the doctor says her life's not in danger, and after all Sir Frederick is on his way now to bring her home from the infirmary.

Buck up now and get on with the dinner, we'll need lots of chicken soup and other delicacies." Without another word the cook wiped her face on her massive apron before turning away, absently patting the puzzled Ellie's cheek as she passed. Yes, work was the best thing. Sheila sighed deeply. She had not told Nessie all of Sir Frederick's words. His voice had faltered slightly as he added.

"Doctor MacLeish says she is in no immediate danger of dying Sheila, but he also says the blow has damaged her brain and she may never regain her senses!" She had reached up to pat his shoulder.

"We'll pray that the doctor is wrong sir, or if he is not then we'll pray the Lord will take a hand, He is the Great Healer you know." Sir Frederick had turned away quickly and Sheila wondered if her own faith would be equal to whatever they all might have to face.

Sundays were usually quiet days in the servants' hall. Denny would be on his day off as would the two under maids. Cook usually retired to her room immediately after church service as did Sheila and any of the family spending the day at home in the mansion. Cold meats and breads along with fruits and cheeses would be set up on the giant sideboards for all who cared to help themselves. On this dark day though Sir Frederick had ordered Denny to get the carriage ready and the maids had been warned to prepare for a possible influx of guests. Hannah happened into the kitchen just as the upstairs maid was speaking to her friend from the dining room.

"'Tis they two tramps giving us even more work and me wanting to go and see my granny the day!" The other maid laughed.

"Aye, your granny is it? Does she wear trousers and take you for walks in the park? But you're right enough about the strays. More work than they're worth but anyway, if Miss Flora dies they'll be for the workhouse!" Hannah waited to hear no more. The maids were right. They had enough to do without having to bother with her and Ellie. Everybody else appeared too busy to even see them. She turned and ran for their room, but first she grabbed Ellie's hand from where she stood outside the big green doors leading to the kitchen, and a short time later, clutching her map and her

Ma's precious cushion, she pushed a loudly protesting Ellie along the lane behind the mansion. Earlier on she had made note of a gap in the hedge. Hannah's plans were simple. The Cowgate for the Sunday Hiring Fair and a farm job for her as long as she could bring Ellie.

"I'm awfy feared Hanny. It's dark and I'm hungry!" Impatience along with shared feelings of fear caused Hannah to reply sharply.

"Shut up Ellie, we'll be there in a wee minute," but she was not at all sure of this. Her roughly drawn map made no mention of some of the dark streets and lanes they had passed through since leaving the safety of the grounds of Craigiehaugh. Ellie's sobs became louder and Hannah took pity.

"Awright, we'll go up this close and eat our pieces. Save some for after though. 'Tis further than I thought."

Emerging from the close some fifteen minutes later Hannah glanced up at the sky, or as much of it as she could see between the dingy tenement buildings. Surely it couldn't be night already? It was not night but dark storm clouds blotted out what light there might have been and before long giant drops of rain began to spatter on the pavement and soon both girls were soaked to the skin. Hannah pushed Ellie into the next close mouth but as she did the parcel with the rest of the food slipped from her cold fingers to land with a sickening plop in the filth of the gutter. Ellie's sobs became screams as she saw the black scummy water immerse the bread and biscuits.

"I should 've et it all. Oh our Hanny. What'll happen to us now? Can we no' go back to Cookie and Miss Sheila?" Thinking that she wouldn't be able to find her way back now even if she wanted to Hannah slapped her sister.

"Did I no' tell you to shut up! The rain'll stop soon and then we'll find a chip shop and we'll coorie doon inside and get dry." Hiccups replaced Ellie's screams and Hannah huddled up close to her sister. Maybe she had been in too big a hurry to leave Craigiehaugh but . . . "We couldna' stay there Ellie they've enough bother the now withoot us and ye heard the maid say Miss Flora was too kind for her ain guid. You'll see Ellie, when thon rain stops we'll go into the chip shop. I have the shillin' that Miss Sheila gave me for being good at my lessons and—" But the mention of Sheila, along with Hannah's unusually softened tones sent Ellie off again. Her cries brought reaction.

"What's this then? What are you lassies doin' here?" At first glance the shadowy figure entering the close appeared to be a man. A battered workman's bonnet almost hid the wizened face and the blackened clay pipe clutched between stumps of broken teeth added to that impression, but as the bent figure shuffled closer Hannah recognized this was not a man but an old crone of a woman. Wondering how much the tattered individual had heard of their talk Hannah drew closer to Ellie and did not answer.

"Is it a wee dummy then but no, I heard you whining awa' in here. Ye canna be feared of auld Biddy surely?" The speaker reached down to touch Ellie who cringed and Hannah grasped the clawlike hand and sank her teeth into it.

"Ye wee bitch. A'll teach ye to bite auld Biddy who was only givin' a helpin' haun!" Hannah didn't wait for more, but grabbed Ellie by the sleeve to haul her toward the back entry. However, Ellie was going nowhere for a while. The small girl slithered out of Hannah's reach to lie in a limp heap on the filthy cobblestones at the close mouth. Her eyes rolled back in her head as her legs and arms began to twitch. The crone took one look before beginning to screech.

"A witch, we've got a witch in this close!" Within moments the place filled up with people all yelling and screaming until one voice rose above the others. Oblivious to all but her sister now Hannah knelt on the ground and Ellie opened her eyes for a second as another yell echoed in the gloom.

"A Bobby!" Ellie reached a feeble hand up for Hannah.

"Don't worry Hannah, I see Jesus up there in the light. Thon meenister was right Jesus does love me an' He's comin' to take me to Mam!"

"Och no Ellie, dinna go to Mam yet, I need you, Ellie. . .Oh Ellie, I'm that sorry, I didna' mean it!"

"What's all the commotion then? Make way in the name of the Law, oot the road or I'll run you in." As fast as it had filled, the space emptied until only Hannah and the policeman were left to stare helplessly down at Ellie. Suddenly the man was galvanized into action. "The wean's in a fit. Here I'll lift her and you come wi' me. The infirmary's just round the corner." As good as his word, the bobby did that and very soon they reached the place of refuge.

"You wait here Hen and I'll—". But Hannah was having none of that.

"I'll not wait here, I'm going with ma wee sister." The policeman carrying his inert bundle rushed on and a helpless Hannah followed at his heels until stopped by a large figure in a starched uniform. Hannah recognized the habit and covered headdress having seen plenty of nuns at the convent next to the carpet factory. This one would stand no nonsense.

"Where do you think you're going?"

"Wi' ma wee sister. She'll be needin' me!"

"We will take care of your sister. You come here and tell me your names and whatever happened." Hannah's frantic gaze had already lost sight of the bobby and Ellie. She gave up.

"She says their parents are dead and they have nobody else to turn to, she was trying to get work at the hiring fair. What shall we do with them Mother?" The Mother Superior sighed as she replaced her pen on the desk top. What indeed!

"Well Sister Winifred, we'll not be turning them out in the street. We both know what could happen to as bonny a lass as you describe. The young one is in the charity ward. Doctor Burke tells me she is an epileptic, and to make matters worse the child has a weak heart. Take the other one to the kitchens and tell Sister Benedict to feed her. You say they're both quite clean, although their skirts were muddy. The bundles too are clean enough although skimpy. Dear knows what they've been up to or what they've run away from. Do your best." Sister Winifred echoed the sigh as she realized further decisions would be left to her. Now for the hard part. As she had guessed taking Hannah Stoddart anywhere without

Ellie proved more than one sister could handle but between Sister Benedict and herself, they at last half dragged, half carried the loudly protesting girl into the kitchen. She stubbornly refused to eat however and at last they gave up and left her seated on a plank form in the bare scullery. Sister Benedict insisted on locking the door as the questions about Ellie still poured thick and fast from Hannah. Questions no one who heard could or would answer. Exhaustion took over and at last Hannah slept. Toward morning she awoke to the sound of key in the lock. She jumped to her feet but before she could begin her questions again the nun spoke.

"You're to come with me to the Mother Superior."

"Who's that and whit for. What's wrong Missus, where's Ellie? She'll be oot of her fit by now and we'll need to just get on oor way." They reached the Mother Superior's office, a big name for a small cubbyhole of a room housing only a wooden desk and two chairs. Frantically Hannah searched the room with her eyes but no one else appeared and some kind of inner wisdom stopped the questions as her voice descended to a frightened whisper as she said.

"Ellie's deed as well, ma wee sister's deed noo is she no'?" The kind but overworked woman turned away. She had witnessed many tragic moments only too similar to this one but she would never get used to what she must do now.

"Yes Hannah, I'm sorry to have to tell you that Dr. Burke did all he could for her but he could not start. . .He could not save her I'm afraid." Hannah's knees buckled and she collapsed at last on to the chair but she did not faint or cry out.

Hannah still did not faint or cry out two days later as she watched the men lower the plain wooden box into the cold ground. Between them the doctor and the nuns had arranged for the simple funeral and after it was concluded and Hannah still stood beside the grave as though stunned until Sister Winifred came up and touched her arm.

"Come away Hannah, we'll get a place for you, but first we'll teach you a bit about housework if you are to be a scullery maid." Hannah started.

"What, oh aye, a place!" But she still did not move. A cold drizzly rain had started but she gave it no attention. The kindly sister tried again.

"Come on lass. You can do no more for Ellie." With a final glance at the raw earth being shoveled into the hole Hannah shuddered before turning to obey. The nuns had been nice enough to her allowing her to sleep in a wee room and giving her hot soup and porridge, even if she hardly touched the food. Belatedly now she remembered some of the manners Miss Sheila had taught her.

"Thank you Sister, but 'll not be needing. . .I mean. . .I was on my way to the Cowgate for a farm job. I dinna want to be a scullery maid." They had reached the back door of the convent and another nun hurrying to get in out of the rain heard the last remark.

"Well well, she disn't want to be a scullery maid, beggars canna be choosers miss and ye'll take whit ye can get." Hannah's head went up but the first nun broke in before she could answer.

"We've just come from her sister's funeral Sister Rebecca, I think Mother Superior will be making the decisions, but not until the morning. Come along Hannah, you need some hot tea and maybe a scone." Rebecca sniffed but held her tongue. If that proud wee besom was to stay at the convent then she would soon learn proper behaviour and she, Sister Rebecca, would take great delight in showing her.

"I hear you can read and write Hannah?" Sister Winifred had told Hannah a few basics about the way to speak to the nuns.

"Aye, I can Mother." The woman behind the desk gave one of her rare smiles. It was the day after the funeral and Hannah had been summoned.

"Did you know we run a school here for bairns with no means to pay?" Hannah shook her head, she had no wish to hear all this it had nothing to do with her. But the nun kept talking. "Sister Benedict will give you a wee test and if you pass, and you like the idea, maybe you could help us to teach the baby class to read.

What do you say?" For the first time since she and Ellie had run
from Craigiehaugh, Hannah's face sparked with interest, not a smile
exactly but the beginnings of one.

"I think I would like that if you—" But apparently the inter-
view was to end there. The Mother Superior gave her signal to the
nun at the door and she entered to be given the instructions for
the test. As she shepherded Hannah out the door the girl turned
back to say.

"If I pass the test could I start the day, I owe you an awful lot?"
The nun who held her arm in a firm grip gasped, but before she
could speak her superior interrupted.

"Yes Hannah, I'm sure it can be arranged, if you pass you can
start today."

So Hannah remained for a time with the Sisters of the New
Covenant, to be taught and in turn to teach, for the most part
happy enough. The order of sisters with whom she entrusted her
life was not a strict order but when, in due course Hannah was
asked if she wished to enter the novitiate she politely declined.
Nothing of their unadorned zeal for their Lord had penetrated her
inner being and if asked she would again have said, still politely, If
there is a God then he doesn't like me, he took my Mam and my
brother, then my wee sister Ellie who trusted him. I'll not be
needing that thank you. Besides I would make a very bad nun as
my life's ambition is never to be poor again!" Following consulta-
tion decided to send her to typewriting school and when she turned
sixteen a live-in job was found for her with a couple who worked in
the inner city, a man and wife by the name of Dunbar, serving
officers in the Salvation Army. By then though Scotland, along
with the rest of Britain and most of Europe, was in the midst of a
bloody war.

With their experiences on that day trip to Dunoon long forgotten, the Lamberts continued with the life of a Scottish suburban household. Talk of war was kept to a minimum in Sophia's

hearing. In spite of that Sophia's deep sighs often fell on the family's ears as time inexorably passed bringing the inevitable. On the surface the individual members kept to their activities. Sophia's sigh this time held a note of relief as her husband sat back to admire his finished project. Normally she hardly noticed the scraping of chisel, or the scratching rasp of sandpaper as Robert worked, but for the past few weeks the sounds had started to get on her nerves. How could he remain so calm when the world was in such turmoil, trying to keep the truth from her as if she were another Lizzie?

Robert had noticed the sighs and pointed glances but had wisely held his tongue, nothing soothed him as well as his woodwork. The beautiful chest of solid oak, formed out of one piece and carved so lovingly by his own hands, was worth putting up with a bit of disapproval for during the long winter evenings. Although he would not say it aloud Robert knew the design was exquisite and each inch of intricate carving showed how he so loved the task. Engaged into this work of art, cutting each detail with precision, Robert had brought the story of Exodus alive around the sides of the kist, beginning with the finding of the baby Moses in the rushes, to the Tabernacle in the wilderness. The lid, a masterpiece by itself, showed Miriam fairly leaping from the wood as she led the children of Israel in a victory dance before the Lord, to the tune of clashing cymbals and tambourines as the scene unfolded. The railway platelayer moved his work roughened hand lovingly across the grooves and ridges, etching them in his mind. Suddenly he laughed.

"That's that then Sophia lass. A bottom drawer for our Maggie, if she ever stops dreaming long enough to look at a lad instead of always having her head in a book, that is." His eyes crinkled as he glanced at his daughter, seated at her desk in the corner, another bit of his handiwork meant for the use of all his children, but no one used it as diligently as Maggie. The subject of her father's teasing paid no heed to either of her parents. Lost in the pages of the volume, she moved her hand to jot something in a notebook, but she did not look up. Her mother's concerns also flowed over her head as Maggie concentrated fully on her studies for the final exams next week. For a good passing mark at Normal School even Maggie Lambert did have to work hard. The talk continued to flow round her as Sophia stopped her knitting to follow her husband's fond glance.

"She's in no hurry for a hope kist Robert. She'll do fine as she is for a while, and she should have a year or two at the teaching first. My own mind is on our Robert, now that he's an officer, an' with all this talk of war!" Robert frowned. He knew all about the war talk having heard nothing else in the bothie for weeks. His one desire when he reached home each night being to forget it and enjoy his simple pleasures. It was his turn to sigh heavily.

"Now! Now! Sophia, remember how he said not to worry so much as he's too stubborn a Scot to be—" His wife almost screamed.

"Don't you dare say it Robert!" Maggie looked up from her book in time to see her mother tug so hard at the knitting that the stitches on one needle slipped completely off. The closest the family ever heard to a swear word left Sophia's mouth.

"Botheration and twice botheration!" Father and Daughter looked at each other before quickly looking away. This must be bad but they could never allow mother to see their inner glee. Maggie decided she should say something.

"Robert's Balaclava helmet's nearly done Mother?" Slightly mollified and ashamed of her outburst Sophia answered.

"Aye it is Lass. If I can get the stitches back on without making a mess of it. I want it to be finished in time for Robert coming home next month." A sound at the door saved the others from remarks and Willie entered. Quickly he removed his Boy's Brigade cap before any mention could be made of the new badge adorning its brim. The sharp eyed Maggie noticed but decided to wait until he mentioned it before saying anything. Willie stopped to admire the woodwork.

"'Tis done than Father? We were sharing about Exodus at the

meeting. Maybe I could take this some night to show my troop."
False humility had no place in Robert so he nodded before saying.

"Nice idea Willie. Sometimes we can learn more from a picture than—" But they had forgotten Maggie's opinion on that
score.

"Pictures are fine Father but they need words as well. The
power of the written word far outweighs the power of a picture!" It
was the men's turn to exchange smiles. Maggie's vendetta that too
much was made of picture books and not enough about words,
which she gloried in, would follow her through life and no doubt
be taught to every unsuspecting youngster to ever grace her classes.
Sophia finished picking up the stitches and with the knitting for
the night.

"Time for some cocoa and then bed. Mornin' comes soon
enough!" As she said this every night at the same hour expecting
no response except a nod from Robert, it happened exactly like
that and soon the house settled into sleep along with the occupants. Lizzie had already been in that blissful state for many hours.

Not every occupant slept. Maggie tiptoed to her own side of
the big bed she shared with Lizzie. Nothing would wake her sister,
but the walls between the boy's bedroom and theirs were thin and
she didn't want Willie to hear her. If he did he just might try to
tap on the wall with his Morse code. The new badge on his cap
showed that he had successfully passed the strict final test for the
code and although Willie was another Lambert who didn't brag, if
he thought she was awake he would begin tapping. Maggie had
not been so engrossed in her studies as she allowed her parents to
believe. She had her own deep concerns about Robert and she
knew that her mother's worries had some foundation. Robert made
light of his danger but she felt she knew both of her brothers well
enough to recognize when one of them put up a false front to gull
mother. That mother was not so easily gulled this time did not
escape Maggie either, or the fact that father was party to the cover-
up. She shivered and reached under the bed for her warm slippers,
another product of Sophia's busy knitting needles. Would the time

never come when they could discuss things as a family, things that went below the surface to real feelings. Maggie felt her father, rightly or wrongly, always wanted to protect their mother from reality. Reality being that most of the young men training to be teachers alongside Maggie Lambert and the other young women, were eagerly awaiting the finals next week, not to get into schools to teach but to get into uniforms and be ready for the coming conflict. She turned back to the bed. Obviously worrying and staying awake would help nothing. Maggie blew out her candle and climbed in beside Lizzie.

What felt like only moments later she jerked awake. At once she realized the awful shrieking noise came from Lizzie. Shriek after shriek left her mouth before Maggie could twist around to stop it. Their door was thrown open with a crash and Willie, followed by Sophia and Robert, dashed into their room.

"What is it? What's wrong?" The screams subsided into a loud sloppy sobbing as poor Lizzie tried to talk. Robert gathered his youngest into his arms, his poor retarded lass, before saying.

"Tell Daddy what frightened ye Lizzie!" Lizzie shook and shivered for another minute, at last words started to come clear.

"They're hurtin' our Robert, they threw him into a big bonfire and they'll not let us get him. They threw mare sticks in the fire and the sticks are makin' big bangs. Oh Daddy, they're makin' Robert deed like Granny Cowan." Glancing over Lizzie's head her father saw that there would be no way he could stop Sophia from hearing these words. But he would try.

"Bring her a drop of the medicine Mother, and Maggie, make some tea." Maggie, about to ask why, caught the glint in his eyes and decided to obey instead. Both women moved toward the kitchen, had her mother heard, Maggie wondered? She soon found out.

"'Tis a warnin' Maggie, I knew all the time that Robert was in danger. 'Tis the cowl. The midwife told me the day she was born that our Lizzie, although a shuttlewit, would have the second sight."

"Mother that's ridiculous, Lizzie only had a nightmare, and I thought we were never to call her that, anyway she's been hearing all this talk and picked up that we're all worried about—"

"No No Maggie, she hasn't heard the talk at all. She hasn't been out either. Lizzie has had a vision of what's to happen to Robert. No two ways aboot it. What'll we do now?"

"Even if that's true Mother, and let me assure you it is not, there would be nothing to do. Robert is an officer in the Glasgow Highlanders now and if war comes we know he'll be among the first to go, but don't kill him off with just by what Lizzie saw in her nightmare, and don't say any of this to father or Willie or they'll think you've lost your mind. Father would be awful angry as well, you know how he is on anything against what the Bible teaches." Sophia leaned weakly against the stone sink. Yes she did know how Robert felt about those things. In fact these were the only time she ever saw him riled up. She must pull herself together. Willie stood in the doorway.

"Father wonders if you went to China for the tea Maggie, or if the well has run dry. We don't need the medicine Mother, for Lizzie's sound asleep again, but I think we all need the tea and some straight talking. I didn't say when I came in from the meeting last night but the time has come. Word came, and the source is dependable, while the leaders were sitting discussing the camp for next year, that war had been declared with Germany. It happened because some madman assassinated Ferdinand the Austrian." Maggie made no effort to continue with the tea as she faced her brother. He would never had said such words if he were not absolutely convinced of their truth. She opened her mouth to ask why he thought he could keep quiet about such a thing but a sound from her mother stopped it.

"That's it, that's what Lizzie saw, she does have the second sight but at least we know it wasn't Robert after all."

* * * * *

Tearing up what must be his third attempt at writing a letter, Robert Lambert groaned aloud. His problem, too many clever readers at home in Eastkirk. Maybe he could gull his mother but Willie and Maggie, and his father as well could see right through any pretences he might be tempted to try. Censorship would excuse some of his reticence but he could say a bit more than-'I am just fine, how is everybody in Parkhall Street?'-If he remembered his geography at all he was on the French Riviera but at this time of year and with concrete slabs and barbed wire barricades along the beaches it resembled any other war torn coastline. He smiled grimly at the thought of adding 'wish you were here, ha ha!'.

He glanced round the drafty hut, part of the so-called rest area, it was not much warmer than the trench where he had been less than two days ago, when he had been up to his knees in mud or worse. A few rickety tables with chairs like the one he sat on at the moment were scattered around the room along with some flimsy shelving enough to give the place the name of Library. A sign outside the door confirmed this with the hand printed words 'Reading and Writing Room, Quiet Please.' Giving up his attempt at letter composition for the moment Robert decided to pay a visit to the canteen. A nice cup of tea and a Sally Ann bun would keep him occupied for a half hour or so, and maybe he would find some inspiration there. He picked up his greatcoat and hat and made for the door, but the years of training where you learned never to leave yourself without a weapon in hand, made him turn back to pick up his officers cane. His holster cradled a service gun but surely in a place like the Salvation Army canteen, provided for the Allied servicemen on leave, he would not need a weapon. Robert smiled again recalling the Sergeant major who had dunned into them never to presume a place to be safe until you had thoroughly inspected it and even then—" His recollections were cut short abruptly as a uniformed figure catapulted into him, knocking him to one side of the flimsy wooden door. He picked himself up and ran quickly to where the figure now lay prone. Noting the strange uniform he spoke his thought aloud.

"I wonder why these Yanks always have better uniforms than we do?"

"Canadian!"

"I beg your pardon?"

"You should too, I'm a Canadian, not a Yankee, but help me up and let's hurry back inside. Some wise guys in there are hasslin' a young lady volunteer and—" Robert leaned over, and grasping hold of the fellow's collar he heaved him to his feet, then together they rushed through the canteen door. Tobacco smoke swirled in the draft from the swinging door and it took Robert a few moments to get his bearings. When he did he saw what appeared to be a heap of uniforms of every description wrestling and writhing on the floor between the rough wooden tables. On top of one table a young girl stood screaming. No one seemed to be in charge. Discerning quickly that he was most likely the senior officer here he called out in his most authoritative voice.

"Attention!" Magically it had the desired effect and within seconds the unruly group had assembled themselves into an orderly troop of soldiers. Privates and non-commissioned officers alike came to full attention and all, except the girl on the table, now waited silently. She continued to scream albeit not at such a high pitch. The Canadian who had almost bowled him over at the door reached up to the girl and lifted her down. The screaming ceased as she turned and slapped him. The response to that amazed everyone.

"Gee you're welcome Ma'am anytime!" Robert spoke up.

"Will someone please tell me what's up here?" Ten voices began to oblige and again he had to shout for silence. "Maybe the young lady would be so kind as to explain?"

"Aye I will Sir. I was serving tea and buns when this corporal here began to, began to—" Suddenly shy she turned away mumbling: "Do I need to go on Sir, I slapped his face for him and he. . .he. . .well anyway this other one here decided to come to my rescue, but before I—" The corporal stepped forward.

"I meant no offence Captain sir, all I done was pay her a wee compliment and this fella came buttin' in with his big rescue act. They think wi' their fancy uniforms they're such heroes and that we canna manage withoot them, as for our lasses—" Robert decided it was time to bring this to a halt.

"As you were men, and I believe you are wanted at the counter Miss." Hannah Stoddart, almost completely recovered put a hand up to smooth her hair before walking off in the direction of the kitchen. The soldiers quickly dispersed, some all the way out the door, and others to the bench seats as far away from the captain as they could go, all except the Canadian. He spoke to Robert now in a voice at once respectful but not subservient.

"Private Gilbert Parker sir, Gil for short, at your service and in your debt for—"

"At ease soldier you owe me nothing, except possibly a better explanation than I've had so far. Would there be a cuppa tea anywhere abouts do you think? By the way I'm Robert Lambert. Captain through no fault of my own but, as we are on leave, shall we forget ceremony for the time being?"

"Tea it is sir, although I prefer coffee myself, I wonder if Miss Hannah feels up to serving us?" An older woman dressed in the smart uniform of a Salvationist now stood beside them. Clearly she had overheard Gil's remark.

"Miss Hannah is finished for the day gentlemen, but my husband and I would be honoured if you would join us in our private sitting room, I believe we have you both to thank for avoiding a near riot. Usually this is a quiet hour or Hannah would not be alone. We do understand the exuberance of men returning to the front lines but every now and then they get out of hand and we have to call the M.P.s. We dislike doing that as we are here to comfort not censure but—" Both men had stood to their feet when the lady began to speak and Robert inclined his head,

"I would be honoured to join you but there is no need for thanks I merely—" Catching his new friends frantic eye signals he changed his tone to say mildly. "It would be nice to have tea in your sitting room and I thank you in advance. I am Captain Robert Lambert." He held out his hand as he said his name and it was taken in a firm grasp as the woman spoke again.

"I too am a captain but in a different army. My name is Dunbar, Mistress Oliver Dunbar. This way please." The first person they saw as they passed through the connecting doors was the same Hannah, and yet not the same. Dressed in a simple grey wool suit that emphasized her slim figure she now resided with great dignity over a small table, set with rough army mugs and plates that could have been the finest rose patterned china equal to any his mother used for best, and Robert would hardly have noticed. The food could also have been such as Sophia would provide for their Sunday afternoon tea.

"If all is to your satisfaction Captain we will ask the Lord's blessing and then Hannah can pour the tea and we can begin." Robert shook his head to clear it and to bring a semblance of decorum to his thoughts he spoke.

"Aye, everything is just grand, but I don't think we've been introduced."

Mistress Dunbar had preceded him.

"Hannah my dear, your gallant rescuers. You know Private Parker of course and this is Captain Robert Lambert, Captain allow me to introduce our ward, Miss Hannah Stoddart!" The handclasp was warm and seemed to Gil Parker to last too long. His sigh brought Hannah's attention and she blushed as she said.

"I'm sorry for slapping you Gil but I—"

"Say no more Miss Hannah, I understand!" But as he accepted his mug of tea from Hannah, Gil Parker's hopes towards the lovely girl faded and disappeared. Captain Lambert and Hannah Stoddart had eyes only for each other, it would merely be a matter of time. Half an hour passed and the plate of scones and pancakes had vanished along with the butter and jam. Robert apologized for both men but their hostess merely laughed as she gathered up the dishes. Hannah moved to help but was kindly excused.

"No my dear, you know no one but myself is allowed to wash my best china!" The woman and the girl chuckled at the shared joke and Mistress Dunbar continued. "You entertain our guests until my husband returns. I am sure you all have much to talk about." As the soldiers resumed their seats Gil remarked.

"Now this is what I call civilized hospitality except that it leaves me the odd man out here although I'd better stay around as chaperone." He might have been addressing the wall for all the attention the other two paid him. They just sat gazing at each other until finally Hannah, the pretty rose blush staining her cheeks once more, addressed Gil.

"Tell the captain what you were telling us yesterday in the canteen Gil."

"Eh, What? Oh yeah, about Canada. Well my home's in Vancouver, that's in British Columbia by the way, with my Mom and Dad. Dad is an invalid though and I'm an only child and—" Hannah stopped him with an uplifted hand.

"Not that Gil, I meant about the Pacific Ocean and the plans to build skyscrapers to make, what did you call it again, the prettiest skyline in North America."

"Oh Hannah, Captain Lambert won't want to hear all that stuff I'm sure." Robert managed to drag his gaze away from the lovely expressive face long enough to put a word in. He had already noted the curly hair, the dark flashing eyes and the mobile mouth that had etched in it, for all her youth, not a few pain lines. 'She must have had some bad experiences already in her short life, but I'll make that up to her someday if I get half a chance' he thought as he turned to respond to the Canadian.

"As a matter of fact I would very much like to hear about your country Gil, my brother has a hankering to go there after the war. He talks of the prairies though and some place called Saskatchewan." Hannah laughed.

"That sounds like quite a mouthful, have you been there Gil?"

"No, at least not to stop there, Saskatchewan is not just a place, it's a whole province, we steamed through it on the troop train on our way to Montreal to be shipped overseas." His eyes took on a glazed look for a few moments before he continued. "We did stop off in Edmonton for an hour or so, that's in Alberta, the next province to my own. My uncle came to the train to see me. I never could figure out how he knew but I suppose, as he is a big shot business man with connections." That he was trying to keep bitterness out of his voice became obvious to Robert but he made no remark as Gil had more to say. "Yeah! Uncle Henry had just gotten married and he brought his new bride to meet me too but still—" His audience of two listened politely but Gil had said enough. "That's it for me, how about you Captain, I mean Robert. I already know that Hannah is an orphan who stayed with the Catholic sisters in an orphanage for a while until the Dunbars took her under their wing, then when the war started she volunteered along with them to come to "Somewhere in France". They serve us heroes with tea and buns, and a feeling of home about as close to the front lines as they can go, but what about you Captain, sir?"

"Me, why I am a very ordinary fellow who happened to be in the Territorial Reserves when war broke out, and who, instead of finishing my education at Glasgow University came straight into the army instead. Actually I would have made a career out of the army but who knows what will happen when this lot is over even if—" Hannah jumped to her feet.

"Don't say it! Nobody here says it at all. Tell us some more about your brother and have you any sisters?" His gaze softened as he saw the near frenzy in her eyes. Poor wee thing, she was an orphan and she needed to hear about other folks families. His resolve to make it up to her strengthened.

"I have that, two sisters, Maggie and Lizzie, the brother I mentioned is Willie, he has a bit of bother with one ear and could not pass for active service. He works on the railway with my father. He also does volunteer work with the Boys Brigade. Maggie is a school teacher and the oldest next to me but never tell her I told you or I'll be roasted alive. As for our Lizzie. . .well—" His face clouded slightly. "Lizzie is the pet of the family being the youngest. Mother knits scarves and mitts and anything else she can get wool for." If his listeners had only known it they were hearing more words from Robert Lambert than he was wont to say on an ordinary day. But this day was far from ordinary, as for the circumstances. . .Well! Just then a face appeared round the door jamb and the men rose as one while Hannah gave a chuckle.

"This is another Captain Dunbar, of the Salvation Army, we seem to have a hut full of captains tonight." The smiling older man came forward and ushered the men to sit down again while be seated himself on the chair closest to Hannah.

"No ceremony men, my wife has explained your presence and I add my thanks to hers for your preventing what could have been an unhappy occasion." He turned to Gil.

"Nice to see you Gil, I'm sorry to tell you this but your hut seems to be having quite an Exodus, in case you don't know or have forgotten!" Gil leaped to his feet with a muffled exclamation.

"Didn't forget but lost track of time. We were supposed to be ready by. . .Excuse me ladies, and Captain it was great meeting you but duty calls, Goodbye Hannah, goodbye Captains Dunbar. 'Til we meet again eh?" the door thudded behind him leaving a stunned and saddened group of people to stare at it in some bewilderment. Hannah spoke first, repeating the last statement.

"'Til we meet again indeed Gil."

Several more hours elapsed before Robert Lambert got back to his mother's letter. During the interval the Dunbars, after a few futile attempts to join in their conversation gave up and retreated to the furthest corner of their humble room. Understanding perfectly but at the same time determined to stay within the confines of propriety. Two single people meeting for the first time within the context of these frightful days. The man whispered to his wife.

"My dear, this is not an idle flirtation!" She smiled having discerned that at once.

"Hannah is like a precious daughter to us, we must first pray and then, when they tell us about it, we can give them our bless-

ing." Captain Dunbar nodded, in complete agreement with his
spouse. At that moment a loud knocking on the outside door of
the canteen brought all four to their feet and Robert was first to
reach the door. A soldier he barely recognized as the corporal he
had encountered earlier stood there. Streaming out behind him a
long line of stretcher bearers could be seen heading for the opening.

"Beggin' your pardon sir, Captain, but we have to bring the
casualties in here. the hospital unit is overflowing and—" Robert
caught his sleeve to stop the flow of words.

"What happened man?"

"A lorry full o' troops got a direct hit from a sniper. The bullet
hit the petrol tank and then. . .they had grenades and—" Captain
Dunbar spoke now.

"What lorry, corporal?"

"The Canadians, Oh my God, I'm that sorry—" A scream
interrupted him and Robert turned as Hannah's scream formed
the words.

"Och no! Not Gil. . .Please God, not Gil!"

＊ ＊ ＊ ＊ ＊

The Dunbars quickly brought Hannah out of her hysterics as the
canteen began to fill up with casualties from the explosion and as
the stench of burned cloth mixed with that of scorched flesh
enveloped the room. Soon the tables were covered and what had
been a scene of comparative peace became that of a charnal house.
As Hannah joined the other willing able-bodied helpers, too
stunned to know what to do next, she jumped when a figure,
smoke-blackened like the others but obviously in charge, beckoned
to her urgently.

"If you have nothing to do pull yourself together, go outside
and help the nurses list the dead, that'll relieve them to help those
who can still be helped." Before she could protest the figure disappeared again and she reluctantly made her way to the yard. The

GILD THE MORNING SKY

sight to meet her made her gorge rise but she fought the feeling as her arm was grasped from behind and a rough voice spoke.

"No time for squeamishness here Lass, I'll read the names and numbers from the dog-tags while you write it down, that way it'll take half the time. The sooner we can bury these poor beggars the better." He pushed the clip-board at her and so began one of the worst hours Hannah Stoddart had ever experienced. Hannah's responses became automatic until she heard the man read out, in his monotone, "Gilbert. . ." She gasped and her knuckles whitened as she clung with all her strength and fortitude to the clip board. Her senses swam as she forced her eyes away from the still form to write the name and her self-appointed partner complained how the tags were almost impossible to read or the string had deteriorated so that it came to bits in his hands.

"I thought they said the tags and ties were indestructible, well, I suppose they must be up to a point or. . .Anyway Miss that's the last one thank God and here comes the burial detail with their lorry. Give the corporal your list and then we better go inside, no doubt more there and—" Meekly Hannah did as she was told thinking that she had not spoken a word during the whole ordeal. Actually she hadn't needed to as her erstwhile companion had not stopped. At the same moment she realized this must be his way of dealing with the terrible tragedy.

Inside proved to be only slightly better, the difference being that here the rows of bodies moved and breathed. She glimpsed Mrs. Dunbar at that moment as she too straightened up from her grim task for a brief respite. Noticing Hannah she came toward her saying.

"We've done all we can for now Hannah. The doctor has ordered us to go and wash up and prepare some food for the survivors and the workers." Hannah still did not speak but she nodded as she started to follow the Captain. Suddenly the room began to sway round her but before Mrs. Dunbar could catch her another form detached itself from the melee and grasped her, roughly pushing her head forward and down until it almost reached her knees.

She came up gasping but no longer feeling faint. Her rescuer spoke and his words almost caused her to faint again.

"Tony Avery at your service Miss, I hear from my batman that you have rendered a great service here today, although unpleasant, the job must be done, and done well so that the relatives of the unfortunates may be informed, I beg your pardon as you very likely knew some of them. . . Now I know I look a sight, but so do you and everybody else here, so why are staring at me like that?" Hannah gulped and at last found her tongue, grateful that the subject had changed and for a time she could try to forget the sight of Gil.

"Did you say Tony Avery sir? and are you a doctor?"

"Yes to both your questions, should I know you?" Hannah blushed.

"No, I don't know, maybe not. . .I just thought—" Captain Dunbar caught her elbow and addressed the man.

"Excuse us Doctor, but we have duties." Puzzled Tony Avery scratched his head before turning back to his patients. This had been a long hard day for all of them and judging by the groans from every corner, a still longer, harder night loomed. He resumed his task with no further thoughts of the young woman's strange remarks until the call came for refreshments. Assuring himself that the orderlies had everything under control as far as it could be for now he gladly obeyed.

The way matters turned out the telegraph system had been busy and within a very short time the Canadian administration had commandeered a work detail to transfer their casualties, dead and alive, to a central debarkation area well away from the proximity of the fighting. The lone sniper had been dealt with, hopefully taken prisoner and not lynched as Hannah had overheard one of the stretcher cases threaten. When all was done and the Dunbars turned to each other to take stock of the situation, only they, Hannah and three others remained in their sitting room. All were sorry sights as attempts to wash up had resulted in white faces and hands except for black rings round eyes and necks. Under different circumstances this would be amusing. Suddenly everyone began to talk at once until Captain Dunbar held up his hand for silence.

"We know Captain Lambert here, having met him only today, or was it yesterday, this awful time has made it seem like weeks, anyway Doctor, could you tell us who you are and how you came to be in our vicinity at such an appropriate moment for us?"

"Yes of course, I'm Tony Avery, M.O. with the 2nd. Cameronians, on a three-day pass along with my batman, Jamie Degnan here, now I'm not sure how much of our leave is gone already. We had heard of this canteen and the Scottish element, so we decided to stop here for our leave and were driving toward this place when we saw the doomed vehicle going in the opposite direction. We witnessed the whole thing." No one spoke for a few minutes and the doctor continued. "You can accommodate us I trust Captains Dunbar?"

"There are some huts available with a few cots I believe but the Canadian contingent left in such a hurry—" A stifled sob from Hannah and a nudge from his wife stopped him and Robert took up the tale.

"The hut I'm in has three cots and I've had it to myself until now. It seems that not only the Canadians left today but some of the other units as well including the bunch who were in the canteen when I arrived." Dr. Avery nodded before turning to Hannah.

"May I speak with Miss Hannah. I believe we have met before!" Hannah heard her name but before she could reply Mistress Dunbar spoke up.

"We have all been through a shocking ordeal in the past ten hours or so as you are aware Doctor so, although you soldiers may be immune, we are not. I must insist that we retire for the night, but if Hannah agrees you may speak to her in the morning, you too Captain Lambert. Oh, and would you be good enough to take the others to your hut and show them the facilities. I believe there is a stove in the hut and you can heat water to bathe. Goodnight Gentlemen!" With that she whisked Hannah out of the room while her husband ushered the men out the other door.

Although consumed with curiosity about where and when Hannah and this uppity doctor could have met Robert managed to contain it as he pointed out the various necessary details for their comfort. As the lady captain had said tomorrow would be soon enough and he, Robert Lambert, was not going to leave this fellow alone with Hannah if he could help it. Amazingly, after all that had happened since he had walked out of here, his writing kit and other belongings were exactly as he had left them and as sleep seemed far away he decided to finish the letter home while his room-mates were at their ablutions. If he could have told them at home about the happenings of the past hours it would make quite a story but for many reasons he could not do that. Maybe he could just tell them about Hannah! He finished his letter just as the others re-entered the hut so he decided to go for his own wash-up and soon the only sound in the hut was Jamie's snores. A loud banging on the door brought a rude awakening in what seemed only moments later. A kilted Cameronian complete with dispatch pouch stood there.

"Medical Officer Avery." That man was already on his feet with a sorry looking batman right behind him. It appeared they were recalled.

"May I have a sheet of your writing paper and an envelope Captain?" Robert complied without a word as the other man continued. "Please be good enough to hand this to Miss Stoddart with my regrets to the Dunbars, Thank you." and they were off leaving a stunned Robert wondering if he had not just had a very strange disturbing nightmare. The cots had scarcely been disturbed proving that those two were no strangers to life on the move so all he had to show here was the letter in his hand. He gazed down at it and then his glance moved to the stove. The dying embers could be stirred up and the letter swallowed by the flames and who would be the wiser.

"I would be," He said aloud to the empty room, "and I couldn't face my father if I did such a thing. It was tempting though."

Forever after Robert was glad he had resisted the temptation to destroy the letter. Hannah's face as first she read it to herself then at her exclamation of joy as she handed it to mistress Dunbar he had a moment of doubt but when that lady began to read it aloud his doubts cleared.

"Dear Miss Hannah" she read "If you are Hannah Stoddart from Govan Hill, as I believe you are, then I have a message for you from your brother Lachlan. Too short of time here for all the details of how I met him. Suffice to say he, Lachie, followed your movements to the home of Sir Frederick Crawford but no one there could direct him further and he had to return to his ship as the war was already underway. I enclose an address where letters can be held for him. Sorry I could not speak with you but I trust this news brings you some comfort. Yours Truly and in haste. Tony Avery M.O. 2ND. CAMERONIANS. S.I.F." Having no tears left as she clutched the letter to her chest. Robert spoke first.

"Should you want to write to the address the doctor gave you I will be pleased to post it for you along with my own to my family. It will go in the dispatches no later than tomorrow night." Hannah's smile was brilliant with the unshed tears and his heart skipped a beat.

"You are kind and I will do it at once if—" She glanced at Mistress Dunbar who smiled her assent. So the two life-changing letters began their journey inside the same dispatch pouch.

* * * * *

Reading aloud some excerpts from Robert's letter Sophia stopped with a gasp of amazement. Lizzie glanced up from her scrap book.

"Dinna stop Mammy, read me some mair." Shaking her head Sophia slipped the letter into the pocket of her apron.

"Not just now Lizzie, it's time to peel the tatties for Daddy's dinner." She pulled the rough sack apron she wore on scrubbing days from its hook behind the scullery door. Lizzie gaped. They had done the scrubbing yesterday. But Sophia relentlessly began to fill the tubs with water from the boiler, the words written by her first born son seared across her mind.

"Dear Mother: This letter is going to be so different from any letter you ever received from me. No, they have not made me a field-marshall yet, and I've not dug up any gold mines in the mud and glaur here, although it would be //////[censored] in this place and no, I'm not being drummed out of the army. What I have to tell you is better, much better than any of that. Today, Mam, I MET THE GIRL I'M GOING TO MARRY, THAT'S RIGHT! In fact if I can get her to say yes when I ask her tonight then I'll be bringing her home when I get my next leave."

Sophia had glanced at the wag-at-the-wa' clock and then the calendar, before noting the date on the letter. He had written it four weeks ago. Despite censorship the family knew that Robert was somewhere in France, but this sounded like he had been on a short leave. It must have taken place in France, and oh my could her laddie be tangled up with a foreign lassie? The envelope was post-marked in Hamilton, but that could just mean somebody posted it there for him. Quickly she pulled the letter from her pocket to read the other page again.

"Sorry Mam, I had to leave the writing for a wee while, I can't explain except that I managed to wangle some leave now and I'll be arriving home one day very soon, bringing my surprise. Love to everyone until I see you. God bless. . .Your son. . .Robert. PS: Don't say anything to the family then it will be a surprise." Sophia almost collapsed on to the chair as the last few words sank in. Lizzie, sensing something very strange, began to moan pitifully.

"Be quiet Lizzie, have ye finished the tatties?" Lizzie sniffed but her answer came clearly.

"Aye Mammy, will I put them on?" Soon the pot was boiling merrily on the stove, but still Sophia sat on, the scrubbing forgotten. To see her there, not knitting or sewing, or doing anything for that matter, was more than Lizzie could understand. She sat opposite Sophia tying and untying her hanky after being ordered once more to be quiet. She sniffed again and this time Sophia gave her a faint smile.

"Och you, the family will be hame for dinner in a wee while. Dinna you tell them about Robert's letter, he wants it to be a surprise." Lizzie brightened, she loved surprises. Her mother talked on. "I'll just put the letter inside my best teapot, we'll no' be using it 'til—" She removed it from her pocket again, gazing in some surprise at the sacking apron, then shrugging she walked toward the front room to find the teapot, but at that very moment a knock sounded on the outside door.

"Tut, tut! Who can that be at this time on a Wednesday mornin'?" The usual tradesmen had made their regular calls long since. Once more the letter went into her pocket as she went all unsuspecting and unguarded to open the door, her mind on Robert's intriguing news, that still hadn't really told her anything. Jack Sweeney, Eastkirk's station master, stood on her doorstep. A different Jack from his usual jovial self, and the next hour was to etch itself on her memory for all time.

"I'm that sorry to have to tell you this Mistress Lambert, but there's been an accident on the line!"

"Is it my man? Is Robert hurtit?" The questions fell over each other as her heart began to hammer alarmingly and her mind tried to deny the answer she knew must come.

"He wouldna' have felt a thing Mistress. Instantaneous death Dr. MacDuff says. Hit from the back as he walked the line."

"But Robert kent every train time. My man would never walk on the line if a train was due." The bearer of ill tidings still stood on the step rubbing nervous fingers along the inside of his uniform cap.

"This was a munitions train, top secret, not a usual run!"

"Somebody should've telt my Robert!" Agreeing silently that indeed someone should have, but as station master, Jack Sweenie must be loyal to his job and his country. Besides,

although all the linesmen did it, it was against the regulations
for them to walk inside the rails. Jack went on to relate the
facts to the newly widowed woman. She was still in a daze but
he had to get this over. Lambert, while walking the line as he
did every day at that time, checking each point, had been
blissfully unaware of the chariot of death as it hurtled toward
him on the same track. The driver of the other train, the regular
express coming down the opposite track, saw the lone man
striding along the sleepers. He began to wave frantically, but
Robert, who knew every driver and had shared many a can of
tea with this one, returned the wave in his usual friendly manner.
The noise of each engine drowned out the other and seconds
later, as both trains ground to a halt, Robert Lambert was no
more. Mercifully he never knew what hit him and he left this
world as he had lived it with a wave and a smile.

A great rush of pain swept through Sophia before the world
blotted out and she sank to the floor. Only moments had elapsed
and Lizzie had not moved although she knew something
dreadful was happening. She began to sob into her hanky and
her garbled words reached the ears of the kindly man even as
he lifted her mother's inert form on to the sofa. He understood
only the name.

"Maggie, Maggie, I want Maggie!" Before long Sophia
roused and her deeply engrained inner strength began to
surface. She sat up and, seeing the unhappy look on the man's
face she gave him a faint smile as she said.

"Thank ye Mr. Sweeney, we'll be right enough now. The
rest of the family will be in for their dinner, Maggie from the
school and Willie from the station." Sweeney left gladly, his
awful duty done, somebody else would have to tell Willie and
Maggie Lambert the terrible news.

They called Maggie to the headmaster's office. Her thoughts
before the message reached her had not been about her father
walking the line, nor any other member of her family. In fact
she had been wondering how she could take back her hasty

refusal to join the new teacher at the dinner break. Surely she could have sent one of the bairns to tell her mother she would be eating at the school today. It would not be the first time. Actually Grant MacAuley had asked her to go to the pictures and that too had received a curt refusal. Maggie had always been taught never to judge folk by outward appearances, and always to give the benefit of the doubt, so just because the school gossips said the newest elementary teacher was a conchie didn't mean she had to believe he was. They knew nothing about him and what if folk, who didn't know her brother Willie, thought of him that way when the truth was he didn't pass the medical because of his deafness in one ear. On her way along the corridor she berated herself silently.

"When, oh when, will I ever stop being so high and mighty, especially with men, and more especially when I like them?" Putting it behind her for the present she tried to concentrate on why Mr. McLean wanted to speak to her privately. The janitor who brought the message to her class had been noncommittal. Could something be wrong at home? Could it be Robert? The headmaster bade her enter, his voice and manner most solemn. He indicated a chair and she sank into it gladly as her knees gave way under her.

Eastkirk did indeed turn out in full force to bid a last farewell to Robert Lambert, even if Nellie Trent the postmistress had a few choice words to whisper to her friend Nessie who ran the fruit and flower stall in the market.

"Fancy, an' him just a ganger on the railway. A team o' high steppin' Clydesdales wi' all the trimmin's, if ye please." Her friend agreed adding that although Sophia Lambert was stuck up, Robert had not been like that, in fact he had always had a good word for everybody. The small sensation about the funeral entourage faded to nothing as the gossips espied the stranger. On the front pew in the kirk, between Robert Junior and Maggie, there sat a bonnie young woman, just a lassie really but clinging to the soldier tightly with clenched fingers, the third finger of the left hand sporting a solid gold band. The guessing game continued until the mourners returned from the cemetery to partake of Sophia's sumptuous funeral high tea and Robert stood up to announce.

"Ladies and gentlemen, I would like you to meet Hannah, my wife of exactly one week today!"

* * * * *

Spring, 1918

"THE PORTRAIT"

"Watch the birdie now, and sit still if you please!" Lizzie could not very well do both so she turned to look for the birdie. The wee man muttered a curse into his velvet camera cover. "All right, let's try again." Sophie fidgeted, she thoroughly regretted giving in to Robert's pleading this morning, but as usual, he had a way of coaxing her into anything. Especially today, the last day of his leave. At breakfast time, when she tried again to get out of coming by saying she had too much to do, he had caught her arm and swinging her round, shouted:

"Come on Mother, leave off the mournin' clothes! Where's yon nice brown frock you had before. . . The war'll be over soon and this might be your last chance to be in a picture with your dashing officer son!" That settled it and here they were. She wondered again if the wee man would take much longer.

"Right you are then, that should do it. Expect the photos in the post in about a fortnight." Then as they trooped down the narrow stairs to Sauchiehall Street, Maggie and Willie found themselves leading the way with Sophia and Lizzie close behind them. The married lovers came last, Hannah clutching tightly to Robert's arm as if she would never let go, Robert preoccupied with the memory of those words to his Mother.

"Why did I make that idiotic remark to her. This might be our last chance to get a picture together? What melodrama! I could kick myself."

"Aye, why did you Robert? At first I thought you meant Willie's plans about going to Canada but now I'm not so sure." The strange feeling, when he had said the words this morning, came over her again and she shivered, the possibility of him not coming home from the front was all too real. The war raged on, rumours that it would be over by Christmas long ago silenced. Last night when she had tried to talk seriously to him, suggesting that he pray to God as she had learned to do through her dear friends the Dunbars, he had laughed. But waking up later she surprised him reading from her Bible, a tiny bit of candle his only light. Reluctant to disturb him she quickly closed her eyes again but he noticed. Seconds later he cuddled up to her in the bed whispering in her ear: "Hannah, Oh Hannah!"

"Hannah!" She jumped and he laughed quietly as the tell-tale crimson stained her cheeks. He knew very well where her thoughts had been.

"Never stop blushing my love! It suits you." Robert teased as he helped her up into the back seat of the roadster. Maggie could drive today, he had better things to do. "Drive on MacDuff, to Ferguson's for mince and tatties and a' the trimmin's, Eh what Mater?" He liked to mix his Lallans with the refined talk from the officer's club and Sophia enjoyed it fine.

Willie Lambert also noticed Hannah's blushes. From the first moment of stunned silence following their father's funeral, as his brother calmly introduced Hannah as his bride, Willie had recognized her as one of those very special women who could be everything any man ever wanted in a wife. After the shock of first recognition, Willie released the thought. She belonged to Robert and there the matter ended. If he suffered in silence when she innocently smiled at him no one else noticed. Without rancor or bitterness Willie conceded the fact that his brother always came up with the best prizes, at school or in sports, and when the war began and he went straight into Officer's training instead of University, it surprised no one. Following his father's fatal accident Willie had scarcely mentioned his plan to go to Canada after the

war, but this morning he had brought the subject up again knowing as soon as Robert was discharged and came home for good. . .
No one else need be any wiser regarding his own deep reasons for
getting away, except Maggie, who always saw through him and
could read his mind like a book.

Concentrating on driving from the photographer's studio, and
down crowded Renfrew Street to Ferguson's, Maggie fervently
hoped they could find a place to leave the motor. Ferguson's loomed,
and as Robert had said he would pay for the tea, she decided to
splurge the ten shillings for a driver to park the car. Might as well
do things in style for today! As they trooped in to the restaurant
by tacit consent, Robert took charge. The handsome Army Officer
had no difficulty acquiring a table for six and Maggie's thoughts
continued their disturbing pattern. Tomorrow Robert would be
on his way back to that "unknown destination" somewhere at the
battle front, while those left at home would settle down as well as
they could to the daily activities of a Scottish suburban household
in wartime. Maggie's job as school teacher to a class of snott-nosed
first year pupils kept her thoroughly occupied during the day, and
she deliberately busied herself with volunteer war work at nights.
She stifled a yawn. Since Robert came home on leave this time,
she'd hardly slept at all.

"Tonight I'll not have to listen to them through the wall so I
should get some sleep. I hope by the time the war is over they'll
have their own house. I'll not need to hear their whispers and
laughter even once more." Chiding herself inwardly for such un-
worthy thoughts she sighed as the ancient waiter came for their
order. She liked Hannah just fine and could not account for this
feeling of heaviness. Maybe Willie's talk of Canada had caused her
depression, because if he did go, who else but Maggie would be
left to care for their mother and Lizzie.

Lizzie's excitement mounted. After all that waiting and fuss
with pictures at last they were to have their tea. She could keep
still and quiet no longer!

"Maggie, don't forget you promised me a bag of sweeties if I was good. I was good wasn't I Mammy?" Sophia, with her eyes glued to Robert nodded absently. "See, there I told ye Maggie, I want the tablet kind we got last time we came here. Wasn't it funny Willie, watchin' that wee man takin' our photo? But I got so fed up. Still, if he hadna' been so crabbit I would have liked it fine." Willie toyed with the cutlery on the snow white cloth as he answered his sister.

"Aye Lizzie. What makes you think he was crabbit?"

"He swore at me and I only wanted to sit beside Mammy but he made me stan' behind Robert!" Catching a glimpse of Maggie's face, and remembering the sweeties, Lizzie stopped talking. Maggie might still get upset and change her mind. She had asked in the photo place to go to the bathroom, and Maggie had pinched her, then the funny wee man had said a swear word, but now here she had to go again and she could not help it , sweeties or no, she had to ask. Looking across the table to her soldier brother she broke the silence with the correct saying she had learned during her brief school days.

"Please Sir, may I leave the room?" Stunned looks passed round the table before Robert exploded. His great laugh filled Fergusons. One by one the others joined in. Red faced Sophia, trying hard to keep from laughing herself, dragged poor Lizzie to the ladies room. Her laughter turned hollow and changed to tears when the inno-cent Lizzie, knowing nothing of all the undercurrents of thought asked. "Mammy, why are ye greetin'? Is it because Robert is a soldier and goes away so much? We could all be so happy at home if only he wouldn't go away. . .and this mornin', when I asked Willie if Canada was further than Edinburgh, he laughed like that as well. Anyway he said he would send me a lot of postcards even one of the big ship he's goin' on. Mammy, is a ship bigger than yon steamers we saw at Dunoon?" Sophia gave her a little shake.

"Lizzie, stop yer bletherin', och I'm sorry. . .when we finish our tea I'll buy ye a book of ship pictures as well as yer sweeties. But, wheest the now, no more talkin', I mean it." Mammy had her

Queen Victoria look on and Lizzie knew too well when to be quiet. A new picture book would be nice. Maybe she could ask for some scraps too. Later on as Sophia settled herself, indeed regally, in her place beside the driver for the journey home, Lizzie recalled every detail of her great day in Glasgow town, for after they finished eating their tea Robert had said:

"We'll all just go to the pictures, we've plenty of time 'til my train goes!" The Charlie Chaplin picture had been funny but the news wasn't. Lizzie didn't like the news, and Mammy had started to greet again. . . Then, at the Central Station, she had got to watch the trains until Robert went on one of them. For a minute they all thought Hannah wasn't going to leave go his arm, but when the guard blew his whistle she had to. What a funny day, even Maggie was near greeting, but Lizzie would not think any more sad things for here they were at home safe and sound and she had her sweeties, her new picture book about ships, and a whole packet of scraps, maybe the morrow Hannah would help her sort them. Lizzie liked Hannah, she never told her to wheest when she blethered a lot. In fact she would ask Lizzie to talk about their Robert. After dinner when Maggie and Willie went back to work, and Mammy was having a wee sleep in front of the fire, Lizzie and Hannah would sort the scraps or Hannah might tell her a story but mostly Hannah would just listen while Lizzie talked about Robert.

The motor stopped then and a quiet and subdued Lambert family followed Sophia through the front door.

* * * * *

Hannah stared blankly at the envelope in her hand. Surely it must be for Mother Lambert! They often mixed up their letters, with Robert and his father having the same name and all.

"Oh God! Even if it's meant for her the message is the same for both of us." How can a single bit of paper, bearing a few wee black

marks on it, have such power? Still in a daze she walked slowly
back to the table where the family sat awaiting breakfast.

"It isn't true, it can't be true! Will somebody tell me I'm in the
middle of a nightmare again." Knowing it must be true though
her voice rose to a near scream. "Oh help me. Please dear God,
help me!"

"What is it Hannah?" Sophia spoke sharply, fear tightening
her throat. At the tone Willie laid aside the 'Daily Express" and
Maggie stopped buttering the toast, the knife held aloft as she too
waited. Even Lizzie, dreaming as she played with her porage, knew
something bad was happening. Seeing the yellow telegram clutched
tightly in Hannah's hand, Willie cursed himself silently for not
answering the door a few minutes ago, but Hannah, thinking there
might be a letter from Robert, always beat him to the door anyway. Maggie knew instantly! Of course a telegram could mean
other things than sudden death but Hannah's stricken look told
the story plainer than words. No tears came but an anguish, far
deeper than tears flowed out of the dry sockets as she handed the
piece of paper to his mother. Sophia read, uttered one strangled
cry before giving it to Willie. He passed it to Maggie without so
much as a glance. The whole drama lasted no more than five minutes and yet eternity's time pattern was closing another era for the
Lamberts, including Hannah the latest member. This breakfast
scene would be set forever in their minds, vivid in each detail, and
Lizzie, ever sensitive to the intensity of the suffering, wept softly as
the 'wag-at-the-wall' clock ticked on.

"It didn't even stop for a second!" Hannah thought irrelevantly.
Walking over to it she began to move the pendulum back and
forth in the familiar winding-up motion. "This wall could do with
new wall paper!" The thought, equally irrelevant made her realize
how her subconscious mind was frantically trying to protect her
from the raw scalding pain waiting in the wings to engulf. At last
Maggie voiced her thoughts.

"I'll never hear him and you through the wall again!. . . and
what'll I do with that pullover I was knitting for him, it's too big

for Willie?" The others, engrossed in their own sorrow, ignored her. Willie, terribly aware of his heart throbbing and of the life blood pulsing through his body, spoke quietly.

"Robert, my brother is gone? How can he be dead? He's my brother and I don't even know where he is. What can I do?" He looked down at the paper lying in front of his untouched plate of toast.

"MISSING, PRESUMED KILLED." "They can't tell us either!"

Sophia still sat as if moulded into the large winged chair that had been her husbands. Robert got to sit in it when he came home on leave but nobody else ever did.

"He'll not be sitting on it again!" She too spoke her thoughts in a soft whisper. . . "What does that mean, 'missing, presumed killed'? Missing could mean he was just a prisoner of war?" They all heard and understood the last remark. His mother, along with them, sought escape from the dreaded reality of the telegram. Knowing, as she did from losing her other beloved Robert, that time would do its healing work, nevertheless the knowledge gave small comfort at this very minute. The merciful numbness ebbed away as she found herself living again that terrible Friday.

Her recollection took scarcely a minute and Sophia felt another rush of pain as the memory of that time mingled with the raw hurt of now. Her other children still sat round the table and Hannah walked about in a daze winding the clock and what not. Maggie had a faraway stare too, and Sophia guessed she also thought of that other time. Her father's death had been hard for Maggie.

On that other terrible morning, Maggie recalled her thoughts just before confronting the headmaster of Eastkirk School. "Could it be about Robert at the front?" It was not Robert then but it was Robert now. Coming back to this day she could hear Hannah's soft whisper. The words sounded incredible.

"Thank you, Heavenly Father, I'll be all right now!"

"The shock's been too much for her." Maggie thought. Rising from the table she walked over to stand behind her sister-in-law and with one of her rare gestures of affection put her hand on

Hannah's shoulder. Hannah reached up to cover the hand with her own and immediately the hot scalding tears, awaiting release, overflowed down her cheeks. They were healing tears and although the pain gripping her throat was no less real, she realised she could bear it after all.

"Mother Lambert, and the rest of you too, I've been waiting to tell you. I'm expecting! Your first grandchild should arrive early in the new year God willing!" For the second time within the hour every eye focused on Hannah as she finished her announcement. Different expressions flitted across each face, but Lizzie voiced her own thought, as only Lizzie could.

"If Robert isna' comin' home, who'll be its Daddy?"

* * * * *

"Who'll be its Daddy indeed?" Hannah gazed entranced at the fuzzy black head resting on her arm. Her two hour old son, her's and Robert's, lay there. Now she had him to herself she'd better examine him thoroughly. His protectors, Mrs. Williams the mid-wife, and Mother Lambert the proud new Granny, might come back any minute from enjoying a cup of tea in the kitchen.

"My goodness, Mrs. Williams talks a lot!" Hannah thought, "But she knows her business inside out." Smiling as she recognized the mild pun. Robert would like it. The smile quickly dimmed as memory returned. Funny how she still tried to share her waking thought with him. An amputee must feel like this as he tries to us a hand or leg no longer there. On the day of the 'telegram', mere seconds after its arrival she had heard his whisper in her ear. She could tell no one else about this but it still brought her a trifle of comfort.

"It's all right Hannie, my wee darlin'!" Not understanding she had responded nevertheless with a prayer of thanks and from that time on she knew that everything would be all right even if she knew nothing else. She also knew some of the family members considered her a bit 'off!' even hard hearted. Hannah felt sorry about that but it didn't matter really. Nothing mattered at the moment but this precious child. Sophia's pleasure in the coming infant, and her unhidden delight now that he was here safely, could forgive Hannah anything, even being 'religious'.

"Am I religious? I don't think so. Not in the sense of being sanctimonious and preachy I hope." Her father had been a religious hypocrite, and Sheila at the mansion house had been a zealot, if a genuine one. Hannah squirmed inwardly at the thought of both these people. Her father because she had openly scorned him, not even trying to understand his terrible frustrations and Sheila, who had shared the true gospel as Hannah knew now, but she would not listen then. By the time she met Jenni and Hector Dunbar, her dear Salvation Army captains and having learned about unconditional love from some of the sisters at the convent, she had softened considerably. In fact her hard heart had melted completely one day when she had been overwhelmed by Jenni Dunbar's way of talking to a young soldier who had been crying for his mother. She had watched fascinated as the compassionate woman had cuddled the boy, for that was all he was, and soothed him until his rending sobs had ceased. Hector had joined them and led the boy away. The two woman had sat in silence for quite a while before Hannah said.

"Tell me what it is that makes you like that Captain Jenni?" Without pretence the older woman had shared her secret. There and then Hannah had responded with: "I want that too!" There followed a most joyful celebration when Hector had rejoined them.

Aware that her thoughts were rambling Hannah brought them to the present joyful occasion and she felt again that deep sense of inner peace, the same inner peace which had brought her through the months of waiting, and which stemmed from more than a fleeting sensation. This new wisdom allowed her to ponder all these things in her heart and even the celebrations for the Armistice Day last November had failed to upset her new tranquility, as well meaning but tactless friends and neighbours had bombarded her with.

"If only Robert had been spared a wee while longer!" or "It's awful nice for Mrs. Lambert you're expectin'!"

Sophia materialized at the foot of the bed again gazing fondly at mother and child.

"Mrs. Williams says I can hold wee Robert for a minute!" Hannah bit her lip to keep from crying out. This would tax her new tranquility.

"Mother Lambert, I thought we agreed on John, Robert's his middle name?"

"Oh Aye, I just forgot." Not emotional and never apologetic, the new granny struggled to hide her pleasure as she slipped expert hands under the baby , taking him from Hannah.

"What a braw lad! Just like his daddy". Seating herself on the rocker she prepared for a long session of adoring. At the movement the baby woke up with an indignant yell. "I love the sound of a new bairn greetin'!"

"This is getting downright ridiculous, if not fatuous." Thought Hannah but her tone was gentle as she replied.

"I hope you'll still say that a month from now Gran'ma!" The nurse had heard the cry and bustled in importantly.

"Time's up Granny! Come on now, they've both to rest. That was quite a struggle we all had through the night". Reluctantly Sophia handed her treasure over to the midwife. Placing him expertly in his new cradle, prepared and waiting, Mrs. Williams admired for a minute, before the baby yawned and closed his eyes, instantly asleep. She turned to Hannah.

"Now Mother, try to sleep for a wee while yourself." Being addressed as mother for the first time in her life startled Hannah and she glanced quickly at Sophia with such an expression of shock, then as the full impact of the title struck all three women at once, they exploded with laughter.

Willie heard the laughter as he opened the back door. At first he thought he must be imagining the glad sound but no, it was real enough. Blethering Mrs. Williams he could believe and Hannah too, but his mother! Could she really be laughing so hearty. Not sure whether to join them or call the doctor back he tiptoed further into the big front room. The merriment abated and the two older women moved on to discuss the very important fact that the new arrival weighed more than any of Sophia's own at birth while Mrs. Williams openly admired the piles of lacy knits and delicately hand-sewn garments adorning the dining room table. Slipping out again without being noticed, Willie left the women to their gloating.

At the station this morning Willie had completely forgotten about old Sonny Logan's habit of relating all happenings, good or otherwise, to the 'Laird' as he called God. Upon hearing the news of the baby's arrival, the old man had greeted it with.

"Och Aye, I trust yer thanking the Laird for him. He's the gi'er o' all life ye ken?" Still full of the news Willie said.

"Thank Hannah and Robert you mean Sanny. When yon man from the army brought our Robert's clothes and his medals, along with bits of personal things I gave up believing in a God who cares about us mortals. How could a God, supposed to be kind and good, take away two such perfect specimens as my father and my brother and leave the likes of me to carry the brunt of a family? The older man stared at Willie blankly.

"But ye all attend the Kirk every Sunday do ye not?

"We do that, but it's just to please my Mother and Hannah, Robert's widow. They have some kind of faith."

"Ye're a hypocrite then!"

"Call me what you like Sanny but at least I'm not telling lies now." Fair minded Sanny reached a hand out to Willie.

"Ye've been badly hurtit' man, I ken how hard it is, but believe me, there'll come a day when ye'll thank the Laird God yersel' for yer mother and a' her bairns, and yer good wife, for when ye win her, she'll lead ye to the light, Jesus Hissel' is the light. Blessin's on the new life." With those words of unintended prophecy Sanny had resumed to his job of sweeping up the station platform.

Wondering if his mother intended to admire baby clothes all the rest of the day, or if she could be persuaded to cook him a meal, Willie slowly made his way back to the house. The last few months of cozy family times, preparing for the new life, had been good. While the women clicked and stitched with their needles he had hammered and sawed and sand-papered and carved. The cradle how holding wee John was his handiwork. No more mention had been made of Canada but Willie thought of it often and his talk with Sanny today had brought it to mind again. Last Sunday the minister had described the promised land and the sermon upset Willie. Didn't Moses have to wait and work forty years and then still not get into it himself? If God could do something like that to a man who believed like Moses it just confirmed his own ideas. God must be a tyrant who played with tiny humans as if they were pawns in a monstrous chess game. Shaking his head to clear it of all this foolishness Willie called.

"Where's the cook about here? I'm hungry!" Sophia reluctantly dragged herself away from the interesting discussion about her grandson and got busy with the frying pan. She had some important questions for Willie.

"Were the trains busy the day Willie?"

"Yes, this being Saturday, half the town seemed to be off to Glasgow this morning."

"Did you mention to anybody aboot the bairn?"

"Och aye, I just told Mrs. Driscoll when she asked me." Sophia nodded her satisfaction. If Mrs. Driscoll knew the whole town would hear soon.

"Who else did you tell?"

"Just old Sanny and Jimmy the Dray. Sanny gave me a sermon and Jimmy thought we should go to the King's Arms for a pint to celebrate." Sophia searched his face. Sometimes she couldn't be sure if her staid dependable Willie was teasing her or not. Deciding he must be she placed his favourite Saturday dinner-time treat, a giant plate of sizzling ham and eggs, in front of him. Pleased enough with his answers. Between Mrs. Driscoll and her sister Mrs. Williams, the Kirk folk would soon find out and Jimmy the Dray could be trusted to inform the rest of the town. She sat down to drink a cup of tea with Willie who pulled his chair closer to his mother's. Here was the perfect chance to talk about Canada and to tell her part of his newest plan.

Meanwhile Eastkirk was finding out about the new arrival, and not only from Mrs. Driscoll and Jimmy. Lizzie Lambert had been dispatched by the midwife to go to the chemist's shop for a few needed items. Maggie, in one of her rare moments of visible generosity, and partly to escape the house, cranked up the motor and they set off together in style. Lizzie couldn't wait until they stopped. She called out regular bulletins from the car window to her many friends. Tom McWhirter the town tramp, who much to Maggie's chagrin was standing talking to none other than Grant MacAuley, were among the first to hear the news.

"We've got a bairn at our house! His name is John and I'm his Auntie and so is Maggie and our Hannah is his Mammy and my Mammy is his Granny and Willie is his Uncle!" Long before the great event itself, Lizzie had learned her relationships well. In the chemist shop they met up with Mrs. Driscoll who had already spread the news, but that good lady had some more news for Maggie, and she repeated it with a certain amount of malicious glee.

"Aye Maggie, I suppose ye heard at the school about the engagement. Grant MacAuley and wee Aggie Henderson! The waddin's to be next June I hear!"

* * * * *

Torrential rain drummed on the roof of the attic in Parkhall Street as the heavy clouds, threatening Eastkirk for days, finally burst on the town on this late September afternoon. Sophia Lambert, deep in the throes of deciding what she would take to Canada and what would go to McMillan's Auction Mart, sat back on her heels to survey the havoc she had just created in her tidy attic. Although they would not 'embark', that was Hannah's fancy word for the sailing, until next Spring she did not believe in leaving things to the last minute.

"I must be soft in the head traipsin' halfway across the world at my age, as for Maggie, I wonder what transpired to make her so keen on goin' to this place, Saskatchy. . .well anyway!" She picked up the box of family pictures once again. The 'Portrait', which she had tucked away at the bottom of the box, now lay on top. Glancing at the calendar on the attic wall Sophia noted that it was exactly a year ago today since they received the telegram about Robert, and The familiar shock of pain stabbed her as she gazed down at Robert. Only a year ago, and so much had happened since. For one thing that terrible war was over, thank God! and Sophia had watched the soldiers with mixed feelings as they gradually integrated themselves back into the everyday life of the town. If she looked askance at some of them as they lounged about the street corners or staggered out of the taverns in the middle of the afternoon, she could be excused for wondering why they should be spared and Robert taken. Then the great day of January twenty-fifth, Rabbie Burns day at that, when wee Robert was born. She would always think of the bairn as "Wee Robert" although she did not say it out loud any more. That was the one thing that got Hannah all riled up so Sophia, along with the others in the family, always called him John. My, he was a clever wee laddie though, whatever name you called him. Why he could walk round the furniture already, any day now and he would be talking, and all before his birthday.

"Will you come down for your tea, Mammy?" Lizzie's voice broke Sophia's reverie and she turned to see her youngest gazing at the portrait still clutched tightly in her hand. "Oh, I mind the day we got that photy took!" Lizzie cried excitedly, "Robert was so handsome and he bought me some extra tablet to eat in the pictures."

"Considerin' how quick ye are to forget a message and ye can remember things about sweeties that many months later is beyond me Lizzie. 'Tis no wonder I get cross with ye at times!" Lizzie fixed her big puzzled eyes on her mother, but she said no more. When the immigration authorities had made a fuss about Lizzie's medical report, Sophia had raged at them. "Mentally retarded indeed!" Lizzie might be a bit slow and glaikit, saying daft things at times, but she was a long road from an idiot. When Sophia finished her raging the papers had been promptly stamped. Lizzie still held the portrait and the ever ready tears coursed down her face. The mother relented.

"What's for tea Lizzie?"

"Hannah and Maggie went for fish and chips, and I masked the tea and Willie set the table and the tea will be cauld if we don't hurry." As they made their way carefully down the steps Sophia glanced at the wag-at-the-wall. She had been upstairs for three hours without getting anything done. The sight now of her family seated cozily round the table, a nice fire in the grate, and the good smell of the food as the younger women filled the plates from the newspaper wrapped bundle, suddenly overwhelmed her and she almost choked. All eyes turned to her as she took her place at the head of the table. Different degrees of surprise and concern showed on each face but Sophia smiled.

"These old boxes are that dusty, I must have a tickle in my throat." She offered by way of explanation for her temporary lapse.

"What's that in your hand Lizzie?" Maggie drew in her breath sharply as she recognized the portrait even as she asked the question.

"It's thon photy we had took the last time we were, Robert was. . .Do you mind that nice tea at Fergusons after and Robert bought us some tablet an' we all went to the pictures?" Fortunately Lizzie did not expect an answer and none of the others in the room tried to give her one. Hannah, who had wakened very early in the morning to her own stab of memories on this day that was the anniversary of the telegram, turned white. Willie who had been wondering abstractly if they would have fish and chip shops in Canada, glanced up as he heard Maggie's gasp. Catching sight of the picture in Lizzie's hand he too paled slightly. but he recovered quickly to say.

"Give it to me Lizzie." Speaking quietly but firmly Willie went on, "I have a nice bit of plywood, just the right size for a frame for this, I'll get started on it tomorrow and then we'll put it in the trunk to take with us when we go." The women said nothing to this although Maggie raised her eyebrows slightly. This was a long speech for Willie, he must be up to something. She would find out soon enough.

For weeks now Willie had been building himself up for just the right moment. . .This was it. Tonight he would ask Hannah to marry him!

"What did you say?" Hannah could have bitten out her tongue immediately she said the words, but it was too late. With his face the colour of beetroot, Willie stumbled over the question as he repeated it.

"Will you marry me Hannah? I would be good to you and the bairn; we could all stay together as a family, if that's what you would like, and I've always thought you to be a right smart women." For the second time that evening Willie Lambert made what for him was a lengthy speech. But of course Maggie could not hear so she could not make sarcastic remarks about him becoming a regular chatterbox. The rest of the family had retired, leaving the coast clear for Willie's plan. Hannah's first response, 'Oh no! I could never do that!' faltered on her lips and second thoughts came swiftly: 'Why not!' It would solve some problems, and would actually be a very sensible move to make. He had not said he loved her, and that was a relief, as no one could ever replace Robert in her heart, but there was something about Willie that appealed to Hannah. They seemed to agree about most things and after all, a year had passed since she received the official notice of Robert's death. Hannah forced herself to stop all this justification to just say it.

"Yes Willie, I'll marry you!" Delight flooded his face, mingled with shocked surprise, and could that be a bit of fear as well? It was his turn to ask for a repeat.

"What did you say Hannah?"

"Oh no, please don't ask me to say it again!" She groaned inwardly.

"I said yes, I will marry you Willie, but first I want to tell you some things about myself and if you still want me, then..please listen, and don't interrupt!" This last as Willie, overwhelmed by her answer, began to protest. "I won't even let you kiss me until I tell you." Shyly Willie withdrew his arm from round her waist, then deciding to risk it, he grasped her hand. After all she had said yes. "I was born in the worst of Glasgow's slums, actual date, New Year's Day 1900. Yes, you may as well get comfortable as this could take a while, consider it a real life story, only straight out of one of Mr. Dickens novels." Hannah tried to hide a shudder as she began the story of their early struggle, holding nothing back about her fathers drunkenness, her mother's attempts to teach her children, Lachie's disappearance or the events leading to Ellie's death.

"I was fourteen years old by that time. Some of it is not too clear but I remember the nuns took me in to the orphanage. They were the Sisters of the New Covenant and they treated me well enough. When you hear how some orphans are treated I was well off. Many a good slap I received for disobedience, usually deserved Willie! Oh yes, there's a lot about me you don't know." Willie made another sound of protest but she held up a hand to stop him.

"I ASKED YOU NOT TO INTERRUPT WILLIE AND I *was* stubborn. I still am so be warned, but I am getting better with the Lord's help. When I ran away from Craigiehaugh mansion, I made a solemn pledge to myself. I resolved never to be poor again. The first chance to get on in this world to come my way, I would take it. One of the sisters discovered this in me and she openly accused me of the sin of pride. As a penance for this they took me out of the classroom and put me to work as a scullery maid. This only made me more thrawn and things got even worse for a while, but I was determined not to give in. Even when they told me I was in mortal sin and must repent I still would not confess. Threats of burning in the everlasting lake of fire terrified me but not enough. Until the particular night I will never forget. It was during Lent and we were in the chapel for 'Stations of the Cross'. We went round them on our knees, I can still feel the pain where my knees were all skinned and sore with the unaccustomed scrubbing. Anyway when I reached the picture of Jesus being crowned with thorns I stayed in front of it for a long time. What a heart wrenching picture it is. Jesus' brow had these great drops of blood oozing out of the holes made by thorns as thick as pencils. Everyone else had gone away but I couldn't leave. I cried my heart out as I knelt there and the thorns seemed to pierce into me and not the face in the picture. I heard a noise behind and then the voice of the priest spoke to me. He was making the rounds of the chapel for the night. I remember how nice his voice sounded. 'Well now and what have we here?' when I did not answer he went on: "A pint sized penitent with all the mortal sins of the world on her shoulders?"

"I'm fourteen!" I sobbed, forced to answer the insult even in my distress.

"I beg your pardon, fourteen year old shoulders. Do you want to tell me about it?" He wiped my tear stained face with a big red hanky telling me to give a good blow. After hiccupping a few times I managed to speak:

"When they put they things on his head, would it not be awful sore?"

"Yes, my child, awful sore, but He tholed it for our sakes!" Before he could say more I started again.

"I was so proud and wantin' to be rich and marry a toff so I could be better than everybody else and not have to obey the sisters and scrub floors and—" I sobbed it all out while the good priest lifted me up from my knees and told me I was forgiven. I'll not forget the relief when he took me to the last picture, the "Ascension", where he explained how everything turns out all right. After that he gave me a wee medal on a string and he was putting it round my neck when I remember the dormitory sister walked in looking for me and I did not get to talk to Father Scanlon again. The next day they put me in training for the Academy. I won a bursary and was put through to Secretarial School. I never knew for certain but I still think Father Scanlon managed that change. At the Academy and later on at the Secretarial School, I forgot all about Father Scanlon. When I left school with top marks and my old ambition to be rich came back, maybe not as strong and determined but still there. When I was sent to work for the Dunbars, Robert and I have told you quite a bit about Captain and Mistress Dunbar and how they told me to call them Captain Hector and Captain Jenni. Anyway that was a good job as a clerk in their office until the time when they volunteered to go closer to the war front with the canteen for the men as they came and went to the trenches. You know about the whirlwind courtship with your brother of course." Her eyes began to glaze over at the mention of Robert and Willie moved uncomfortably.

"Aye, we've heard all that, but not from your point of view." He had not intended to sound impatient but something got through to her and she continued her narrative.

"Working and living with the Dunbars was good except maybe that Captain Hector was inclined to make a sermon out of everything. When he said the name of Jesus I would see in my mind the picture of the Thorny crown. One day I told him I didn't want to hear his sermons any more. He listened politely but he still kept placing little tracts under my typewriter cover and in spite of myself I became interested. When we got to France as well as doing the books I helped in the canteen. 'Twas not a religious place but a place where the soldiers and sailors could come for cups of tea and a place to write home and such. Then one night some soldiers began to torment me about the medal I wore round my neck. Next minute I was surrounded with soldiers and sailors, all jeering at my 'Holy medal'. I burst into tears as I recalled Father Scanlon and the picture of the thorns. One sailor grabbed the string with the medal and before help could reach me he wrenched it off my neck. I was yelling and screaming that he would surely go to Hell! Remember Willie, I was not yet seventeen! Then from nowhere this tall handsome officer appeared, and without even saying a word at first, he took control The soldiers jumped to attention, and when he gave the order they all seemed to vanish, except for one Canadian who had also tried to help me. I forget a lot of what happened after but I'll never forget that officer, his name was Robert Lambert!" Hannah stopped for breath and to gain some composure. Her memories still brought pain along with the thrill. This time Willie waited. He had his own painful memories.

"We got engaged on New Year's Eve, the day before my seventeenth birthday. On the same day as your father was killed, although we didn't learn about that until the next day, we got married by special license. Robert had visited the Canteen every day and again at night until the Captains realized he was not philandering. Captain Jenni then took the place of the mother I had lost, telling me the facts of life, with no details of course, but she did tell me the whole business was part of God's plan. I listened but I was in a dream world of love." She gazed over his head again and Willie stirred.

"Then!"

"Captain Hector talked to Robert, I think, and they gave us a bonny wedding considering everything. You know the rest but I just wanted you to be sure of my feelings. I loved your brother. He became the reason for my life and no one can take his place, but I believe God has another plan for me in this family. Looking back now I see where I had many foolish ideas about religion and some other subjects too. Basically selfish, yet I knew and still know, there must be more to living than what my mother had, or the priest or even the Dunbars had. So to fulfill my ambition for riches, I wanted more education, and if the war had not come I would never have met Robert or the Lamberts, as I feel certain I would have fought tooth and nail to go on to University instead of Secretary School."

"You have a very different set of ambitions now Hannah."

"Aye I do but I may as well tell you Willie, while I am about it, I believe women should have the same chances as men, to do what they want in life, or be what they want to be. So if you still think you want to marry me here is what you will get. A child who never had a decent father but resolved not to be poor spirited like her mother. A young girl who scorned religion but who by age sixteen had determined to find out all about God and why life is like it is. That's a search that never ends. A would-be scholar who, upon receiving a small globe of the world as a prize, made up her mind to see more of the world than just the streets of Glasgow." She stopped and Willie made no move knowing there was more. Hannah's eyes had become even more distant as she continued.

"Never forget too, although it may seem I have no family of my own I do have a brother out there somewhere. I feel sure I would know or have been told for certain if Lachie was dead. I have never given up expecting word from him and I never will until I learn one thing or the other." As quick as it had appeared the distant look cleared and she returned to the topic of describing herself. "A young bride still, who until her wedding night knew nothing about how babies came. A young wife who adored your brother and learned from him what love can really be like. A young mother whose small son you will acquire along with me, and who is utterly spoiled, but adorable." Willie sighed, pretending horror.

"Aye, I'll have a job surviving that!" but Hannah kept on as if he had not spoken.

"I've come a long road since I ran away with Ellis through those bleak Glasgow streets Willie, and beneath it all I'm still Hannah Stoddart who is also a very young widow with most of life still to live, but who has seen to much of death already and now, after having suffered the loss of my love, I begin to see glimmers of what might come to pass. Seeking and finding truth through whatever means I can. More education as far as I am able to go. Possibly even in theology but I want to write a book too someday! The Bible says. 'With God all things are possible' and I do want to go with God!"

They were seated side by side on Sophia's couch in the parlour. The fire had died down to a few faint embers. No other sound than the coals falling could be heard. Echoes of Hannah's words reverberated through both their minds. Suddenly Willie started

to laugh. Softly at first and then gaining power. She put a finger to
his lips thinking of the baby and the others but he would not be
silenced.

"Let them get up. We have some great news to tell them, but
first let me tell you this, you're just the most special thing that
ever happened to the Lamberts and to me, how my father would
have loved you. . .Marry me Hannah, I've asked you three times
now and I mean it more than ever! If you are going with God,
doing all the other things you mentioned, I'm going with you"!

The mixture that comprised Maggie Lambert included her
mother's strong character and her father's quiet nature 'still waters
run deep' had been used to describe her many times.

Willie and Hannah's news was not truly news to Maggie but
when she heard the plan put into words her thoughts flew off in a
different direction and they spelled escape! The idea to break away
to a life of her own at the very first opportunity took seed at that
moment. Could it just be possible that as early as the end of the
first school term in the new place would see her free to explore life
in her own way. The following night she and Willie took stock of
the family's financial position and the disclosures proved most grati-
fying. They seated themselves comfortably in the front room and
the high pool of light from the lamp illuminated the lists and
figures on the table in from of them. So as not to disturb the
others who would hopefully be asleep, Maggie whispered.

"What with the estate left to us by Grandfather Cowan and
the money we got from the auctions, we won't be so bad off Willie!"

"Yes, I know we got a good price for the stuff, but mind you,
we don't know the value of things in Canada yet, so we will be very
canny until we find out what it's like over there." Embarking on a
new life could not change the practical Willie overnight. The lamp
sputtered and the brother and sister glanced at each other. Neither one being emotional as a rule made this time together even
more special. After Willie's marriage nothing would be the same
again. On impulse he reached over and covered her had with his
but she turned away quickly to hide her feelings although she did

not remove her and at once. Did Willie guess her underlying motives for agreeing to go on this life-changing journey? When she made the announcement in the school staff room Grant had come over afterward to wish her bon voyage, his fiancé by his side. Maggie had accepted their good wishes in the same manner as she had all the others, never showing for a moment the deep ache inside. Briskly now she had began to gather up the papers to tuck neatly in the steel strong box, another of Grandfather's Cowan's legacies.

"That's settled then. We'll save on the journey and have more to spend on land when we arrive in Saskatoon. That way we'll have a cushion for emergencies. There are six of us and only two will be in a position to earn!"

True, their finances might be stable enough to allow her to go on her own within a year, but somehow the satisfaction she hoped for didn't came. Something other than money nagged at her mind, but that, along with her resolve to live her own life, would have to wait.

* * * * *

Being Johnny's daddy proved quite a challenge for Willie Lambert and being Hannah's husband even more so. That sweet woman had a definite mind of her own as she had warned and he soon discovered for himself. Wedding plans had really been her plans and he had known a few moments of doubt when she went over the marriage ceremony with him. Unable to find anything actually wrong with the service, or the fact that she wished them each to speak the vows for themselves, identical words at that, the minister took Willie aside to say.

"I see nothing against it Willie, although 'tis most unusual and unorthodox, but I suppose we should be thankful Mrs. Lambert wants to be sure of what the words mean. Both of you should talk about the truth of them together." But Willie could not bring himself to mention the subject again. So many other matters needed discussion. Like getting jobs in Canada, the Railway promised his, but Maggie's would be a different story. Whether Maggie truly wanted to leave her good position here to come with them. Some day Willie would ask her what had caused the sudden decision. Whether to take a lot of furniture or start all over again when they arrived was another important consideration. His mother would have packed the house itself in a box if she could. They would leave the very next day after the wedding and. . . Oh he had a good many legitimate excuses to not bother her with questions about the ceremony. On their wedding night however, he made further discoveries about Hannah.

"I'll be a good wife to you Willie. There are certain things about being married I enjoy!" She blushed as she said it and Willie felt fire course through his veins to flood his own face with the same telltale colour. "We can be happy together just as long as we don't expect too much from each other at first, who knows what the future is going to bring. I'm so excited!"

Later, as she lay sleeping peacefully by his side, curled up like a kitten with her head on his arm, he still wondered what she had been trying to tell him. The sheer delight of the last two hours had removed all else from his mind, but now that the tumult inside was quieting down, his ability to think things through to the end, returned.

Gently, so as not to disturb her, Willie leaned on his other elbow. He still found it difficult to believe Hannah was now his wife. Her hair, spread out on the pillow, was of that deep chestnut brown. He had come into the kitchen one day to hear his mother's horrified exclamation following Hannah's announcement that she was going to cut her hair.

"You are not surely meanin' to cut it off?"

"Not yet, Mother, I'll wait till we're settled in Canada first. Who knows I may change my mind, I have not cut it since—" Willie had moved away then and so missed the rest of the discussion. One thing he knew she would not cut it if he could stop her. For once he would put his foot down. Still very much awake the new bridegroom continued to admire his bride of less than a day.

Below the widow's peak, as he had heard that little point on her forehead described, her smooth brow dipped gently to the curve of an almost perfect nose. It was Hannah who complained about her nose being too big. He considered it not imperfect at all but an addition to her character. Maggie would have a name for it. Maybe that's what they meant by Patrician. Her eyes had been closed in sleep so he could not admire afresh the fathomless pools, almost the same colour as her hair, where he came so close to drowning in their depths a short time ago. The lovely fine skin, dark for a woman, only added to her attraction for Willie. She must have true Celtic origins. Maggie, of course could have told him again that Celtic could mean anything from whitest fair to raven black hair with eyes of different shades from the blue of the summer sky to the black of pitch.

Willie left off admiring his bride at this point and began to go over in his mind the plans for the next day's departure. Their trunks were all packed and waiting in the front room to be picked up by Jimmy the Dray. Perched on the largest trunk was the adjustable sleeping apparatus intended to hold wee John. Justly proud of his invention, Willie had produced it one day and the four women watched breathlessly as he carefully strapped the baby into it.

"He'll not stay in that!" Sophia's scornful comment was echoed by Maggie's hearty agreement. Lizzie, second only to her mother as John's devoted slave, secretly planned to unfasten the straps first chance she got. Hannah, approving anything that would keep her active son in one place, merely smiled. Then, to everyone's surprise the main character settled the matter by shrieking his pleasure at this new position. Ruler of all he surveyed in his hammock throne he shouted.

"Johnny wants his din-din!"

Willie's arm began to cramp and he moved slightly to ease it. Hannah turned over on her side without waking and he was able to retrieve his arm completely. It was not so much her announcement that she intended to seek a higher education when they got settled in Canada, although that was disturbing enough; but rather

her constant mentioning of God in everyday conversation bothered him more than he cared to admit, until now. They all knew
Hannah read her bible a lot and that she had spent hours talking
to the Reverend Hamilton before the wedding, but Willie was
only beginning to realize how seriously she meant it. The Bridal
suite of the King's Arm boasted a giant four-poster bed. Earlier on
this, their wedding night, Willie had retired to the small dressing
room, discreetly allowing his wife time to do whatever brides do.
Surprised to hear Hannah's voice coming from the other room, he
had hurried back to find out what she wanted. She was kneeling
by the side of the bed deep in prayer. Unsure what to do next he
had just stood helplessly waiting until she finished.

"Father, bless this union and make it to your glory I pray. You
know all about Willie and me and about this family and our future plans. May your will be done in all things and I put the
Lamberts into your hands now as much as I am able. Help me be
a good wife to Willie and thank you for the special gift of joy we
will have as we come together as man and wife. In Jesus name.
Amen!" Willie, not knowing whether to retreat or stand still had
felt like an intruder on her innermost thoughts, but when Hannah
turned and saw him standing there, she smiled and beckoned to
him. After that he forgot everything else for a time.

As he stood now on the second class deck of the "SS Caledonia",
Willie Lambert's thoughts returned to that night and he still was
not sure whether to laugh or cry. He gazed at the speck on the
horizon, the first sight of a long awaited land of his dreams and he
marveled again. After many days of endless ocean, some of them
spent looking through portholes at torrents of rain, his appreciation
of today's warm sunshine and brisk breeze, with it's scent of land,
became even more pronounced. Suspended, as time on shipboard
must be, between the old life and the new, put him in the perfect
position to take stock. Just then a deck steward approached him.

"Can I help you with something sir?" Startled he shook his
head and then laughed. Had the man thought he was ready to
jump in the ocean? Willie's life was so full that such a notion was

more than ridiculous. A sudden longing for his wife came over
Willie. Where could she be? She had promised to meet him here
for a few moments of privacy, something he sorely missed. Sleeping in a bunk cabin with five other men, starved for her company
throughout the long days and nights of travel, had proved much
more difficult than he had ever imagined. True they had talked it
over and decided this would be the wisest way to go, but that was
before he had tasted what life could be like married to Hannah.
Once in a while she would catch his eye and wink at him, or if
they sat together at meals, she might squeeze his hand. Thinking
of that seemed to cause it to happen, and his heart leapt as he felt
her hand slip under his on the deck rail, a rush of gladness filled
Willie's heart.

"Sorry love! But I have just met the most interesting person.
He is a retired minister on his way from the Hebrides to join his
daughter in Canada. He is going to a place called Edmonton in
the Province of Alberta. See, here it is on the map; Not so very far
from Winnipeg when you measure—"

"Hannah, will you stop your blethers for a minute to catch
your breath? I've been standing here waiting for an hour or more
and all you can talk about is another man and his plans. What
about our plans?"

"Oh Willie, I do believe you're jealous! Reverend MacAlister,
that's his name, is older than your mother I would say. Anyway I
just want to mention some of the things we spoke about and then
we will discuss our own affairs. Reverend Bruce, he says I may call
him that, he has a really lovely Highland brogue and he knows the
Gaelic too, is going to this city to teach for a year in a new Bible
school there. I told him about my far-fetched dream of taking
lessons at a place like that and do you know, even if he seemed a
bit surprised, he still sounded encouraging. He has the most expressive eyebrows, they're snow white and seemed to rise right
into his hair, it is white too and thick and—" Willie choked:

"Hannah will you get to the point, I know there is a point,
even if we hardly see each other these days I still remember that

you don't usually speak like this without a point!" Still too excited
to sense his sarcasm Hannah rambled on:

"Reverend Bruce then made the most astounding offer!"

"Wait a minute Hannah, where did you meet this man, I'm
not sure I like the sound of all this!"

"Oh, it was all very respectable Willie, I had left Maggie and
Lizzie telling stories to John, I wanted to surprise you by wearing
my new shipboard outfit, it's been too cold to wear it before now.
Do you like it? It's in the latest style!" She pirouetted as she spoke
and Willie looked about quickly, shocked again. Other passengers
strolled round the deck but no one paid any attention to them.
Willie had already taken note of her new dress. He had seen pictures of similar clothes and thought they were riding habits. The
divided skirt seemed shorter than customary and Willie just knew
his mother would not approve, it was a bit too daring. She easily
read his mind.

"Och yes, your mother frowned a bit until I explained how I
would find it more convenient hopping around the ship—" Daring outfit or not she did look most becoming and Willie, trying
not to gloat, smiled at last. Her cheeks were pink with excitement
and health, and that inner glow mingled with the exhilaration of
the day, made her a lovely sight for a man to behold. "I do have a
most active son to run after, remember? Do you want to hear more
about my new friend or should I put it all out of my mind?" Willie
shrugged.

"You might as well tell me, you will anyway, and as for putting it out of your mind, would that be possible?" She flashed him
a pleased smile before continuing:

"Reverend Bruce's offer was this: 'Come to Edmonton then
and you'll have my support at the college.' We were sitting in the
First Class lounge where he had invited me as his guest for afternoon tea. Remember Willie I still had half an hour before coming
here to meet you?"

"I remember, and I'm sorry I cannot take you to tea on the
First Class deck, you may recall how we agreed to save the extra

money from the stateroom in the light of what it will buy once we are settled." Some of Hannah's animation evaporated. That her husband did not share her excitement, at the prospect of some of her personal dreams and hopes coming true, had not occurred to her until now. Sure in her heart that her meeting with Reverend Bruce MacAlister was more than coincidence, and sure also that it would not end here, she sent up a quick prayer for wisdom. It was then the beauty of the day, and the land coming ever closer, bringing all the promised it held for them, helped her make a decision. Everything else could wait. She leaned close to her husband, this man who was beginning to catch hold on her innermost soul. Finding his ear she nipped it with her teeth.

"Och away wi' ye Hannah, dinna do that out here, somebody might see us!"

"We're married, are we not? Well then, I'm so happy I don't care who sees us!" Her laugh was pure joy as his face took on a deeper shade of red. In a twinkling, the answer to her prayer for wisdom came and she stopped her teasing. Willie's clenched knuckles, clutching tightly to the deck rail, told their story plainer than words. Contritely she spoke.

"Oh Willie dearest, I'm sorry! I didn't mean to upset you."

"I'm not upset Hannah, I just want—" The tight control that made up Willie Lambert would not allow him to speak his want aloud. His wife needed no more words. The dinner bell clamoured and echoed over the water, but Hannah, still leaning close to his ear, whispered.

"When we get to Montreal we'll have our own room in the hotel. It won't be long now!" As Willie still did not speak she went on as she tucked her hand into the crook of his arm. "Can I at least take my husband's arm as we go to the dining room?" For answer he pulled her closer to his side allowing himself to smile down at this child/woman/wife who, by some mysterious workings of, Willie knew not what or who, was his, and yet not his at all.

Their room in the Montreal hotel was just another beautiful memory for the wedded pair and now the Lambert's found themselves in the middle of another ocean. An ocean of golden wheat that stretched far into the horizon, billowing out on each side of the ship-on-wheels, as far as the eye could see. The rich dark green of the forests of Ontario, pleasant and restful to the eyes at first, had palled after whole days of gazing at nothing else.

Maggie had listened to train talk all her life, first from her father and more recently Willie, so she knew at once that the shiny iron monster, pouring out clouds of smoke and flames as it leapt along, barely touching the two very fragile steel rails, traveled faster than any other mode of transport she had ever known. Even so, after four days, the novelty had palled and everyone was tired, everyone except John Robert. On boarding the train she had asked Hannah.

"What will we do with John?" Smiling at the thought of doing anything with him Hannah answered.

"We'll allow him to run until he is so tired he'll be falling off his feet, then we'll put him in his chair by the window till he falls asleep. Each of us can take turns to adjust the chair and—" Lizzie had interrupted here.

"Oh, can that be my job Hannah, I know how it works and Johnny likes me to do it?" Hannah and Maggie exchanged glances before Hannah replied.

"Of course it can be your job Lizzie". So Lizzie cherished her privilege of unclasping the chair-bed to make it lie flat, and would brook no interference as she solemnly carried it out. Today Lizzie sang softly to him as he slept. Maggie, gazed intently at the wondrous tableau of green and gold rushing past her window, so she did not hear her sister's song at first, but after a few minutes the words began to penetrate.

"Speed Bonnie Boat, like a bird on the wing, onward the sailors cry, carry the lad that's born to be king, over the sea to Skye."

"Where did you learn to sing that song so perfectly Lizzie?" Lizzie turned shining eyes to her audience. The whole family sat up to listen

"From Reverend Bruce, he learned it to me!"

"Taught it to me!" Maggie corrected automatically.

"Oh, did he learn it to you as well Maggie, that's nice, we can a' sing it the gither." Maggie chose not to pursue the futile grammar lesson at this point but Lizzie continued." He learned me some more, will I sing ye another one?" Maggie nodded absently. This man MacAlister seemed to be influencing the whole family, First Hannah, then Willie even if he grumbled a bit, and the biggest surprise of all, her mother. Lizzie was no surprise, she liked everybody. As her pure sweet voice filled the coach, Maggie found herself joining in with her contralto to harmonize. To everyone's delight Willie added his deep baritone along with Hannah's soprano, and even Sophia began to hum the melody. Other occupants of the coach caught the spirit and soon the chorus swelled to fill the space. Song followed song while John Robert blissfully slept the summer afternoon away. Hannah's heart was full as she thought the angels must also unite them as thee glorious words of the old hymns echoed throughout the air.

"We shall gather at the river, the beautiful, the beautiful, river!" The train puffed it's way into the huge melting pot that was Winnipeg's station, while hearts had been mellowed and softened with a memory that, for many there, would last a lifetime.

* * * * *

Reverend Bruce MacAlister, in truth the one responsible for the impromptu singsong, would have been there, singing the beloved songs along with his new friends had he not been otherwise engaged.

"I am surely much obliged to you Henry." He said now to the pale, rather austere gentleman seated opposite him in the train's Club Car.

"Think nothing of it sir," Henry Parker replied in his distinctive Canadian drawl. "Happened to have business in the East at this time, thought I'd enjoy your company on the trip back west." Henry almost had the grace to blush as he spoke, remembering his wife's firm instructions to meet the Reverend and invite him to share his private car.

"Well, I'm still obliged to you and you can tell me what I may do for you in return."

"No need for return favours man, you're family are you not? Just don't go prayin' for me, that's all I ask!" Bruce made no reply to this but his thoughts were busy. Stop praying! May as well ask him to stop breathing, but wisely decided to change the subject.

"This club car has seen better days, I mind it fine, the first time we came to visit Mary Jean in 1905 if my memory serves correctly." Henry Parker lit a fresh cigar before settling himself more comfortably in the deep plush cushions. The old minister was famous for his stories, and even if he was a bit long winded at times, the stories were usually worth listening to. He was not disappointed this time either.

"They've done away with some of the ornate decoration they used to have, why the carpets on the floors alone must have cost a good few pounds." Henry could have related much on that theme as many of his own investments had been in railways. At the beginning of the century the tendency had been to build first class passenger cars with even more luxurious detail than the reverend had just described. Henry brought his attention back to the present story.

"There was a terrible fuss being made and we just could not understand what a' the kafuffle was aboot." Reverend Bruce tended to allow his speech to fall into the Highland brogue when he became excited and he was not above hamming it up a bit when he had an appreciative audience as now.

"It was so in 1905, I recall it exactly, because that was the year the main railway line reached out to Edmonton. Anyway there was a stoppage on the line somewhere just West of Lake Superior. I don't remember why now but I do remember it lasted a whole day. We left the train for a breath of fresh air and a walk and—" Coming from Henry, the interruption was not rude as he held up his hand.

"Pardon me Reverend, but you did say we, did you not?" For a moment his guest's face registered, along with surprise, a look of such sorrow that Henry wished he had kept his big mouth shut, ashamed he had to glance away.

"Aye Henry, I did say we, my dear wife Kirsty was with me at that time. She's with Jesus now, this twelve-month. Oh 'tis all right Henry, we had a some glorious years together before, but that's all another story, maybe I'll tell it to you one day. Now where was I, och yes, we got out the train for some fresh air and a stretch, when I glimpsed these folks further down the line a bit. They where dressed quite a bit different from any folk I had ever seen before, except in pictures. When we got within hearing distance I recognized a foreign tongue, not French either, because I do have a smattering of that myself, and would have understood it. Well, here we were then, out in the middle of nowhere, and being very curious as to what would happen next. We hadna' long to wait before one wee fella broke away from the rest and came toddlin' toward me yammerin' away. Without thinking I put my hand in my pocket where I always keep some peppermint sweeties, but before I could do anything else this stout lass came up and snatched the laddie away, skelping his hand and yabberin fifteen to the dozen. Deciding we might not be that welcome here, I turned to go back when I must have had a dizzy spell The next thing I knew I was lying on the ground and the same stout lass was waving a coloured hankie in my face while a man, I found out later on he was a priest and could speak English, tried to force some spirits between my lips. As you know Henry, I never touch spirits and so, I'm feared I sat up and spat it out in a very rude manner. Well, to make a long story short." Henry smiled to himself at this remark:

"This priest Nikel, of the Greek Orthodox persuasion, was the leader of a whole town full of people who had just up and left their Ukrainian home one day to come to Canada en masse. Their desire to keep their free way of worship one of many reasons for the journey. The wee boy was Nikel's son, and the stout lassie his wife. She soon realized I was harmless and when her husband explained I was a man of the 'cloth' too she relaxed and let the wee lad have a

sweetie. The group had been preparing for a makeshift picnic before we came along. So overjoyed were they to get out of their
crowded "Colonial" car that they decided to have a worship service
as well as a party. We had been told the delay would be at least
eight hours so the upshot of it all was they invited Kirsty and me
to join in their celebrations as soon as I felt recovered from my
indisposition. At that stage they would have found it hard to get
rid of me as I was having a rare time by then. Kirsty knew me well
enough to just resign herself."

"I bet!" Henry thought but he did want to hear more so he
prompted.

"Then what happened?"

"After that we began to have one of the most enjoyable times
I've ever had in many a long day. The worship part was very meaningful indeed, and even if we couldn't understand the words, we
understood the reverence of the worshippers. Their rituals were
beyond us as well but meant a lot to our hosts. As soon as the
service concluded the food was served. Having no chairs or tables
didn't bother them. The women spread out their shawls on the
ground at the side of the tracks thereby providing chairs and tables
at one go. Food appeared almost by a miracle and I was reminded
of the story of Jesus and the loaves and the fishes." Henry smiled
as he thought. I knew he wouldn't miss a chance to mention
religion!

"There was no hot food but the cold sausage and pickles and
cheese along with their chewy, but very tasty, bread was awfully
good. Some enterprising individual had set up a small campfire a
safe distance from the train and we had our first taste of Ukrainian/Canadian coffee. Mind you, I'm fond of coffee but this stuff,
well at first I was tempted to spit it out the same as the spirits, but
even as I thought on it I glimpsed Mikel's wife watching me closely,
waiting for a sign, so we both swallowed politely, to be immediately
rewarded with a lovely smile and a refill. A display of Ukrainian dancing followed that and we were delighted with that too, until one
young woman thought I should do more than spectate. . . I de-

clined that invitation in a hurry, reminding them of my recent fall. All too soon the time arrived for us to re-enter the train and this is when I got into trouble with the conductor. It hadn't taken me long to discover how cramped these folks were in their "Colonial" car. I had noted the inside of it and could see nothing else but what resembled the long wooden benches on the old station platform at Aribaig. I looked my question at my new friend who shrugged helplessly as he said, in his broken English.

"We have the cheapness. Then have money left for land in the Alberta!" That was when I got the idea of having them as our guest in our car. By now I also realized why his wife was so stout. (Their second son was born two weeks later and they named him Bruce!) It took a fairly lengthy discussion with the conductor and I had slipped him what I thought to be a half-a-crown, but later learned it was really a silver dollar, before he left us alone for the remainder of the journey. The quarters were rather cramped but the lap of luxury for the couple and their wee lad, compared to what they had before and they were truly grateful. Kirsty and I had made new friends for life. Six weeks ago I received a letter from Nikel. They have prospered in a small farming community about eighty miles east of Edmonton. I plan to pay them a visit as early as possible."

Henry had closed his eyes during the last part of the tale but he was not asleep. His thoughts had reverted to the old familiar pattern of bitterness as his companion mentioned the young woman's condition. When the flow of talk ceased he sighed. The sigh was deep and long, almost a groan, and Bruce, a student of human nature for so many years, immediately sensed the need.

"Are you all right Henry?"

"Yes, no! Oh I don't know, what's the use? I suppose your Nikel and his stout wife have at least a half a dozen kids by now." Bruce peered closely at his relative by marriage before answering in his soft brogue.

"No no, as a matter of fact they had no more children after that. Just the two boys Andrew and Bruce. The first boy was called

after their patron saint, who of course, is ours in Scotland too."
His sensitive spirit had quickly discerned the true reason for Henry's
questions. The train slowed down for its entry into the Winnipeg
station, and Bruce glanced one more time toward his travelling
companion as he breathed a silent prayer. "Oh Father, by Thy
Grace and Mercy, give me wisdom for silence now and the words
to speak later when he asks. I know he is about ready to ask. Nevertheless Lord, you know best and your will be done, In Jesus
name. . .Amen."

No further opportunity presented itself during that journey,
or for many days after. A business associate of Henry's met him
unexpectedly on the station platform at Winnipeg, and Henry
invited the younger man to join them for the remainder of the
trip. Bruce experienced a sharp thrill of disappointment until he
remembered his prayer. He had asked for wisdom and words to
speak, he had also asked for God's timing. That must not be yet.

* * * * *

The monstrous engine shook itself to a standstill in a great cloud
of smoke and steam. One final shudder and the coach doors flung
open, erupting human beings as flood gates spill forth their waters
in springtime. Idly watching the exodus from the window of their
compartment Hannah Lambert pondered the latest development
in the family chronicles. As soon as the crowd dispersed Willie
would go to the ticket office. Exactly when the decision to travel
further westward to Edmonton had been agreed upon she could
not be sure, but except for having to spend two more days and a
night on board the train, no one mourned Saskatoon. Lizzie carefully explained the change to John Robert and the simplification
pleased all as her explanations usually did, bringing matters into
perspective.

"Now Johnny, we're not at Edmonton yet so don't worry?"
She assured her nephew as Hannah in honesty confessed to herself
that even if he had said the deciding words, Willie would not have

thought of the idea of going on to Edmonton on his own. Ever since the Reverend MacAlister had planted the thought in her mind, it was she, Hannah, who had cherished the desire to go to Edmonton and she had said as much to her husband more than once. When he telegraphed to the railway officials in the Alberta capital that he had changed his mind and would now travel there instead of Saskatchewan it had all been surprisingly easy. Setting aside her feelings of guilt Hannah turned to smile at Willie as he re-entered their compartment with a handful of brightly coloured folders. His voice betrayed his excitement.

"The main thoroughfare in Edmonton is called Jasper Avenue and it crosses at One Hundredth Street which is the centre of the city!" Reading aloud from the detailed map he had just obtained. Willie's greatest difficulty at this moment was curbing his own amazement. Soon now they would arrive in Edmonton and the adventure, a vague dream in his mind that morning when they had all posed in the Sauchiehall Street studio to have their picture taken would become a reality. Although on that day his dream had not included the whole family, still here they all were. He glanced at Hannah again. She made no effort to hide her excitement, and she did look bonny with that extra glow in her eyes.

Hannah's own thoughts tumbled over each other. Only this morning Reverend MacAlister had mentioned Jasper Avenue, and here was Willie showing them pictures from a folder of that very place. As the train hurtled them closer and closer toward the new destination she prayed the decision was the right one. The old minister had given her a slip of paper with his daughter's address and it was now nestled safely in her handbag. She glanced again round the coach at her family. Sophia snored quietly in the corner now recognized by the others as her own. Across from Sophia in the other window seat, blissfully unaware of any significance in the invisible border they had just crossed, slept Lizzie and John Robert. Maggie had slipped out to investigate along the corridor, leaving Hannah and Willie virtually alone and unobserved for a few precious moments. In one accord they moved toward each other. Willie placed an arm round his wife's shoulder and she settled into the space sighing contentedly. Tomorrow they would begin a new life with all its responsibilities but this sweet moment she would savour to the full.

"Happy my dear?" She whispered. For answer he kissed her cheek.

This cozy domestic scene confronted Maggie as she rejoined the family group and her first reaction registered disapproval tinged with resentment. Although she chose to go off on her own for a part of each day knowing that her mother and her sister would be engrossed in caring for the baby and the married pair in each other, she still struggled with that old underlying resentment. Not so much against Willie or Hannah as with her own feelings. Otherwise she could have enjoyed the journey quite well. The spare time and all the new sights and sounds had at first been rather nice but it had begun to pall.

Scrupulously honest Maggie searched out the reasons for these feelings. "I started resenting Hannah over again, the night she married Willie, even more than when she was Robert's wife. The woman has such an easy way with men. Why even that old preacher seemed to have fallen under her spell."

The train steamed its way into the terminal at Edmonton, and Maggie put aside her inner searching for the time being as Lizzie summed up the situation, her trusting eyes turned full upon her sister as she said;

"Now we can a' get back to livin', eh, Maggie?"

* * * * *

"It's so big and flat, Willie, and have you ever seen so many motorcars, even Glasgow never got this bustlin' and busy?" Sophia's son paid no attention to her words. Willie's thoughts were winging high as his eyes followed a light plane where it cavorted and spun out far above them.

"I wonder if I could ever learn to do that?" He spoke softly to himself but Hannah, coming up close behind him, heard.

"Of course you could Willie, why not?" Before that discussion could develop further the porter, who had snatched the luggage tickets out of Willie's hand just moments before, appeared now with his iron wheeled cart trundling behind him. The Lambert clan instantly became absorbed in re-acquainting themselves with tin trunks and leather valises not seen for many days. The larger crates and barrels would not come to light for many more days but the containers on the porter's barrow contained articles most necessary to get them started. Pleased that he had thought of sending a wire from Winnipeg for a hotel reservation, Willie painstakingly tried to explain their destination to the taxi driver while that enterprising individual piled luggage and people into every available crevice of his "Model T". The open space in front of the railway station swarmed with humanity and the motor traffic was indeed thick as Sophia had noted earlier. Excitement filled the air.

"There must be some kind of a fair on?" Exclaimed Maggie and immediately Lizzie clapped her hands in glee.

"What great fun! Can we go to it Mammy? Please?" They had no need to 'go to it' as it was coming to them.

"We ain't goin' no place for a while!" The cabby spoke in a Western drawl new to his listeners.

"He talks just like yon cowboys in the pictures Maggie!" Lizzie whispered excitedly into her sister's ear, causing Maggie to resolve afresh that Lizzie had seen enough 'pictures' for a while if she had anything to say about it.

Three hours later the exhausted Lambert family woefully took stock of the most recent developments. Seated on trunks, and other miscellaneous articles of luggage, they surveyed their situation with incredulity stamped on every face. Hannah broke the spell as she began to laugh. Five pairs of eyes swiveled in her direction. Could the strain have been too much for her? Her laughter became louder and soon Maggie could not help joining in. At first cautiously but as she caught the infection, and the whole ridiculous scene came back to her and then to the others, suddenly they were all engulfed in helpless laughter.

"Willie, if you could have been your face when the man asked you for five dollars for a half mile hurl!"

"Well that's a whole pound, and Hannah if you could have seen yourself when that box on top of the taxi burst open, right in the middle of your famous Jasper Avenue!" When this last had happened the Exhibition crowd, many of whom were still milling about idly after the parade had passed, began to good-naturedly help them put their belongings back together. Pink blushes had adorned the faces of the women when one husky fellow from the crowd had removed his wide brimmed hat and replaced it with an item from John Robert's nursery equipment. Those around him roared, and thus encouraged, the same fellow had proceeded to try on several other articles scattered on the road. After some more clowning the box was secured more firmly and replaced on the taxi roof. Continuing on their way along the parade route toward the hotel the newcomers had soon realized they now had a royal escort as well as an advance guard and a rearguard. From a nearby hostelry, some kilted pipers had appeared, leftovers from the parade, and well primed up. Commandeered at once by the crowd to lead this impromptu procession the convoy soon arrived at the Kensington Hotel about a hundred strong, with one brave chappie perched on top of the errant box where it teetered on the taxi's roof. Sophia's laughter now verged on hysteria as she proclaimed to all and sundry in that hotel lobby.

"My, I was black affronted when yon awfu' man was carryin' on!" Her tone sounded stern but her eyes belied the stern words. Changing the subject, thereby sobering the others, she continued. "Where *will* we all sleep the night Hannah?" Neither Hannah, nor anyone else knew at that moment what their sleeping arrangements might eventually be. The clerk at the Kensington had shaken his head and looked at Willie blankly when he insisted they had made reservations. He was sorry but every room was filled, not only the rooms but the lobby too. In fact, every available inch of space, held a body. Their friendly, but rapacious, taxi driver had gone long ago, leaving the heap of luggage just inside the swinging door. The pipers and retinue had retired to the adjoining hostelry. The Lamberts were alone in a strange land. Sophia's question brought home the predicament. Suddenly a voice, friendly and accented with the merest flavour of French, spoke up, softly but clearly.

"Could I be of some assistance to you?" The tall stranger gazed at Maggie as he said the words but it was Hannah who answered him.

"Only if you could rent us a couple of rooms sir!" He smiled ruefully as he turned to her.

"Not a couple of rooms I am so sorree, but I may be able to arrange for you one, wait 'ere a second." Having little choice they sat still for the time it took this new acquaintance to exchange something with the desk clerk.

"We've arranged for you to 'ave my room for the women and the child, also another cot 'as been found where *you* can sleep sir." The last was addressed to Willie who came out of his dazed state to thank the man.

Shortly they were all gathered in the said room and Hannah once again found herself in charge.

"Mother Lambert, if you and Maggie will share the big double bed, Lizzie and I can do the same with the smaller one. J.R. can sleep on his hammock and Willie will be quite comfortable in the lobby with the other men for the duration of this crush." Willie sighed resignedly as his wife continued:

"Oh and Willie, I noticed a shop on the corner, not that far away, they call it a 'delicatessen', please go there and get us something to eat that doesn't need cooking and some milk for John, while we look for the box with the dishes and spoons. Thank goodness there's a bathroom next door. When we've had our tea and washed the dishes we can take turns at having a bath.

Maggie volunteered to be last in the bath. Enveloped in her old dressing gown, with a towel wrapped round her head, and a pair of her mother's old slippers flapping on her feet, she was glad

of the late hour and that hopefully no one would see her as she
padded back along the corridor. She need not have worried about
how she looked. The lone watcher saw no flaws in Maggie Lambert. Sensing her shyness he kept hidden behind the banister. A
few tendrils of jet black hair had escaped the towel, curling round
her brow and neck, making her all the more endearing, but Claire
LeTourneau scarcely even noticed that as he exulted.

"La belle petite! She is for me, Non!"

"What a bonnie view!" Willie and Hannah had escaped for a
while and having walked a short distance from the hotel they now
stood on a high embankment overlooking what they had discovered to be the North Saskatchewan River. Far below, and to the
East of where they stood stretched the pylons of the High Level
Bridge. However although that wonder of engineering drew Willie's
fascinated gaze, it was not what caused Hannah's gasp of admiration now. Clouds streaked across the sky changing it from a pale
pink to deep vermilion even as she watched breathlessly. It was
nine o'clock in the evening the same day of the epic arrival and the
westering sun still rode high in the heavens.

"We cannot be far away from the land of the midnight sun
you know?" She chattered on to an unheeding husband. Getting
no answer she pinched his arm and he started, speaking for the
first time since they left the hotel.

"I wonder if a person could fly one of those planes to the North
Country?"

"I don't see why not! Oh Willie, isn't life exciting? I feel as if
we were all just starting life over again." Some of her enthusiasm
began to spill over on Willie at last, and as he answered her he
recognized that same excitement welling up within himself. This
had been a most eventful day, although he did not relish the thought
of spending the night on a cot in the hotel lobby, still there were
compensations. Some of the conversations he had overheard there

already intrigued him more than he cared to admit. With her usual quicksilver change of mood Hannah followed his thoughts.

"The crowds seem awfully big, even if there is a fair on!" She remarked.

"I think it's more than that Hannah, I overheard a few remarks in the lobby just now and it seems we've not only landed on a fair week, or "Exhibition Days" as they call it, but the whole place is buzzing about an oil strike somewhere close by!"

"That would have the same effect as a gold rush, would it not Willie?"

"Yes it would Hannah, but nonetheless I believe we have come here at a good time for us, I'm pleased and I know everything will be all right." Hannah, never having doubted this for a moment, was wise enough to nod as she tucked her hand under the crook of his arm. Willie, for once not bothering to look round to see if they were observed, bent over to plant a quick kiss on her velvet cheek.

"Thank you Operator, yes, I will hold the line!" The telephone was not new to Hannah so she had given the operator the number Rev. Bruce MacAlister had furnished her with the other day, and she waited now in the telephone booth provided by the Kensington Hotel for its patrons. Set up in the alcove at the far end of the lobby made it possible to watch the people as they passed without yourself being seen. Hannah was keeping a sharp lookout for stray members of the family. Willie and Maggie should be back any minute from their land-scouting jaunt.

"Hullo!" She jumped as the voice resounded through the wire very loud and clear. Bruce, like many another of his generation, seemed to think one must yell to be heard that far away, so he did. "Oh, it's you Hannah!" He boomed, "I've been wondering about you."

"Yes, so much has happened in the few days since we've been here I don't know where to begin."

"Well, don't worry, as I thought about you I just prayed that everything would go smoothly for you and your family so I have not been too concerned." Hannah welcomed Bruce's easy manner of praying as it resembled her own style.

"Yes, I've been missing our daily talks and discussions quite a lot." She did not add that her own ideas as they sat and talked of the bible truths had been that this must be like sitting at the feet of the Master Himself. Actually she had mentioned this to him one day on the ship and he had hastened to assure her it was indeed the very presence of Jesus in both of them that she sensed. Suspecting he did not wish to blow up his own special relationship with his Lord she merely waited, eager and ready to listen and learn as much as she could. Each time he had shared a memory story with her she sensed a different kind of joy, more than his natural joy, which was in itself contagious and which she could not name. Lizzie put her finger on it one day.

"Reverend MacAlister has shining lights round his head like the lamps on the Parkhall Street on a rainy night!" Hannah had taken a closer look next time, and sure enough, there was indeed a glow about the man. It was another one of those things Hannah kept in her heart, the time was not yet. She held the telephone away from her ear as she remembered those thoughts. He spoke on.

"Yes, my prayers have been with you, I'm glad you called. Tomorrow I will speak the message in the service at McDougall Church and I want to invite you to attend. James, my son-in-law will call for you in his car, the rest of the family too, of course." Hannah did a quick count in her head before agreeing.

"Thank you, I would like that very much, what time should we be ready?"

"Oh, about half past nine o'clock and I'll see you after at the reception." A loud click announced the end of the conversation and Hannah, asking herself how she would get around this one, slowly replaced the receiver. The hotel was more crowded than ever this Saturday night and although Willie had been trying everything possible this past few days to find a more permanent place for his family to live, there just did not seem to be any places available. Changes in terminology were happening overnight and phrases like 'real estate' and 'deals' and plans to buy a 'lot' were being bandied about between Willie and Maggie. All this new vocabulary simply meant that the possibility of buying a bare piece of ground and building a house on it was more than just a far away dream. From other scraps of conversation and something she preferred to ignore as ridiculous, the word 'tent'! Surely they would not ask that of her. Not Willie. Thinking about him brought him on the scene as often happened and it seemed that Willie would. . .Well not a tent exactly but. . .He watched her leave the alcove where the telephone was situated and he followed her to the first landing before he began to speak.

"It wouldn't be so bad Hannah and at least we can begin to have some privacy." Hannah at last came out of her own dream, she had missed some of the conversation, but she picked up the obvious conclusion.

"A tent! You want us to live in a tent like gypsies? Oh Willie." The last came out as a wail of despair but she had heard aright. It seemed that as Maggie and Willie had visited the fairgrounds, strolling along somewhat idly they had silently absorbed this vastly different scene and Eastkirk's Annual Cattle Show day paled in comparison. The sights and sounds of the various booths and exhibits, the smell of the popcorn and other strange foods, concocted by the endless variety of ethnic groups represented here from every corner of the globe, fascinated the brother and sister, newly arrived from Scotland. Never had either one encountered anything quite like this. Stopping to look closer at a shooting gallery that didn't appear to be doing much business Maggie was startled to hear the sound of angry voices from behind the gaudy display of prizes.

"You bought a what?"

"Hush! Hush! Not so loud Hannah, we bought a caravan and a big tent, it was dirt cheap at the fairgrounds this afternoon and Maggie and I just could not resist it, we—"

"But I thought we were to have a family discussion about such matters before coming to any big decisions, Oh Willie, I'm upset, that I am!" Her voice had risen to a wail once more.

"I know we agreed on that, but Maggie and I had to decide there and then , as this circus family are leaving tonight and they had to sell out. It is a rare bargain Hannah, at least wait until you see it before you judge." Willie gazed at her with such pleading in his eyes that Hannah began to soften.

"What does your mother think?" she asked.

"Maggie is telling her now, but I'm more concerned about what you would think. Mother will likely think the same as you until she sees for herself."

"When will that be?"

"Just now if you want. I paid a boy a quarter of a dollar to hold the horses for a few minutes."

"Horses!" No doubt now about the wail as she continued. "You'll be telling me next that you bought a menagerie or a side-show to go with it. Oh Willie, nothing will surprise me any more." Willie laughed nervously but with a touch of relief as her dimpled smile replaced the frown.

"Oh no, not a menagerie, just a wee spaniel pup for John Robert, it came as part of the bargain!"

The Lambert family sat in church, an ordinary enough occurrence except that inwardly each personality experienced vastly differing degrees of pleasure. From sheer delight on Hannah's part through measured neutrality in Willie, typical of him until he had time to form an opinion, to Maggie whose feelings registered anger. The last had agreed to attend the service in a moment of weakness following relief at Hannah's amiable reception of the news about yesterday's purchases. Now she thoroughly regretted the too easy agreement. Not that the old man wasn't a good speaker, in fact, if she didn't know better, he could almost convince her there was a God somewhere who cared about people, but. . . Deliberately Maggie set her mind to blank out the gentle, penetrating voice coming forth from Reverend Bruce MacAlister where he stood on the high pulpit platform, and concentrated on thoughts of the events yesterday. What an incredible piece of luck to be passing that booth just when the violent argument, leading to the termination of a show business partnership, had reached its climax. For consolation, she recalled the words Willie spoke as they made their way back to the Kensington later.

"If they fight like that it's about time they separated anyway!" She had agreed, adding her own observation that the partnership wasn't even a year old. This reminded her of the comparative newness of the miniature house on wheels and she continued her inner exulting. It was certainly worth gloating over. Only an extremely creative person could have dreamed up such a contraption. The additional bonus, as far as Maggie was concerned, woven out of heavy duty canvas, fitted right over and into the side of the main wooden part, custom made they explained, producing an extra room and a cooking area as well as a porch. The wooden floor on the extension clipped into sections to the underside of the caravan itself providing as neat a little home as any family could ever wish for. At least until they could see a bit further into the future when they might be able to build their own.

In her enthusiasm, the idea to strike out on her own for the moment completely forgotten, Maggie continued to plan for the whole family, ignoring the stream of eloquence flowing through the old church. On Monday morning she and Willie would attend a land auction. According to the fancy handbills posted up all along the street where their hotel was situated, one could bid on a plot of ground or a lot as it was called. She and Willie had one already picked out from the advertising material, situated two blocks west of the "Kensington" overlooking the river at 100th. Avenue and 117th. Street.

"I'm becoming Canadianized already, using all this strange terminology, even in my thoughts!" Aware now of a stir in the pews as the people in the church had risen to their feet while the

last hymn peeled out of the organ. She stood with the others thinking it will be soon over. Instead Maggie received a further surprise
as the music picked up tempo. Could they really be going to sing
that Salvation Army chorus? Yes, it seemed they could.

"When the Roll is called up yonder—" Trilled Hannah, clapping her hands in accompaniment. Lizzie was in her element, war-
bling in her childish soprano while John Robert jumped up and
down in sheer delight. Hoping for a semblance of sanity Maggie
turned to her mother.

"They've all gone mad!" She whispered. But Sophia disagreed
with Maggie. Although her own participation in the service had
been moderate she did not consider Bruce MacAlister mad, in fact
she was totally enthralled by him. Not only his good preaching
either, but by the man himself.

"What a fine man, yes, I never noticed on the boat that he
is such a fine man!" Her daughter was speechless and her anger
grew.

But the 'fine man' was jubilant. Surrounded by family members, and many friends old and new, his eyes picked Hannah and
the other Lamberts out of the crowd of well wishers as they politely accepted a cup of coffee from one of the hostesses. The special reception, planned in his honour, was well under way. He
chuckled now as he spied Sophia sipping the coffee, it must taste
terrible to her as it once did to him, and he sympathized. The
crowd of admirers thinned momentarily and Hannah seized the
opportunity to speak to him.

"So, Reverend Bruce, if it's not too presumptuous, I would
like you to see it and say a prayer for it, as you told me you did for
the similar place you and Hamish Cormack lived in at one time
during your Scottish revival days."

"Telephone me at Mary Jean's in the morning Hannah, I'd
come over today but they have plans for the rest of the day. But
I'm intrigued with your description of—"

"Oh the caravan is not set up yet, we still have no grounds for
it, but I know it's going to be all right soon. Yes, I will telephone

you as soon as I know more." The last part was said to his departing back as someone snatched him away to his other guests and Hannah had to be content with that.

"Surely she can't mean it Mother!" Maggie, not sure whether to laugh or get angry again, mocked Hannah's latest idea. "What next? Hannah's goin' fair daft these days, that Highland preacher has her bewitched!" If this were so then her mother had been bewitched also. It all began the day when Hannah met the man on the boat, or, maybe not. Come to think of it, on the day the telegram arrived at Parkhall Street, announcing Robert's death, Maggie had noticed that faraway look in Hannah's eyes as if she listened to something or someone. Thoughtfully she walked away from her mother now, Sophia paid no attention to her words anyway, and she continued with her summation. "She does mean it and I must be extra careful it doesn't get to me!" Willie's voice cut in softly for Maggie's ear alone.

"Yes, she means it, and maybe it's not such a bad thing, a bit like a house-warming Mother thinks, it canna do any harm."

"Och no Willie, not you *and* Mother, am I the only sane one left in this family. House-warming indeed. . . I'll not be going to that Willie, I'll just stay here in the hotel and finish packing. I can watch John Robert while the rest of you go."

"No thank you Maggie." Hannah joined them in time to hear the last part of Maggie's speech. This was typical of the kind of thing they suffered from with such close quarters, but soon now they would be in the new place, even if it too were small, it would be better than this.

On moving day the family members had all risen at dawn, each with a specific job to do for the move. Willing hands had helped set up the tent on its wooden base, and advice regarding insulation and other technical details, quite beyond Hannah, had flowed freely. Willie accepted it all having no experience of how to prepare for the Canadian winter. The result, a neat, compact, self-contained home that would become quite a show place. Obtaining the chosen lot had been amazingly easy, and all that remained was the arrival of Reverend Bruce to proceed with the ceremony. Hannah, not sure what the blessing service entailed, knew only it would be something good and she had more to say to Maggie who still glared at her.

"I want my son to be included in the blessing service Maggie, and I wish you would come as well."

"Sorry Hannah, but I think it is so much nonsense and I refuse to be a part of it or seem to condone it in any way, so if you will excuse me I am going for a walk. Later I'll return here to do the last minute packing." Maggie deliberately stepped between Hannah and Willie as she spoke and an involuntary shiver passed through Hannah. For a moment she felt cold and clammy but it quickly passed and she reached for Willie's hand.

"Shall we go dear, we don't want to miss anything, do we?" Willie, watched his sister flounce off and he too experienced a moment of unease, but looking at his wife's radiant face he pushed it aside. Maggie would get over it and for the present life's promise held only good!

"In the Name of Jesus, we take authority over all the power of the enemy and Satan we rebuke you and command you to leave this consecrated place now, in Jesus name I pray, Amen!. . .. Now that this home has been purged and cleared of all evil we invite the Holy Spirit to come in and fill the empty spaces with Himself. Every corner to be filled with the love of Jesus by the Power of the Holy Spirit. Thank you Lord that you are blessing this home now and all who will live here. They shall prosper and be in health even as their souls prosper according to Your Holy Word. We apply that Word to the lives of this family and we thank you that we can Jesus, Amen!"

As the powerful verses flowed about them Willie stole a rather fearful glance at the other guests. Some curious onlookers had gathered outside the open part of the tent and more joined even as he noticed. The minister had spoken loud enough thought Willie and there had been moments during the service when he wondered why he had agreed to Hannah's suggestion. Maybe Maggie was right after all. One glance at Hannah's glowing face and he realized anew how she did not think it nonsense and a glimpse of his mother's smile confirmed how they both considered it all very real.

In the hush that followed the prayer many other faces mirrored Hannah's. Mary Jean and James Douglas for instance. Introduced to Willie on Sunday as the daughter and son-in-law of the Reverend MacAlister they already seemed like old friends. Their daughter Jamie emitted the same glow he was beginning to recognize as she pounded away on a small portable harmonium, brought along for the occasion, and her beautiful face could only be described as ecstatic. Behind her stood a young man whose face also shone but his held another, more earthy form of ecstasy. Introduced as Jamie's fiancé' George Boswell had eyes for none but Jamie. She, a music major attending the University of Alberta, used no sheet music as she played, softly now, a fitting background to her grandfather's words. The ceremony drew to a close and Sophia urged all and sundry to stay for a 'cup of tea' that turned out to be a feast in the true Scottish tradition. The miniature oven had been put to the test and she had been busy since the early hours producing such delicacies as her special griddle scones and the tiny feather-light pancakes the members of her Women's Institute in Eastkirk would have recognized. Not content with that, an immense plate of shortbread, without which no tea of Sophia's would be complete, graced the table's centre.

Mary Jean Douglass had brought her contribution in the form of a dish of home made strawberry jam. Some more new friends stood in the background. Their names still unpronounceable to the Scots. First names were enough for the moment and Sophia knew them as Marta and Nik, whose gift to the feast reminded her of Grandpa Cowan. A container of rich thick cream and another of yellow farm butter. The trestle table, product of Willie's fertile hammer and a few bits of board, literally groaned under the weight of the tea ingredients. No one seemed to miss the absent family member until Lizzie, finished with the job of handing round a

plate of cakes, made a typical Lizzie proclamation. Into a lull in
the conversation her voice sounded a clarion call.

"I wonder if Maggie and that big man are having such good
fun as us?"

* * * * *

If she had heard her sister, Maggie might have blushed but she
could not have denied enjoying herself. Engrossed in her self-
imposed task to clear everything out of their hotel room she failed
to hear a light knock on the partly open door. The original owner
of the room had returned to claim it. Aware immediately of the
pull of mutual attraction sparking between them, although shy
with it, neither one wished to part from the other's company, so,
when Claire LeTourneau suggested they proceed to the almost
deserted hotel dining room for 'petit soupe', Maggie agreed with
only a slight hesitation. At first she paid more attention to her very
handsome escort than to his words but she jerked into enthralled
attention as some of them began to penetrate.

"So, my wife never recovered from the shock of losing both the
children at once, when she got tired blaming me she turned on
'erself. After that she started drinking too much wine and soon
she. . . well she could not live with 'erself or me, any more. . .she
left one day, the weather was so cold. They found 'er stiff body on
a park bench!" Maggie sensed at once that this was the first time
her table companion had told this story in such depth. His words
saddened her and the knowledge humbled her at one and the
same time. It also made her feel privileged and special. Absorbed
in the revelation so far the next shock almost passed over her head.

"You're a what?"

"Not am, used to be. I used to be a Minister. Don't look so
surprised there are a few French Canadian Methodists, you know?"

"Oh, I'm not disputing that, how could I know? It's just your
attitude to all this religion I find myself enveloped in. You seem
indifferent and the connection evades me."

"Well, you know, it seems a long time ago now but at the time of the tragedy, when the utter futility of raising two belle petites to the age of four years and then watch them die 'orribly. Then to stand by 'elpless while my wife suffered a terrible break down which ended when she took 'er own life, has left me with no faith in God. During those dreaded nights of being alone with my awful memories I've thought much. I've even thought that if there is a God after all then he must be even more sadistic than the worst man ever heard of." For some time they both sat silent but it was the kind of silence that speaks volumes. Maggie longed to comfort him but even with the new liberty she was experiencing at this moment she could not bring herself to cover his hand with hers. After all, although this man did not feel like a stranger now, he nevertheless still was one. The food cooled in front of them as he continued.

"All I once 'eld dear, God and the church, marriage and love, wife and children, erased from my life as if they 'ad never been. Deliberately I stayed away from places where a child might be. Your little nephew is arousing in me emotions I'd 'oped buried forever as 'e reminds me of my lost ones." Although his English came through impeccably, strong emotions caused him to slip into a broken patios. Although unspoken Maggie's sympathy was evident, and this became too much for him, abruptly now he changed the subject.

"Your brother, Willie seems very interested in flying!"

"Yes he is, isn't he?" A few days earlier Sophia had told Willie to bring their benefactor to the room for a cup of tea and they discovered that Claire Phillipe LeTourneau came from Anglo-French stock, had been born in Northern Quebec and enticed to move west, in company with thousands of others, to seek his fortune. They had also learned that he was a trained pilot. Maggie showed interest in his career.

"What kind of flying do you do?"

"Oh, you know, some stunting, although my partner does that better than I, delivering newspapers to nearby towns, taking daring passengers aloft for a spin, the sourdoughs like that, and they 'ave the money."

"Yes we noticed a plane above the station one day. Maybe it was you?"

"Ah Oui! It was to show off to your brother but 'e wants to learn to fly I know. When I told 'im our plane 'as gone as 'igh as 3500 feet 'e appreciated the story." Maggie frowned and he noticed it at once.

"Maybe Mademoiselle Lambert, you would not approve of your brother learning to fly? 'is wife seemed not to object to the idea."

"Not disapprove exactly, it's just that if anything—" She stopped, embarrassed.

"It's all right, most people men and women, fear the flying. I could tell you the statistics of the dangers of other forms of transport and even of everyday living and breathing in the North Country, but I will not bore you."

"You don't bore me and I do understand that Willie has agreed to take lessons from you."

"'e 'as. I offer 'im one free lesson and 'e will be our first student in Edmonton. Tomorrow is the day 'e and 'is wife come up for a joy ride." He looked at Maggie speculatively. She smiled but shook her head.

"Oh no, Mr. LeTourneau, I'll stay on 'terra firma' if you don't mind." His laugh rang out and again Maggie felt he had not laughed for a while.

"Please, not so formal. Claire is my name. English, sorry Scottish too , think this is a woman's name but in our 'eritage not so. Could you?"

"All right Claire and I'm Maggie, Mademoiselle doesn't fit me at all."

"Agreed Maggee, I 'ate to say this but I 'ave to leave you now. I promised Ben, that's my partner, I'd check the plane out for tomorrow's flights. We leave for the Peace the day after. First, may I walk with you to your new 'ome?"

"Thank you, that would be kind, the praying and such should be over by now." Some of her normal composure returned just before she joined the company at the caravan, but not before Hannah's sharp eyes discerned the new sparkle, and Lizzie, as usual, voiced it for them all.

"Maggie, are you goin' to marry that nice man? He looks like Maurice.. you know Maurice. . . He's in the pictures?"

"Chevalier?" Said Hannah absently.

"Aye, that's it, the one that sings about the breeze. Can I be best maid if you do marry him. Oh please, can I Maggie?"

No "best maid" attended Maggie Lambert at her wedding less than a month later but a solemn-faced Hannah witnessed at the civil ceremony, while Willie stood up with Claire Phillipe as he signed the register.

"It's mair like a funeral!" Thought Sophia as she watched her lass become Mrs. (or should she say Madame) LeTourneau, in the eyes of the law at least. She had coaxed and pleaded, even resorting to a few tears, to get Maggie to change her plans, but to no avail.

"At least let Reverend Bruce marry you in the house!" Maggie's mouth firmed in the way her mother recognized and so she stopped trying. If she got angry enough she might talk her man into eloping and not have the family present at all. Claire had politely but firmly agreed with his bride.

Married to a Canadian Maggie automatically became one herself, and at once life changed for all the Lamberts. A sense of belonging that otherwise could have taken much longer happened almost overnight. The LeTourneau-Lambert version of the Scots-French alliance took place in 1921, and later that same year Willie signed his name to another form of alliance when he became a partner with his sister's husband in the June Airplane Company Limited. Following his first 'free' flying lesson, Willie had quickly become a proficient pilot. Hannah too was busy making another kind of history, but history was far from her mind on this bright wintry day as she caught up with her friend on the university steps.

"I'm glad you're on my side Reverend MacAlister, otherwise I believe I would have given up my studies after today's debate with Dr. Layton."

"Well we knew it wasn't going to be easy, but we can manage without Layton's class on Eschatology. I'll give you a few private lessons and then prevail one of the other professors to examine you." The two walked across the park toward the street where Willie would be waiting for Hannah. More than one professor had stated bluntly that he would not have a woman in his class let alone a married woman, and another one would only allow her there as an observer. Hannah made the most of what she could get and Bruce became her able champion.

"I have a confession to make before we get too deeply into the New Year. John Robert will have a brother or sister by Easter time."

"Congratulations are in order then!"

"Thank you, you've taught me well that all good things come from God and I'm excited." Hannah blushed as she spoke and Bruce smiled again.

"Never fear, we'll not let you sit idle, you may borrow some books, and continue your studies at home." She groaned.

"Not those heavy tomes you showed me this morning, I hope?"

"The very ones I'm afraid my dear, but if you want your papers, you'll have to face them some time." They reached the edge of the lawn, and as Willie had not yet arrived, they continued their talk.

"I suppose you're right, and don't think I'm not grateful, it's just that, what has 'keeping the church records', the subject we spent most of this morning on, got to do with bringing the love of Christ to a needy world?"

"I admit it does seem rather ridiculous Hannah, but just remember how '. . .all things work together for good', as St. Paul says in Romans, and see if that doesn't make it go down better. Ah, here is your high flying man."

"Just like sugar and castor oil?" Hannah quipped but her dimple appeared as they parted, he to walk to his daughter's home close by, and Hannah to climb into their motor car.

"You're awful quiet the day love, was it a hard one?" She shook her head and smiled at Willie absently.

"Not too hard Willie, but a few things set me thinking." The truth being that the phrase 'if you want your papers some day' still lingered as she asked herself. "Do I?" But something else was on her mind tonight and Willie sensed it.

"What is it then Hannah?"

"Our family is expanding and I feel as if I have no one of my own to share my happiness. Oh, I don't mean anything . . .I'm not sure what I mean except that I keep thinking of my brother. Here I am with a great family and I know nothing about Lachie. Where is he? Is he married with a family too? I have not allowed myself to think he may not have survived the war but if he had surely I would have heard something." Trying hard to suppress a sob Hannah turned away from Willie but he was too quick for her.

"Hush now, I have often had thoughts of your brother but I never wanted to upset you. Anyway I have talked about him to James and he has written to somebody in London who has interests in the Shipping Line his boat belonged to, yes maybe I should have told you but I didn't want to get your hopes up as it seems a long shot!" His wife had pulled away from him and now she gazed at him in astonishment. Excited words poured from her.

"Oh Willie, when did you do that? Has James heard anything? Whatever he may have heard I want to know, then I can—"

"Calm down now, I'm sure James will let us know as soon as he hears, meanwhile—"

"I know, meanwhile we have the present to contend with, and a very good present it is as a rule." Sensing more in the last phrase than the words Willie nevertheless let it pass. He would remind James tomorrow and even suggest using the telegraph or telephone to speed up the process.

Debrah Ann Lambert made her entry into the world on schedule, and without fuss, and a jubilant Willie celebrated by presenting his wife with a two-seater runabout motor car, to mark the double event of his daughter's birth and his own graduation as a fully-fledged pilot. Other factors added to Willie's content. Their home was taking shape and the week before they had moved into the main part of the house, not quite finished yet but certain to be before the 'snow flies', as the workmen had so quaintly phrased it.

One day, several months after the great event, Hannah left the children with Sophia to take a drive alone in her very own motorcar. She felt the need of time to think without interruption, an opportunity she seldom had in their crowded home. A decision must be made soon as to whether she would return to her studies or give up altogether. Changes were imminent in the church organization, including a big amalgamation, and although the thought of the double challenge of herself as a woman invigorated her, she must consider her family and always put them first. Her prayer was fervent as she found a deserted place to stop the car.

"Dear Father God, Your servant Bruce and I agree that something has to be done to change some of the rules and attitudes about women's place in Your church and You need pioneers, but, am I to be one of them? If so, not only will You have to show me but please give me the strength and the fortitude, the wisdom and the true calling. Please Jesus, I only want to serve You and if quilting bees and bake sales are to be how I do that then so be it, Amen!" She maneuvered the car expertly back on to the roughly paved road and made for home. As she drove into the space in front of the house, that would become the garage, the door flew open and Lizzie, who along with John Robert had been watching for her, came bounding to greet her. Sophia, quiet and thoughtful, followed slowly. The dog bounced and leaped catching the excitement. Hannah, her thoughts now on the special meal she planned tonight for Willie's return from the North country where he had been flying the last few days, brought them back abruptly as she realized

Sophia was not just out to greet her, and as always excitement brought out the Lallans tongue.

"Claire telyphoned. He's at the hospital. It's Maggie's time and as soon as you get your coat off I'll be away over there. I can get a taxi so don't worry about me and I'll get Claire to telyphone you when I arrive. Maybe when Willie gets hame one o' you can come over?"

* * * * *

The twin-engined Avro, pointed southward from Fort Norman, had behaved just splendidly and Willie's spirit soared with it. The bit of trouble with the propeller had been adequately dealt with as he, with the help of one of the base mechanics at the Fort, had fashioned a new prop, using a few sled boards and some tough moose hide, produced by the Indians. Like his wife, Willie Lambert also counted his blessings today, even going so far as to say aloud.

"Thank you Lord!" The only human ear within the vast wilderness as far as he could see, being his own, he smiled. A person could speak to himself when flying solo. This was a grand life and no mistake. Anxious to get home to his family in Edmonton he settled down to the easy flight. The indication of further trouble came when a small chunk of the sled board flew past the cockpit and vanished. Things happened swiftly after that and his dream shattered with an earsplitting crack as the remaining bits of the sled board and moosehide thong broke away and disappeared into the distance. For the space of one long minute the plane hovered like a humming bird preparing to settle, before it turned slowly on its side and floated lazily to the ground. The landing was almost soundless and Willie opened his eyes, amazed to discover he still breathed, and more amazing still, he felt no pain.

"I'm not hurt at all!" He put forth a hand to remove a piece of metal from across his legs. It refused to budge! He tugged and tugged until the blood spurted between his fingers. Then he realized he could never move it alone, the truth of his possible predicament flashed through his mind. He voiced the awful thought.

"This wreckage could catch fire any minute!" The last word came out as a scream of panic and in that moment Willie knew the reason for his helplessness. "I'm not feeling any pain because my legs are paralyzed! Oh my God, I'm paralyzed from the waist down! I can move my hands, and my head, but I can't move my legs at all!"

The LeTourneau's apartment in the Douglass block was located in the district of Strathcona. Earlier in the day Maggie had been engrossed in her special delight of polishing the circular walnut table she and Claire had found one day while exploring the second hand shops just North of the railway station on 100th. Street. The table was one of the few very good pieces the tiny home was furnished with. Maggie rubbed and rubbed not satisfied until she could see her face in the marble-like surface. Placing a small doily to protect the finish precisely in the centre, she added a delicate crystal rose bowl with its single bloom. Her contentment showed in her smile, which she wore permanently these days. Sometimes she just couldn't believe her good fortune. A husband whose consideration for her included bringing her a posy every single day. Roses in season, or a peony, a spray of lilac, a carnation or two and even a tiny bunch of forget-me-nots. She never asked where they came from as they appeared on the days he was away from town as well. She accepted them gladly. She stood back now to admire the rich golden chrysanthemum that graced the bowl this morning. Dragging her gaze away reluctantly she stepped into the kitchen. This past few weeks Claire had been coming home at mid-day and she wanted to prepare a tasty bite for them to share. He also called often on the telephone, and as she thought of this, a slight cloud floated across Maggie's happiness. He made such a fuss about her every move that at times she found herself snapping at him. This attitude had only become evident after he learned about the baby. Part of Claire's attraction to her in those early days had been his calm way of dealing with circumstances.

Take that first meeting when he had rescued the family from their predicament. Her sincere admiration of his way of handling problems soon developed into wonder that one who looked like him with his classic Greek profile, smooth olive skin, contrasted against prematurely silver hair, could be gazing at her with obvious delight in his gaze. On the night he had opened his heart to her, relating the story of the life-devastating fire, he had also disclosed the fact that his hair had changed from a perfectly normal brown colour to its present silver white during the ordeal. Maggie came out of her daydream at the sound of his key in the lock. Her sigh was deep, he was early again. At that exact moment a spasm shot through her body causing her to cry out involuntarily. Instantly Claire was at her side, he picked her up without effort, carried her through to their bedroom, and tenderly placed her on top of quilt, before rushing out to the phone to shout at the operator. His wife only realized what was happening when she heard his yell.

"George! It's started, what will I do? Oh what will I do?"

"Richard Phillipe LeTourneau, the name sounds furrain and high fallutin' for such a wee lad, but we'll soon get used to it." Sophia's third grandchild slept soundly after the ordeal of birth and throughout the admiration of relatives. Catching Claire's strained face Sophia hastened to reassure him. "He's a fine healthy bairn Claire and ye're no' to worry about him. Just as braw as I've seen and in a different way from his cousins altogether I never saw such eyes before." Indeed Sophia had been amazed at the baby's eyes. He had opened the lids in a brief moment of introduction while she lost herself in the twin pools of dazzling blue. He had closed them again at once but a link had been formed. As she waited now for Claire to finish bidding his wife goodbye Sophia sent a prayer of thanksgiving to the Lord for this new life, safely delivered. It was then she received a revelation of the knowledge of how God can love all His bairns without taking anything away from any one, and although the profound truth of this went far

beyond her simple faith, she was content with it. John Robert had
his own special place and wee Debrah Ann, who couldn't love her?
Sophia again thanked the Lord there could be room in her heart
for however many he sent her. Claire walked into the waiting room
then and the two left for the apartment.

An excited neighbour met them on the landing and together
they all proceeded up the stairs to number 206. A cloud of smoke
awaited them there and Sophia stole an anxious glance at her son-
in-law. She knew something of his story and how fire had de-
stroyed his family and his home and she wondered how he would
react to this fresh outburst of smoke as it billowed under the apartment door. He appeared to be in a daze however and he allowed
her to take hold of his arm and guide him on through the door.
For such a big man he surely gets sentimental and excited at times
she thought as she ordered him to open all the windows to get rid
of the smoke. An hour later Sophia finished scraping off the last of
the burned on soup stuck to the top of the couple's new gas stove.
Then, following her usual ritual for troubled times, she brewed a
pot of tea. She placed the tray on Maggie's polished table, being
careful to first put a tablecloth on the shiny surface, in the tiny front
room. Claire paced about like a caged lion in the confined space.

"Sit doon and dinna fash yersel' so much!" She ordered. He
obeyed but got up again and renewed his pacing immediately.
"They're baith all right ye ken, even if the baby is a bit early, he's
healthy. Maggie's doctor says she had a 'classic labour' and 'delivery'." Sophia felt her face redden as she spoke the unfamiliar words.
"Whatever that means. Anyway the wee laddie is perfect and there's
nothin' to worry about." Pouring the tea she continued.

"It's a good job the gas was turned doon low or we might've
had mair than a wee bit smoke and a burned pot to contend with.
We'll give the walls a good wash down and have everything back to
usual before Maggie comes hame wi' the bairn. We'll need to give
him his name now and no' always say bairn. Should we say Richy
or Phillipe?" Sophia knew she was blethering but his silence
bothered her.

"I wonder. . .?" The telephone jangled, before she could say more, Claire grabbed the earpiece as it rang again. "ello! 'ello! Oh. 'annah! Oui! It's for you Maman!"

As she related the telegraph message to her mother-in-law, Hannah felt as if she were reliving the nightmare of another time and another telegram. She had been happily engaged in telling the children about their new cousin, while explaining the rela- tionship to Lizzie, when the message came in. Thinking it to be Willie she had held Debrah Ann up to the phone, the baby would gurgle into it as she often did when she heard her daddy's voice, but a stranger cut in instead.

"Telegraph for Mrs. Lambert!"

"She's not here, can I take a message?" As usual Hannah thought of Sophia when she heard the name Mrs. Lambert.

"Mrs. Hannah Lambert." the voice persisted.

"Oh yes, that's me." Her throat tightened.

"The message reads "Airplane accident. . .William Lambert seriously injured. . . conscious. . .will be transported to Edmonton first available flight."

Hannah's automatic controls functioned as she fed the chil- dren and prepared them for bed. After that she would call Mother Lambert, her numbed senses told her all this, but she reckoned without Lizzie.

"It's oor Willie, isn't it Hannah? Will he no' be comin' home?" The last word choked in a sob. John Robert took up the cry fol- lowed by Debrah Ann. Then King Charles decided to add his contribution by lifting his head and howling in sympathy. Trag- edy could have its funny moments Hannah decided as she tucked the sleepy baby into her crib then patted the blankets absently over a very subdued John Robert. The little boy was praying.

"Dear Jesus, you'll not let my Daddy die, will you?" That was the moment when Hannah's hard won fortitude deserted her. She stumbled her way back from Willie's office and the telephone, while a disconsolate spaniel dog followed her closely, his wet nose gently nuzzling her hand. This time Hannah let go. With so much to do and so many people to comfort, she had managed to keep her mind occupied and all the frightening possibilities at bay but now she collapsed into a chair and the tears overflowed. King Charles yelped in protest as he was grasped bodily and squeezed, all the while being showered with tears.

Claire found them like that. Having rallied quickly to the cry for help he burst through the door, a grim-faced Sophia close on his heels.

"I can stay with the children while you two go to the hospital!" He offered.

"Thank you Claire but there's no sense in going yet, and anyway, Reverend Bruce will be here shortly with the others for a short prayer service." At this Claire rose without apologies and left at once. Sophia returned from removing her hat and coat in time to hear the outside door slam. She walked over to Hannah.

"You must have mentioned a prayer meetin' or the like." But Hannah didn't smile. Then Sophia stepped out of her mould, and placing her work worn hand on top of Hannah's curly head she murmured.

"'Twill be all right, I know it lass and now I'll just make us a nice cup of tea while we're waitin'. 'Twill chipper us up a bit."

The present crisis overwhelmed the vague concerns about Claire and Maggie, and when the doorbell rang again the two women had finished their tea. Hannah almost ran to the door.

Bruce MacAlister strode in, quickly followed by Mary Jean and James Douglass. Moments later Jamie Douglass and her boyfriend George Boswell joined them and the prayer meeting began. The expected call came from the hospital just as Bruce said "Amen", and as Jamie and George offered to stay with the children, the others set off at once.

The attending physician took Hannah off to the room where Willie lay, leaving the Douglass's and Rev. Bruce in the waiting room. Mary Jean nudged her husband.

"Should you tell Daddy now about the letter you got today James?" Bruce glanced up but said nothing as he waited.

GILD THE MORNING SKY

"Oh yes, with all this I almost forgot. I received a letter from that detective friend I wrote, you remember Bruce, asking him to make enquiries about Hannah's brother. I know it was over a year ago but these matters take time and—"

"Yes, yes James. What's the news then?" Good I pray, she surely needs some."

"Not good Father-in-Law I'm sorry to say. It appears the ship, 'The Atlantic Brigand' I believe, went down with all hands. It happened just as the war ended apparently. A submarine in the Arctic Ocean, the crew either had not heard of the Armistice, or chose to ignore it. A common enough—" Again his father-in-law interrupted.

"We can't tell her, not now, maybe not ever!" But Mary Jean had something to say about that.

"I agree she has enough to contend with at the moment, but Daddy, she will have to know. A right time will come so that she can put the matter to rest in her soul. We must trust God for that." The men locked eyes and nodded in silent agreement. The Lord would show them.

Willie's guess had been right. He was paralyzed from the waist down.

"You mean I'll not walk again Doctor?" Dr. Mountifield sighed deeply as he shook his head. Not walking is going to be the least of it, he thought but all he said was.

"One never knows with this sort of injury. I've heard of people with broken backs walking again, but I must admit I've never seen one and it's extremely rare. . . My advice to you is, make the best of things, be thankful for your life. You lost some blood but you're strong and healthy so your body will correct that through time." Willie had another question for the doctor and again the answer made no definite statement.

"Who can tell? Like I say just be thankful you got out in time before the plane and you went up in flames. Be patient and let nature do the healing. From what I've seen of your wife she seems a sensible enough young woman. I'll explain to her and I'm sure she'll understand!"

Hannah understood.

"Don't worry Willie, Reverend Bruce called a special prayer meeting and I know the Lord is going to heal you!"

"Heal me?"

"Yes Willie, heal you. God still does that you know. It didn't stop when the Bible was completed. But Darling, don't bother with anything tonight. Rest now. Dr. Mountifield says you'll not even need to stay in the hospital more than a day or two. When we have you home everything will seem much different."

Three days later Willie Lambert was carried to his own bed. Plans were in progress for a wheeled chair and his clever mind already worked on extra helpful attachments.

God would heal Willie, but many tons of water would flow under the High Level Bridge, as the family faced further trials and tribulations, before it came to pass.

"Maggee! Maggee!" Maggie jumped up in bed.

"What is it Claire, what's wrong?" But she already knew the answer.

"Phileep, something is wrong with 'im, Vous ne comprenez pas?"

"No darling. The baby is all right. Go back to sleep, nothing is wrong." She sighed heavily thinking if only he would.

"I'll just go and make sure." Resigned to the routine Maggie threw the covers back, only too familiar with this nightly waking. If I could only reassure him but he doesn't heed me. Baby Phillipe started to cry, and Maggie reached to take him from Claire. She placed her breast to the baby's mouth, and her thoughts tumbled over the reasons for her husband's bizarre behavior. Claire's nightmares held all the terror-filled memories of the fires that had taken the lives of his twin baby girls. When he had first related it to her she had cried along with him at the mental picture of Claire being forcibly held down by no less than four husky lumberjacks, two of them sitting on him, while the log cabin, completed just a few days before, burned to the ground. "If only" became part of his existence from that night and his wife Marie had cruelly echoed the words for years after.

"If only you had listened to me!" She would taunt him as together they traveled back to Montreal, their high hopes of setting up a home and a Mission Station, black ashes to match the remains of their cabin. "I told you that wild frontier country was no place to bring young children or to try to build a church either! Other territories manage with a circuit preacher why—" Pain and shame had washed over him as he turned away and the voice faded.

Tonight as she placed their child back in his cradle after having soothed the baby for most of an hour, Maggie made up her mind. Something must be done about Claire's awful fears. They could not go on like this or all three of them would suffer. Already she found herself yelling at the baby for no good reason. Firming her resolve she faced her man.

"Claire, maybe we should talk to George about these nightmares of yours, they are happening too often now and I'm worried about you." Had she pressed a switch electrifying him the reaction could not have been more startling. He had been sitting on the edge of their bed his head on his hands but now he leaped up.

"Non! Non!" His voice was a screech and as always at these nocturnal sessions he spoke a mixture of French and English. "Nothing is wrong with me. It is Phileep we must watch constantly, every moment, do you 'ear me, nothing ever 'appens to me, only to those I love and admire. Just look what 'as 'appened to your brother because I took 'im as partner. I need no doctor. All that ever 'appens to me is to watch others suffer and die, that it my portion!" His voice had shrilled louder and louder during the diatribe until it ended in a scream unlike any Maggie had ever heard. Thoroughly terrified by now she ran over to the baby's cradle to stand before it in an attitude of being on guard. At that moment a knock sounded on the door. The baby began to cry again so she picked him up and ran to open the door.

On the mat stood a contingent of their friends. Without a word she stepped aside and allowed them to enter. Behind the three Douglass's who lived on the block stood Dr. George Boswell, Jamie's fiancé. This was not a social call. Concerned for some time about the night noises reported by neighbours as coming from the LeTourneaus's apartment, James had confessed his fears to George, a frequent overnight visitor at the home of his future in-laws. As all four stepped into the room, Maggie's tightly sprung control system snapped and she began to sob quietly and hopelessly, but without tears. Mary Jean put her arms around her as the two men walked toward Claire. He turned a blank uncomprehending face to them. Their intentions were simply to offer Claire a hand of friendship, and maybe place an arm round shoulders hunched in an attitude of terrible despair, but Claire's mind, taut to breaking point with his own awful fears, saw the two as the lumber jacks of that other occasion, trying to prevent him from rushing into the burning cabin to save his children. Thrashing wildly he kicked out and caught James with a direct blow on the shin. James yelled with pain as he stumbled back into George. The three landed in an ungainly heap on the rug. At once George's fitness and training surfaced and the situation quickly came under control when he grasped Claire in a powerful wrestling hold.

"Call emergency Jamie!" Three pairs of feminine eyes glared at him reproachfully but he said it again. "Call emergency, Jamie. I'm sorry Maggie, really sorry, but it is for your own safety and the protection of all three of you. At the hospital they'll do what is necessary and he'll be back with you before you know it!"

"Back with you before you know it?" Maggie's mind echoed and re-echoed the words as a question countless times during the weeks, and then into months following that fateful night, but with no answer.

Unlike the many other occasions when Willie and Maggie had sat down together to work out the family's finances, this time proved much more distressing. Willie, an invalid in a wheel chair, stricken down in his prime and not always as thankful to be alive as his wife reminded him he should be, and Maggie, whose husband lay even now, in a special locked ward in the University Hospital, in a state of frozen immobility. Out of the depths of her anguish Maggie cried.

"Willie, I know it seems hopeless now but I also know Claire is going to get better. If I wasn't sure of that I could not carry on. It isn't anything mystical like Hannah believes about you, I simply know. It comes from deep down out of our closeness, you know?" Willie knew but wisely he merely said.

"I only hope you prove to be right Maggie but it is the now we have to face up to. The situation is this. Eight people are dependent on us for their keep. The two main breadwinners almost wiped out in one go. We'll take a look at the assets first though and go on from there." The two heads bent over the mess of papers spread in front of them on the table that served as Willie's desk. It was the focal point of the room known as Daddy's office, and as such sacrosanct. On top of the pile were the books of the June Airplane Company. The decision on whether to keep it going must be reached today. Alex June, the third partner in the company and one of the original owners, wished to sell his share. Drawing up a page of columns preparatory to making notes, Willie failed to notice his sister open her handbag and bring out a small black book until she placed in on top of the pile. From inside the cover he read.

"Joint account of Claire Phillipe LeTourneau and Margaret LeTourneau!" Their eyes met in a glance of complete understanding. In moments like these the family resemblance was startling. They both had the same dark brown hair that tended to curl and wave in a life of its own. Willie's habit of pushing back his too curly cowlick with an impatient hand showed his intolerance for such vanities. Today he had pushed it back so many times it now stood up like a mop. Pain-filled, each pair of eyes reflected the others as in a mirror. Willie took time to note how the sense of apathy, present these past week in all of them except of course Hannah, was being replaced by a spark of interest and the unspoken question. "Where do we go from here?" Surprised at his own thoughts he expressed the next one aloud.

"We'll take up the lance of challenge and face the dragon of change, that's what! We must or else perish as a family." Maggie's eyebrows raised. Could this really be Willie spouting such poetic prose. She did not feel particularly brave. Throughout their lives to the present day she had been the strong one but recently she found herself leaning more on this brother whose own need had reached a dimension where it could hardly be borne. Since that night when Claire, still struggling frantically, had been marched from their apartment with James Douglass on one side of him and George Boswell on the other, she had existed in a state of detachment, taking no part in the family discussions or activities. But today, following a long private talk with the doctor in charge of her husband's case, the doctor had done most of the talking, she had suddenly announced that today she wished to make plans. Floundered in his own problems Willie gladly complied but Maggie had not finished.

"For this Hannah must help us decide!" Willie could not hide his pleasure at this unexpected turn. Loving his sister as he did he had not failed to notice what he took to be her dislike of Hannah. Now, rather than analyze it all, he reached over and rang the little bell placed strategically on the table for this very purpose. To summon Hannah he only had to hit it sharply two times and the tiny gong would echo it's special signal. Even before it stopped reverberating, a breathless Hannah, wiping floury hands on a hastily snatched up dish towel, burst into the room.

"I thought you two would be set to talk for hours yet and I started a batch of—" She glanced from one to the other, then she said without rancour, "What can I get for you?"

"Come in and shut the door, we need you here!" Hannah turned to Maggie, a question arching her fine brows, but a smile etched Maggie's mouth, the first for months.

"Yes, we need your help Hannah." Confirming her brother's words. Without further comment Hannah closed the door as she had been told. Wondering how she could possibly help, other than by her constant fervent prayers, Hannah listened politely for a while. The pair seemed to be concentrating on making a choice between two options. One option being that they should hire a pilot, preferably one that had gone through their own training, to carry on the task of fulfilling the commitments already piled high on Willie's desk, or they should shut the business down. The first would entail acquiring a bank loan while the second would mean that Maggie get a job teaching school. At that moment Hannah made her startling contribution.

"Henry Parker!" Brother and sister stared in astonishment. At last Willie spoke.

"What do you mean Hannah? What has Parker to do with our family business?"

"I know from overhearing Reverend Bruce's family members that Henry is an investor of some consequence and that he has—" Maggie intervened.

"Are you suggesting we float our small company in the stock market?"

"The stock market, I know nothing about that, but perhaps we could ask for his advice at least maybe he could tell us if it's possible."

Two hours later the three emerged to find a harassed Sophia seated on the rocking chair in the kitchen. Lizzie, carefully following instructions, pounded enthusiastically at the pastry, which Hannah had completely forgotten while John Robert sprawled on the floor, deeply engrossed in making words from printed blocks. Debrah Ann sat up in the high chair banging loudly with a spoon demanding attention while Phillipe, more affectionately called Wee Richie by his Granny, nestled contentedly on that lady's ample lap. His mouth showed definite clues that he had just been fed some delicious but forbidden, chocolate 'saps'.

"The tea'll be ready in a minute; or would you rather have cocoa?" Sophia was still in the cuppa tea business and it was with a sense of deep relief she recognized that another milestone had been safely passed. Maggie's quiet laugh, the first for many weeks, reassured her doubly.

"Yes Mother, we'll have tea, I'm sure you're not really serious when you suggest cocoa, although I see the tin is out and my son's face tells me. . . that wouldn't be the remains of a dish of 'saps' now would it?" Sophia's relief expanded to the others in the room and soon they all laughed. John Robert looked up with a puzzled frown and Lizzie nudged him with her foot as she said.

"Come on lazybones we're going to have a tea party!"

The tea party was over and the children tucked in for the night. Sophia took Lizzie off to bed and Willie, sensing that his sister and his wife might want this time alone, wheeled his chair back toward his office. Anyway he still had some details to work out, including how to approach Henry Parker. King Charles sprawled as usual, when John Robert was not available, with his head resting on Hannah's feet. The dog made a grizzled protest when she rose to match her next words with actions.

"I'll make a fresh pot of tea." But Maggie moved faster.

"Let me make us some coffee, Claire taught me how. He likes it better than tea although don't tell Mother as—" She broke off and the familiar pain filled her eyes for an instant but was quickly re-placed by the new resolve. "I must confess I've come to like it myself."

"Good! That'll be very good!" Hannah's enthusiasm bubbled and she cared not if she sounded effusive. Maggie had said his name and in a natural way. Her remark 'good' meant much more than gladness about the coffee and as Maggie filled the pot Hannah sent up a silent but fervent prayer.

"Oh Lord, Thank you for this chance to talk to Maggie, help me say only the right things, using your wisdom, Amen!"

The two women, so tragically pitched headlong into similar pits of suffering, each with a husband so different now from the ones they had married, wasted no time in idle talk. Maggie spoke first.

"As you very well know Hannah, no special wedding ceremony took place for Claire and me, but still we vowed to each other for better or worse, in sickness and in health, so I'm not complaining. I know my man will get well some day, I don't know how or when but I know that when he does I'll be waiting for him in our home. I'll also do all that is humanly possible to hold on to the business that meant so much to him." Hannah's ever-ready tears flowed as the other woman spoke. Silence reigned for a while and then, as the wag-at-the-wa' chimed the midnight hour, Hannah took in a deep breath before saying.

"Maggie, I know you would rather we did not mention God when we talk but I feel I must say this, Oh no please hear me out. . ." Maggie had moved restlessly and Hannah prayed again in her heart. "You just said if it was humanly possible to do you will do it, while I say that 'with God all things are possible!' You believe Claire will recover and I agree. But I believe God, in His own good time, is going to perform a miracle in and through your husband! I believe Claire still has a great work to do for God, and people. I believe that our flying business will prosper even now, and that there will come a day when Claire Phillipe LeTourneau will return to his true calling and again minister the gospel. As for my man, your brother, his time will also come. The Lambert clan is going through a deep dark valley just now but it is only for a season. This too shall pass!" Hannah could have continued but the wisdom she had prayed for came through and she resisted her own impulse. Again the silence in the room pulsed almost visibly before Maggie rose to join her son in the tiny guestroom. Her voice a whisper she said.

"It's all beyond me Hannah. For me I can only go with what I feel myself and that is if a God would let a truly good man like Claire suffer so much as he has had to suffer, and now our Willie too, then I would rather forget about Him. Meanwhile we continue to do our best. I'll say goodnight now!" Left alone Hannah sensed defeat creep in to her thoughts but she resolutely put it aside. She had prayed and she would again.

"Dear Jesus, thank you, at least she listened. Oh thank you Lord. She didn't stop me talking about you or completely deny what I was saying. Thank you, thank you, Amen!" Turning to leave the room she glanced out the window at the other wing. Even as she looked the light in Sophia's window snapped out. As Hannah went to join her husband who had been waiting up for her, he too seemed different, almost as if they had all spent some time suspended in a vacuum until this moment. No such fancies bothered Willie.

"We cleared up a lot of things today, didn't we?" Not expecting a reply he continued. "I'm glad you suggested we pray before we voted and Maggie didn't object did she? Anyway, all things considered, it won't be so bad. From what I've heard Henry Parker is an astute businessman and our track record, barring the accidents, is good. With Mother as sleeping partner I know she's pleased. That was funny when she said she would just keep her feet on the ground and she wanted no free samples of our services. . . It's a pity to discontinue the flying lessons but we can't have everything." In his new found enthusiasm Willie hardly noticed his wife's pre-occupation until he stopped for breath. Then giving her a keen look he went on. "Are you all right Hannah? You seem miles away! Have you heard a word I've been saying?"

"These decisions are long overdue and you'll be happy to know—" He stopped again as she put both hands to her face and began to sob. He had hoped for a better reaction. Just as suddenly it ceased and she leaned over to hug him tightly until he gasped for breath.

"Oh Willie it'll all come out fine, I know it and I love you so much." The last words were muffled as she spoke directly into his bad ear but he got the message. King Charles, neglected all evening, nudged at Hannah's ankles.

"All right, all right Charles, but don't be long, it's time we were all asleep!"

"Definitely not and I'm sorry Mother, but I just will not allow Hannah, or anyone else, to try that healing prayer business on Claire, how can I when I don't believe in it myself? I remember how you got our hopes up on Willie's recovery and the disappointment after. Besides my husband would be very upset and it could worsen his condition." In the silence that followed Sophia glanced over at Willie, but he refused to meet her eyes. Since Maggie mentioned his name he had refused to meet anyone's eyes. His sister spoke the truth. Up until the actual prayer meeting in his hospital room, on the day Maggie talked about now, he had honestly tried to believe he could be healed. Remembering how that group of friends, led by the Reverend Bruce MacAllister closely followed by the Douglass clan, which included Dr. George and the Semchuks, had trooped in to his hospital room. Earlier he and Hannah had discussed it.

"Willie Darlin', please give this a chance, at least listen to them!"

"Aye, I'll let you try it but it's you I am worried about. I don't want you to get your hopes up and then be disappointed."

"We must never lose hope Willie. James and Nik have just come back from seeing many miracles and they say that place in California, Azuza Street it's called, has no monopoly on miracles. The Lord is looking for people to use."

"You've told me that at least three times now. Why do we not wait until they come and I'll hear them out?" She had turned brimming eyes toward the door. The hospital room held four beds. Of the other three one was unoccupied, one held a soundly sleeping older gentleman and in the one closest to Willie a man of about Willie's age lay glaring at them. Hannah smiled at him and asked the age-old question.

"How are you tonight?" He answered by deliberately facing the wall. The arrival of Reverend Bruce with the two professors stopped her from saying more just then. The lively debate between James and Nik suggested a wholesome relationship that seesawed between insult and humour until Bruce silenced the debate with a wave of his hand.

"James, and you too Nik, it makes no difference to us here how many deaf ears were opened in the meeting at Azuza Street. The important thing is it did happen during the revival there. We won't waste time. To quote a great philosopher: "In essentials—unity, In non-essentials—liberty and in everything—charity—" The two learned men glanced at each other, barely able to stifle their glee. Bruce spoke again.

"Right, let's get to prayer."

"Amen!" "Amen!"

"First of all, I'll read from the Book, Acts Chapter nineteen. Then I've a question for Willie, after that we'll pray. '. . .And God wrought special miracles by the hands of Paul..' Now Willie, I have a two-part question, what does the doctor say about you getting better?"

"He says to prepare myself never to walk again. Not to get my hopes up."

"Aye, and what does God say?"

"God did the extra-ordinary miracles, curing illnesses and other maladies, and that we can. . .I mean we should, hope." Willie glanced at Hannah as he said the last few words. She was smiling. He had said the right thing. The others also smiled at him. In one accord they gathered round the bed, and Bruce lifted his hands, already dripping with the precious oil for anointing and began to pray. Suddenly a loud crash echoed through the ward. A vase of flowers, until that moment adorning the bedside table of Willie's neighbour, had hurtled through the air to shatter on the wall beside the empty bed. Hannah jumped up but James grabbed her arm to stop her movement.

"Leave it for now. No harm has been done. We will see to it later."

Later had turned into a fully-fledged revival meeting. Of the men, three were fully qualified doctors, and no one disturbed them as they related the happenings of their trip to California. Admitting, that at first he had gone to the conference only to please his wife, Nicolas with his native curiosity mixed with his sincere desire to believe as she did, made him ready to receive the truths. James's thoughts and feelings were similar to those of his friends. What they learned there was to last a lifetime and beyond. . . So changed indeed that their wives hardly needed to ask what happened. Each man gladly shared his own unique, yet strangely similar, experience. Mary Jean Douglass could not resist reminding James about her father's prayer sessions and healing meetings. Her polite way of saying "I told you so dear." Marta Semchuk had kept her own counsel. Only when seated in front of her organ did Marta feel free to release the vibrant joy she felt, pouring it all out in a symphony of joyous harmony that must have reached heaven's gates.

Willie's thoughts returned to the present, his smile somewhat rueful as he finally caught his sister's eye.

"I'll say this to you Maggie, I'll just say it the once and then leave it to you. Let them pray for Claire, it willna' hurt him and it could help. At least give it a try." The clock ticked through the silence. The others eyed Maggie beseechingly. Her mother, also receiving bible lessons from Reverend MacAlister, knew when to keep quiet. She too had many questions of her own especially concerning her two Roberts but her faith was growing. Lizzie, who had always known and accepted the whole thing without question, walked over to Maggie.

"Maggie, when I talked to Jesus about our Claire, Jesus whispered in my ear that Claire and him were best friends for a long time, maybe if we 'mind Claire aboot that he'll be happy and then get better!" Hannah sobbed into her hankie and King Charles moved in his sleep with a faint sigh. The atmosphere grew tense. At last Maggie spoke.

"Even if I said yes, we'd still need to wait 'til after Jamie's wedding tomorrow. We couldn't expect them all to just leave their plans and parties. They seem to have some strange customs for weddings here, showers and trousseau teas, and what not!" Realizing at once what this babbling might mean, Hannah's sobbing stopped and a look of incredulous delight crossed her face. Willie glanced from his wife to his mother and he saw the same thing mirrored there.

"They've all been praying for months now, as we have, but anyway we can still go as a family to see Claire. Hannah can pray, and as Reverend Bruce would be the first to remind us, it is the Holy Spirit who does the healing, not us. It's important to mind that." Maggie, concerned and desperate had one final query.

"What about you Willie? You're not better and I know you've been prayed for a lot?" His mother took up the banner.

"Other things have been happening to Willie and his turn will come, we're all very sure o' that Maggie. You know the great job he's been doing among the war veterans and amputees this past year since. . . Hannah it's time to stop talkin' and start doin'."

"Yes, I'll phone Marta to come and stay with the children while we go to the hospital, this is the appointed time for Claire, I just know it is."

Delighted to comply Marta arrived so quickly that Maggie, were she not so preoccupied with her own thoughts, might have suspected all the compliance rather too fast, almost as if Marta had expected the summons. Nik eagerly helped Willie out of his wheel chair, and into the car and out again, at the hospital doors. No one expected George to be there on this the eve of his wedding, but there he stood at the entrance to the special ward, as if he too expected them. Later they would learn of the web of plans, set in motion by the nod from Maggie, but here and now no one questioned. Doors, usually closed and barred, opened smoothly before them and shortly the determined little group assembled outside the small, box-like room that had housed Claire LeTourneau for the past two years. A nurse loomed up and addressed herself to George.

"Dr. Boswell, this is most irregular, I cannot be responsible."

"You are right Nurse, you are not responsible, I will take that from you."

Adding under his breath. "God being my helper."

The man seated unmoving on the edge of the bare mattress of the bed, did not so much as glance up when they advanced into the room. In one accord they stopped while Hannah positioned herself directly in front of Claire. Placing her hands very gently on his head she prayed.

"Father God, we bring you Claire, your child whom you love with an everlasting love. We see your rays of healing light pass through my hands to this wonderful brain, we know that this dear man is very special to you Father, being rightly a minister of your gospel. Jesus, You are the same yesterday, today and tomorrow so we ask you to take us on a journey into Claire's past, and heal all those bad memories about the fire, along with the guilt and self condemnation about his children dying and his first wife's disastrous end, for which he blames himself. Fill his heart, mind and spirit with Your all-forgiving love, Your joy and Your peace. All this we ask in Jesus name. Amen." As she said the Amen, Hannah suddenly became aware of an intense yet painless heat flowing through her hands. She could not refrain from an excited gasp, and as the others heard, they at once opened their eyes and crowded in to see Claire, paying no attention to the orderly who stood, as always, by the small barred window, ready to intervene if needed. Nothing stirred for a moment and then Hannah, removing her hands, raised them aloft as she cried out.

"In the name of Jesus of Nazareth, rise and be healed!" Again the hush descended, with every eye turned on the man seated on the cot. Loving compassion flowed toward him in such intensity, that even the guard moved in closer. All within a few seconds Claire's eyes, dull and lacklustre for so long, sparked into life, and shaking himself as if waking from a long sleep he unfolded, slowly at first, and then more energetically he stood up until his six foot frame towered over the others. The once brilliant mind housed within that tall frame, blocked all these months, and blighted for many years before that, was being restored in the presence of these witnesses. Raising his hand to brush away the hair falling in front of his now clear bright eyes he let them rove about the small space. Immediately comprehending the scene he reached for Maggie.

Weeping unashamedly with the others, she moved into his circled
arm. He spoke without faltering.

"Oh my love, I'm so sorry for the waste, but our God is so
good, 'e gives me the second chance and I will teach you and our
child about 'im!" This was the signal. Nik hugged George and
they kept repeating.

"Oh Praise the Lord, Oh Praise the Lord!" Hannah, tears
streaming unchecked down her cheeks whispered to Willie.

"It's you next my dear, Hallelujah!" Sophia did not speak, she
and Lizzie simply clung to each other very tightly waiting for
whatever came next. They did not have long to wait.

"We all go 'ome now, n'est ce pas?" It required some arranging
on Dr. George's part but finally the deed was accomplished. Claire
and Maggie would not be parted, not even for a moment, so as the
men went off to settle details of paper signing, Maggie kneeled
down in the dark, dingy waiting room. No longer doubting, or
questioning, she asked Christ to forgive her and accept her as she
accepted Him as her Saviour. Mother Lambert could hold it no
longer and as George returned, wheeling a jubilant Willie and
somehow keeping a triumphant Nik from dancing ahead of them,
they found four weeping females surrounding a slightly bewildered Claire. Nik summed it up later to a delighted Marta, as he
told her.

"It was Lizzie who finally got us out of there when she asked:
'Could we all hurry up now because I have a ribbon bow to sew on
to my new hat for the weddin' the morrow and then I'll have my
bath and go to bed!' Now we shall do the same Marta my dear."

Jamie's wedding day dawned bright and clear as everyone knew
it would. As Lizzie put it,

"Jesus turned on the sunshine 'cause we asked Him to!"

Bruce MacAlister watched his lovely granddaughter walk slowly
down the aisle of the old church on the arm of her father and the
wedding party moved into position in front of him, then he along
with everyone else, became caught up in the beautiful words as
the ceremony began, simplicity bursting with meaning.

* * * * *

". . .And the twain shall be one flesh!" The words came to Hannah Lambert where she sat at the outside of the pew, to be close to Willie in his wheelchair. She glanced at him quickly wondering if his thoughts matched her own. "One flesh! That phrase means a lot more than just two bodies meeting! It's the melding together of two complete persons into one, body mind and spirit, no wonder they use the circlet of gold as a symbol. Complete in one unit." Suddenly aware that she twisted and turned her own wedding band as she thought these things, Hannah forced her attention back to Bruce as he pronounced the benediction. Willie, his own mind busy with unwelcome comparisons, now found his view of the happy couple unblocked as they turned to the congregation. Both simply glowed with joy. A photographer began to fuss busily then, and Willie continued his inner searching.

"Hannah and I never looked like that on our wedding day although I supposed at the time we were happy enough. I know I was happy." The procession saved him from deeper recollections as it started down the aisle straight toward him. Triumphant music filled all the space, rising in waves of praise to the vaulted ceiling, and beyond, as Marta gave the organ her all. Sophia struggled to keep Lizzie from clapping her hands or even jumping for joy. Her new hat sat askew but nobody noticed or cared. John Robert tugged and strained at his best collar and bow tie, the novelty of being trainbearer had rapidly worn off. Catching a warning glance from his mother, he obediently straightened his shoulders, and followed Jamie down the long, long path to the doors of the church as he had practiced. It wouldn't be long now until the reception and all that food. More pictures and fussing followed but at last the newly wed pair climbed into the huge white limousine, specially hired for the occasion, and suddenly it was over.

Hannah's nightly ritual of helping her husband to bed seemed as usual, but unlike other nights, she found herself chattering incessantly about the events of the day.

"Didn't the bride look bonnie? ..and our JR I was so proud of him weren't you, Willie? He did his part so well. And goodness didn't the couple look happy as they came back down the aisle? That is a marriage made in heaven if ever I saw one, there can be no doubts on that score!" Stopping for breath she realized that no response of any kind came from Willie, not even a grunted "Mmm Hm!" Too late she wished she could bite back that last phrase as a look of sheer anguish crossed his face.

"Oh Willie, I didn't mean. . . I'm sorry love, it's only—" Willie held up his hand to silence her.

"It's all right, Hannah, don't concern yourself about me. I know you wouldn't mean it. I'm ready for bed now if you'll just swing my feet." Although his legs were useless, Willie's fingers had lost none of their skills, and he had fashioned a unique gate-like contraption to fit the side of his wheel chair. He sprang it open as he spoke and Hannah gently picked up the inert feet, placing them on the cot. Some nights he chose to sleep beside Hannah in the big double bed but obviously not tonight. Her voice betrayed her disappointment.

"Oh dear, I had so hoped—" she stopped as Willie, with a great show of finality, pulled the covers up and over his head. His muffled "Goodnight Hannah!" confirmed it. With her hopes dashed again, Hannah sighed her prayers, as she settled into the big empty bed.

"How long Lord, Oh how long?"

"Where is this place Nathaniel anyway, and what a name for a town? Why does Nik want us to drive so far? Could we not just have our usual picnic in the park instead of this barbecue business? Fancy words for ordinary food!" No one paid much attention to Willie's grumbling although Hannah was still pondering in her heart. She too would have enjoyed a quiet day at home to catch her breath after all the excitement of the wedding, and to have a private talk with Willie about a few matters. For weeks now he always had an excuse, some real enough but she guessed most of the time he was merely avoiding discussion. Complaints seemed to be his only conversation and she was worried.

"The wedding has left everybody worn out. Could we not all just stay at home the day and rest." Sophia decided it was time she said something.

"And miss church? Och ye know we couldn't do that! Stop complainin' Willie and say something pleasant for a change." Pleased to have some attention at last Willie prepared to continue the debate. His mother had dished up the porage while Lizzie got on with her job of making the tea. Willie liked everything burning hot and Hannah had his two eggs just how he liked them, the tops must be white with no jelly but not over-cooked either. Until his accident Willie trusted no one to make his Sunday eggs, declaring that only he cooked them right. After months of careful coaching, he now conceded Hannah could serve them at least eatable. Ignoring his continued grumbling the women proceeded to plan the picnic. John Robert was showing off his knowledge of words to Debrah Ann.

"It's Nik's picnic and not pik's Nik, Ha Ha!"

"It is not! It's a babbycue." His small sister shrilled as Lizzie added her contribution to the general hubbub.

"Whit for is everybody so crabbit?" Sophia spoke into the sudden silence that followed this.

"I wonder why Marta doesn't want us to bring anything the day?"

"Not so strange really, Marta has so many relations, why there's eighteen in her own family, not counting Nik's and they all have special traditional dishes they make, and always enough for a regiment."

"Aye I know, and all Ukrainian food too so I suppose anything we might bring like shortie or black bun would seem out o' place."

Not only out of place but ridiculously redundant. The trestle tables, set up for the feast on the front stoop of a most delightful log house, groaned with the abundance of food. Marta's father, the

family patriarch, watched proudly as wife and daughters, grand-
daughters and son's wives plied back and forth with more and yet
more. Every known vegetable plus a few unknowns, some cooked
some mixed into salads. Potato salad, cabbage salad, they called it
slaw and JP planned to have some fun later with that word but for
now he was too busy eating it. Crisp, crackling lettuce, tomatoes
plump and rosy, only out of the garden for a few hours. Dishes
defying description. Neatly packaged cabbage rolls in succulent
sauces. Something strange to the Scots, which Marta called Patihi
and Nik's favourite, a hot hot sausage named Kobasa. All this on
the sidelines to the giant platters containing mountains of fried
chicken, golden brown and crisp. The main dish, a regal turkey
done to a turn awaiting the stiletto sharp carving knife to be plied
by the host himself. This was Peter and all those present knew that
he and Bruce MacAlister were close friends and had been for more
than twenty years. If this was a first time for such a feast for the
Lambert's it certainly was not for Reverend Bruce. A hush descended on the assembly as Peter raised his hand. He spoke the
blessing in his native Ukrainian before asking Bruce to do likewise
in English. Then the feasting began.

Willie Lambert was not eating, Hannah knew it and although
she felt helpless she nevertheless moved in to ask him what she
should bring him. Maggie noticed too and she signaled to Hannah
that she would serve Willie. Ever sensitive to her brother's need
she drew a campstool up to sit in front of his chair, gazing directly
into his eyes before he could put up his screen. She saw there the
twin wells of deep suffering in answer to her unspoken question.
Having been in a similar condition until two days ago she knew it
too thoroughly. Claire's miraculous healing, coming as it did in
the midst of the preparation for the wedding, had left Maggie
breathless. The emotion charged atmosphere enveloped her
completely and the even greater miracle of her own conversion
went beyond her comprehension. Unused as yet to prayer she
still gave a silent one that she would say the right things to
Willie now.

"It's strange about coming through the door of faith into this new life. When you look back only once and see the welcome sign is on the inside of the lintel If you could have seen that before you might have come in sooner but then that wouldn't be faith would it?" He smiled at her. After only two days his sister's quick mind already grasped a deeper meaning as she opened up to the Holy Spirit's teaching. But his smile remained bleak.

"What is it Willie?" Her whisper, soft and gentle touched a chord deep inside him.

"Wheel me over to the burn yonder for a while." She glanced round quickly to make sure Phillipe and Claire were all right. She need not have worried. Her son squealed with delight as his father bounced him around on his shoulder. Claire's very attitude declared his freedom from his old worry that the child would be hurt. Quick tears of gratitude filled Maggie's eyes as she returned her attention to Willie. Her man had been restored to her and their boy, the darkness that had previously filled his life completely gone. Later she would learn how her thoughts echoed words from God's own word, the Bible, but for now she leaned over her brother. Every nerve in her being yearned for Willie's restoration too. Pushing the chair to the spot requested she waited.

"I'm not going to talk about anything Maggie, I just want to escape the noise and hubbub for a while. All that chatter when I don't understand a word is giving me a sore head." The two sat in silence, busy with private thoughts so different and yet so similar, Maggie opening up like a rose in a summer sun shower, while Willie burrowed deeper, refusing to communicate. She would never forget how his quiet talk to her that day had marked the turning point in her persuasion to allow them to pray for Claire, and overjoyed at the contrast in her own life this week from last, she could not now fathom Willie's grief. In blissful ignorance she again prayed silently.

"Bless my brother, Lord, it should be easy for you to make things right for him too and I thank you, Amen!" She had whispered the last word without realizing she had it inside her vocabulary, Lizzie and her mother, and of course Hannah used it constantly.

"Maggee!" Her thoughts switched abruptly as she thrilled anew to the voice of her husband. How she loved the way he said her name.

"You can leave me here Maggie, I'll be quite all right." With one more glance at Willie she left him alone.

The water flowed so swiftly past the wheels of his chair that it fascinated Willie, drawing his eyes to peer closer. He could see a whirlpool where the stream circled round a deeply embedded rock and if he leaned closer still he could catch a glimpse of his own reflection. Wait a minute that was not his own face because he could see the long hair flowing, nor was it the face of Hannah or any of the other women he knew. The long hair reflected blonde and suddenly he drew back. He did know that face! She was no stranger on the night in Peace River. The night before the crash. . .

"Goodness Willie! How did you get away over there? You're far too close to the edge of the creek and it's deep and swift although the whirlpool looks innocent enough. Lucky I happened to be passing. . ." The hearty voice of his friend Nik Semchuk broke through the swirling thoughts bringing Willie's mind back to the present and if Nik noticed the unenthusiastic response he did not mention it. His strong arms grasped the wheel chair handles and he pulled it out of danger. Apparently satisfied he began to speak. At first he mentioned only general things like the quaint customs of his family. The deep traditions of their Ukrainian heritage kept up by his kinfolk and practiced diligently even at so informal a gathering as today. Soon Willie showed a spark of interest in spite of himself. Nik was a born story teller and. . .but could he be hearing right?

"Wait a minute, Nik, are you telling me your own father did that to you?"

"That and worse, I usually never speak of it but I am under orders for some reason only God knows. Man, if I could not say the rote prayer, not only was I beaten with a belt, but I was forced to kneel for an hour at a time in front of the icon of the saint for that day." Willie was incredulous.

"My God!"

"My God is right Willie. My poor mother would try to tell us stories of God and his love but we just could not believe her then and after what happened to my sister Sonja, impossible to believe in God's love." Hesitating to ask the obvious question Willie waited. Nik continued.

"Sonja must have been sixteen at the time, I was only five myself but I remember vividly the scene. Sonja became pregnant and would tell no one the name of the man responsible. After my father beat her with a willow stick until she could on longer stand, he, in his terrible righteous rage, forced the whole family to watch and my older brothers to hold her, as he heated a poker to white hot and printed the letter "F" for fornicator low on her neck just above her breast." Nik paused as the painful memory seared his mind again.

"Later that night Sonja tore a strip off her petticoat and hanged herself from the bedpost in the girls' bedroom." Again Nik paused and then, pain dulling his voice, he finished the terrible tale.

"So you see, for many years the very sound of God's name, and it was in that Name my father claimed to do these things, brought all this back to sicken me anew. God appeared to me as a harsh cruel being not unlike my father who stood over a shivering five-year-old morsel of humanity with a huge leather belt, ready to beat the prayer into my hide if need be."

"No wonder you grew up hating God! . . . but?"

"Yes, it is no wonder. I was bound and determined to be an Atheist until I discovered in philosophy class there is no such thing, so then I went with Agnostic for a while."

"Nik, why did you tell me all this today, or at all for that matter?" As if he hadn't heard, Nik continued.

"Until a night many years ago now, when God made Himself real to me. You know, I'm so glad God is an individualist, He never does the same thing to different people. They might be similar but each one is unique. . . The night I want to speak of now I was walking on the lakeshore finding it too hot indoors. We had a little cabin built right on the water. Hopefully Marta slept on. Dawn's promise glowed in the sky, and I remember thinking ,it is going to be another nice day. Deciding I could very well go to sleep now I began to retrace my steps to the cabin but as I turned I tripped and fell landing squarely on my knees on the sandy ground." His face wore a faraway expression and Willie watched for a while before he asked.

"Then what happened Nik?" The other man shook his head in remembered wonder as he resumed his tale.

"From somewhere deep within me came the prayer in Ukrainian my father had leathered into my being. The words all jumbled together and I had no idea what they meant until suddenly I found myself repeating them in English. 'Every knee shall bow and every tongue confess that Jesus Christ is Lord!' As I spoke the name Jesus I felt a bolt of lightening strike my body, there was no pain, only a glorious thrill and as it passed it left a wonderful feeling of well-being. I was charged with a life force so beautiful that even before I heard the voice say my name I recognized the speaker. I heard my own voice in reply saying. 'Who are you Lord?" and the wonderful voice that was much more than a voice came again. 'I am Jesus whom thou has denied.' "Never again Lord will I deny you, but I will begin from this hour to find out about you!" and I have Willie, I am still doing it. All the conversation we had then is in the bible too but I didn't find that out until much later as I studied. I never did get back to sleep that night and when Marta came to look for me, some four hours later, she found me deeply engrossed in a tattered bible I had found at the bottom of an old trunk in the lean-to shed beside the cabin. This trunk had been my mother's hope chest and had traveled all the way from the Ukraine, but I better not get into that story. . . What I am saying to you Willie, and only God knows why I'm saying it now, is that God is real. The bible says in at least three places, that God may seem to depart for a season but he will always come back to his own. His own, my dear friend, means you and me!" Nik stopped talking and they sat in silence as the crowds milled about across the yard

Willie caught a glimpse of Hannah as she turned to assure herself he was taken care of. Again he broke the silence.

If all that is true Nik, what about my brother Robert. Why did he have to go to war and not come back? He was much better than me at everything. Why did God allow me to be the chosen one, as Hannah and Reverent Bruce say I am, and not Robert? Even now, all these years later, I am still jealous of him, especially with Hannah. You know she was his widow when he got married, don't you?" these questions, or very similar, Nik had heard many times before. Taking a deep breath he prepared to answer but at that moment a small hand touched his elbow. Glancing down he saw John Robert.

"Mum says to come now and Aunt Marta is looking for you Uncle Nik."

Startled both men stared amazed at the scene of the picnic. People were packing up to leave. Some had already gone. The hay wagons that had brought them in from the main road set up for the return trip. This was farmland and folks with animals to be cared for. Nik leaned toward Willie.

"We will talk again soon Willie, but for now we'd better go." He pushed the wheel chair as John Robert ran ahead to tell his mother ad aunt.

"Daddy and Uncle Nik were just talking. Imagine just talking with all these fun things to do!" the women laughed and Bruce joined them saying.

"I would have been more sensible myself to have been just talkin' rather than trying' to show all the young fellows how to toss the caber, or toss the log as they call it. It always amazes me how like our traditions and even our games are. Who would have thought folks tossed the caber away over there in the Ukraine too?" Everyone laughed and Willie joined in . That his laughter sounded forced and hollow would have been detected by Maggie, but at that moment Maggie sat in Hannah's runabout, borrowed for the day, as the LeTourneau's made their way back to Edmonton City. Hannah's eyes still had a question as she looked at her husband, but her questions too would nave to wait for another time to be answered.

* * * * *

Sophia's knitting needles clicked busily at another shawl. She had knitted many shawls of this same pattern since the first one for her son Robert, but as she counted the stitches this time, the task required little concentration, her thoughts flew back to the shawl she had made for John Robert. Strange fancies had invaded her mind, during the waiting period for Hannah and the dead Robert's child yet to be born. For one thing she had known it would be a boy. When she suggested to Hannah that at least one of the given names should be Robert, she had not dared to give her reason. Hannah would not have agreed so readily had she known that Sophia, not accepting the fact that her first-born was gone forever, had allowed herself to hope that this child, already stirring in her daughter-in-law's womb, could be Robert returning to her. Until a night a few years ago when Bruce MacAlister pointed out how this kind of idea was completely against the Lord's way and word, this fantasy had remained locked in Sophia's mind and heart. Even after the child was born she kept the wish within her. Bruce had been the first to hear of it. She recalled now how his brows had furrowed deeply for moments before he said.

"Let's pray about this, and then let it go Sophia. The enemy of our souls preys on heartbreak and loss holding up false hopes to the bereaved ones. Then he takes their ignorance and. . . But we will not dwell on those conditions. Once warned we need no longer be concerned. What the Bible says is that we, as children of the Living God, need not fear the evil one but we must make sure all our armour is intact." Sophia, unsure what he meant, waited further enlightenment but Bruce merely proceeded to the Bible lesson for the day. Gradually as she studied, glimmerings of understanding began to expand to clearer visions so that today, as she deftly spun the strands of yarn to form a lacy covering for Bruce's expected great-grandchild, she could smile at her own foolishness and his wise teaching. The main weapon of our warfare the Word of truth as he had shown and taught many times, and he had then helped her with the other equipment necessary for defense, the armour.

On this afternoon Sophia sat alone in the house waiting for the children to come in from school. A quick glance at the clock showed her that they would be rushing in at any minute now. A door banged and she smiled. Footsteps and then the usual yell.

"Hiya Gran! What's for eats?"

"Wipe your feet and stop shoutin'." Sophia's half-hearted try at sternness would fool no one. Her attempts at discipline fell far short of her rules in her own children's upbringing. But she did keep trying.

"Wash your hands first and then we'll see if there's any biscuits." The sound of running water muffled the next words but she still heard them.

"That's cookies Gran, not biscuits, cookies!"

"Whatever ye name them ye eat plenty." She expected and received no answer to this.

"Gran?" John Robert perched at her feet munching contentedly at a handful of the contents of the baking jar. His word formed a question.

"Aye, J.R. what is it?"

"They said in school that the earth was made by a piece of the sun falling off and cooling and then things started to grow on it. That's not what we were told in Sunday school last week. Who's right Gran?" Sophia groaned inwardly. Why did this question have to come today when she was in charge? Hannah, the Bible scholar, should be here to answer this, or better still Bruce. At this moment both Hannah and Bruce were far away attending a leadership meeting in the city and she had the ball, as Willie would say.

"Where do they get that story about the sun?" She delayed her answer to gain time as she sent a quick silent prayer of desperation.

"It's in the Book of Knowledge." John Robert waited making the most of the opportunity with more of his Gran's delicious cookies. Sophia's prayer of, Lord help me now and tell me what to say to the lad, was answered quickly enough and she amazed herself as her memory clicked like the electric light coming on and a lesson learned some time ago began to unfold.

"The Bible has the right answer John Robert. Does it not say that Christ, the Son of God, our creator, was before all things and by Him all things are held together?"

"Oh yes, but even if it says that Gran, some kids in school and some teachers too, don't believe the Bible!"

"Well we do! If David Livingstone and Bruce MacAlister agree it is true, then that's good enough for me too. The apostle Paul says this: 'Through faith we understand that the worlds were framed by the Word of God. so that things which are seen were not made of things which do appear." Words came thick and fast now, so fast that Sophia could hardly get them out for excitement.

"But Gran, the boys in the class laugh when I tell them what the Bible says!" Sophia had long discarded her knitting and now she leaned over and planted a kiss on the curly cow lick as she said.

"The Bible proves over and over that God exists, but remember we were not sure about that ourselves until we began reading and learning, at least your Gran wasn't. But now we are sure so J.R. never mind what your friends think, just forgive them because they don't know yet. Go by what you and I know to be the Truth. People could not be just happenstance and there's an end of it!" The boy twisted his head to glance up at her, a question still clouded his eyes and Sophia's breath caught in her throat, he looked so much like his father at that age. Suddenly his face cleared and a brilliant smile replaced the frown.

"Oh I see, yes that's it. I'm goin' out to play now Gran, be seein' ya'!" He was off like a flash, doors banged and boots clattered on the porch, leaving a Grandmother so relieved that she paid no attention to the Hollywoodism. The magnitude of the inspiration washed over her as she began to gather up the knitting to put it away for now.

"Thank you Lord, it was Your doing, not mine, why I didn't know I'd taken in so much of those lessons. How true that you are a rewarder of those who diligently seek You!"

Later that evening as she related to Bruce the events of the afternoon he chuckled.

"Och yes my dear, the Lord is good to His own and that we are. What better thing should we study this night than the 'Creation Story'. The bairns will be learnin' the heathen ideas more and more, and if we don't have the Word of Truth to show them we might lose them. Do you want to start by askin' questions yersel'?"

"Aye, that I do indeed, but first let me tell you that my man was a staunch believer. Some day I'll show you the bonnie kist he carved. It's from the Book of Exodus. For the now though I can just see the next question from J.R. bein', 'if God made everything who made God?' What will I tell him then?" Bruce smiled before answering.

"Sophia I can remember asking my Gran'pa that very question. I don't recall his exact words but here is the answer. For some good reason, known only to Him, God has chosen to reveal nothing about Himself previous to his acts of Creation, and nowhere in the Bible does he try to prove His existence. Can it be He feels no need for further proof? As you told J. R. too much proof shows less need for faith?" At that moment Hannah poked her head around the door frame but seeing the two earnestly poring over the giant Bible, one dark haired though with many silver threads showing, the other completely white, she decided not to disturb them. This didn't seem the right moment to suggest biscuits and cocoa. An hour or so later, Bruce quoted to close the session:

"In Him, Jesus, was Life and the life was the light of men." Then, as if touched by the same thought there eyes met and Sophia echoed one word.

"Life! Bruce?"

"Yes Sophia, life!" Together they spoke the name.

"Willie!"

"Aye Willie!" As if on signal the door swung wide and Willie propelled himself expertly into the room.

"What about Willie? Are you taking my name in vain again Mother?"

"Och no son, but Bruce and I have agreed that tonight is the night that God is going to put life back into those legs of yours!" Willie's groan came out in a forced laugh. He has seen too many miracles of every kind to discount them as real but for himself he was resigned that his case would not be one. He would not allow his hopes to rise again.

"Now mother, I thought we agreed to leave that up to the Lord? I'm—"

"That is just what we're doing Willie!" Bruce made the declaration in his soft Highland brogue and he went on to say further. "We believe tonight will be the night, but first I want to ask you a question. It's the same question Jesus asked the crippled man at the pool of Siloam. 'Wilt thou be made whole?" This time Willie's laugh echoed through the room.

"Oh come on now! How many times have we been through all this. To be truthful, I'm tired of it. Let it go will you? I'm one of those who have to be content in this state. If the Lord willed to heal me He could have done it long ago." It was Bruce's turn to show anger.

"Nonsense, man! and you've still not answered my question, be honest now Willie, 'Wilt thou be made whole?" To everyone's amazement, including Willie's own, he put his head on his arms and began to weep, the deep penetrating sobs of a man who had held it in far too long.

Wordlessly Bruce signaled to Sophia just as Hannah entered with a tray of refreshments. Nodding in complete understanding Sophia took Hannah by the arm and almost pushed her out of the room.

"Your mother and Hannah are away out now Willie, do you want to tell me about it?" Willie's words came hesitantly at first and scarcely audible, but soon they started tumbling over each other until they reached a torrent. Bruce waited, not even touch-

ing his young friend as he prayed for wisdom. Agonized phrases
continued to pour out.

"So I thought it to be God's judgement on me for my sin and
I would have to live with it for the rest of my life!" The old clock on
the wall, as always an uncaring witness to another moment of family crisis, ticked into the silence. King Charles, who had followed
Hannah with the tray and stayed on to wait, being more sensitive
than the clock, gazed at Willie with deep sad eyes but made no
sound. At last Bruce broke into the silence.

"I understand you Willie! I understand because there was a
time in my own life when I thought the same things about me.
When my Jeannie was taken from me I was angry with God, but
deep down I didn't really blame Him. I believed I only got what I
deserved. After all didn't the Lord God judge and take vengeance?
Since then however, many times since, He has shown me by His
love that He is able to cover all my iniquities. But on the day they
buried my Jeannie I considered myself to be paying for my own
sin, particularly for a certain night in Glasgow, right at the end of
my term at University." Interested in spite of his own troubles
Willie sat up. Pulling a hankie from the pouch attached to the side
of his wheel chair he wiped his face carefully before settling down
to hear what this great man of God could possibly have to confess
that would resemble his own guilt in any fashion. With a sigh
Bruce sank into a chair in front of the fire.

"Examinations finished, and essays beyond recall, brings such
a sense of relief only those experiencing it can know. Picture, if you
will, the young Bruce MacAlister, so serious and staid in his hand-
woven knickerbockers. My friend Peter argued they could now be
called plus-fours but that matters naught. Each year as I would
prepare to leave my home in Aribaig for the big city my mother
would lovingly roll up the new pair into my bundle before I went
to board the train. On the day I'm telling you of now my thoughts,
still filled with awe for the great Glasgow University even after four
years, were far from my mother or my home. Along with the dozen
or so other students from the class we sallied forth, through the

famed Kelvinside Gardens, and hence to board a tram, we occupied the whole of the upper deck, out to conquer that big bad
'Mean City', or is it 'No Mean City'. Some of my classmates prepared for celebration while others, who knew only too well who
they were, prepared for the opposite, commiseration. I, Bruce
MacAlister, happily ranged in the former category. With hardly an
exception, although I like to think I was one but I doubt it now,
we were bent on 'Saturnalia'." Willie's eyes widened at the word
but he kept silent, wishing the old family friend, Hannah's friend
really, would get to the point.

"Aye well, after surviving a long hard dull term, we set off
exulting in being free from classes and professors. We rattled off
the tram and trooped into the back room of the "Ram & Uni-
corn", a public house on Queen Street. You may raise your eyebrows Willie but this naive fellow talking to you now would never
have, on his own initiative, entered such a place, in fact the whole
area was a new experience for me. Anyway, the "Queen's Theatre'
would be honoured by our presence later as soon as we finished
eating the kingly feast spread before us. Seated in front of a foam-
ing tankard of the strong dark beer native to the place and having
swallowed a dram of whiskey, truth to tell I didn't feel as happy as
the others had promised me, or that they seemed to be themselves. For one thing my first taste of the fiery spirit brought con-
firmation of my mother's warning to never to touch the de'il's
brew. Trying to appear as a man of the world the same as the others
I downed a second glass of the sharp draft in one gulp and followed it at once with quaffing the rest of the beer in two quick
swallows. At once my stomach started to somersault, and my head
seemed to want to separate itself from the rest of me and float away
up into the roof beams. The room started to spin and suddenly
the people next to me were all twins. That girl on my knee was
slowly changing from green to white before my eyes! A GIRL ON
MY KNEE? Leaping to my feet, I rudely dumped her on to the
floor along with the remains of the glass she had been sipping
from. She shrieked and the pandemonium began. More even than

whisky both mother and my gran'pa had warned me about the loose women. Crowds gathered round us as the girl continued to scream.

"He took advantage of my innocence and then he shoved me doon!" She explained to a couple of giant fellows at the inner edge of the crowd. Large crocodile tears flowed down her rouged cheeks and as I gazed I became glued to the spot. One of the giants spoke.

"Whit dae ye haff tae say aboot this me fine sir?" Looking directly at me. I gulped and managed a few words of denial, "She's telling lies. I never set eyes on her until this minute!" The fumes of the whiskey, added to what I thought of as the gravity of the accusation and what it could mean, caused my voice to quiver like a frightened child.

"No, because you were blind drunk when you dragged me off into the other room and—" The other ruffian joined in then saying.

"Aye, that's it, see if he even kens the time!" A dreadful suspicion crept into my mind as I realized that indeed I had no idea of time just then. I could not recall any of the happenings of the past hours. My mind immediately took up a cry to haunt me for days. 'Oh God, what if?' The thought was too much for my overtaxed system and I pushed my way through the crowd to the door, and out to the curb, to lose the contents of my complaining stomach into the gutter. The two men followed me, my classmates all seemed to have vanished. The ruffian who was the spokesman now said.

"My wee sister Biddy, has been insultit' and we demand satisfaction!" At last I managed a few words.

"What is it you want?" My voice sounded hoarse and weak even to my own ears and they were quick to seize the advantage.

"Ten pound would cover it nicely." I must have groaned and almost fallen because the other one grabbed my arm to keep me upright. I came to my senses then and shook off the offending hand.

"Don't touch me. I'll get the money for you on Monday." A bravado I was far from feeling crept in then and. . . the rest of the story is too long to relate now suffice is it to say that it worked out fine. I came back on the Monday with the ten pounds and the landlord laughed in my face telling me I had succumbed to one of the oldest tricks in the book. He said a tip of ten shillings to himself for cleaning up the mess would be sufficient and he would deal with Biddy and her so-called brothers. I left that place walking on air and saying aloud. 'Never again will I set foot in a place like that, and never again will I allow strong drink to pass my lips, as long as the Almighty gives me breath; and I never have!" He finished telling his tale just as the wall clock struck the midnight hour and the dog slept blissfully on. "As for Biddy, I knew later I had not put a hand on her except to push her off my knee the minute I knew she was on it. As I said I'm not for telling the long story on how I discovered that." Willie had not moved during the whole narration and he had one more argument left.

"Aye, that's all very well for you Reverend, it turned out that you never really did too much wrong. Foolish perhaps to take the drink when you've not been used to it but, we both know what I did, and so I must take my punishment and grin and bear it. It's not too bad most of the time. I am quite happy really and Hannah has plenty of other things to keep her occupied. I can still do the bookkeeping and I'm even learning the typewriting, why—" Seldom had anyone ever witnessed such anger in Bruce MacAlister as he displayed now. He broke into Willie's justifications with rage.

"So that's it, is it? Just what I thought! You're comfortable in that chair and in that rut you've dug for yourself and think you're paying a debt to God and to Hannah. Well, let me tell you man, and listen carefully, you could rot in that chair, wearing sack cloth and pouring ashes over your head for the rest of your days if you so choose, proud of your own ability to pay for your sin, but you'll never pay! You could never make recompense to God for your sin or any sin, because He has already paid the price, for you and me at Calvary. If you think you can better His payment think again. He, and I mean Jesus Christ, took our punishment upon Himself that day. He took it for us and we've no right to try to take it back. Don't you see or understand that the words by His stripes we are healed means just that, healed, not punished. Oh I know it seems too good to be true, but nevertheless it is true!" Pausing for breath and praying for calmness, Bruce looked squarely at Willie, his frank blue eyes piercing what remained of Willie's cloak of reserve. "As for Hannah, of course she'll not complain, but did you ever ask her! ' She is suffering more than you, and if you can't think of yourself or your wife, think of your bairns." Sobs again shook Willie as he obeyed the last. He considered John Robert as his own, and loved him dearly, but Debrah Ann was the delight of his life, with her dark curls clustered round a piquant oval face and big brown eyes twinkling at him through their screen of silky lashes, she could get from Daddy anything her heart desired. Allowing himself to think further into what life might be like now if he could walk and run with his children in the park, playing ball or skating on the pond. Only this afternoon, as he watched them chase each other across the yard with the dog yapping at their heels, he had squashed the old familiar pang. Squaring his shoulders he suddenly shouted at Bruce.

"Where in the Bible is it that the man is 'walking and leaping and praising God'?" Bruce was ready.

"That's in Acts I'll read it to you. It's Chapter three, verse eight, but first I'll repeat an earlier question, "Willie Lambert, will thou be made whole?"

"Aye, I will!"

For the past two hours a hushed household had waited expectantly. Two women, sensing this not to be the proper time to weep prayed without ceasing. Suddenly the parlour door burst open and a man stood there in the opening, but only for a moment. He appeared to leap through the air landing in front of Hannah.

"I'm healed, I'm healed. Praise God! I'm healed." Bruce followed more slowly, but no less jubilant. He too praised God as he proclaimed joyfully.

"The God of Abraham, and of Isaac and of Jacob, the God of our fathers, hath this night glorified His Son Jesus, Praise be to God."

Lizzie alone heard the shrill sound of the telephone and she rushed to answer. A moment later she stood in the doorway and Sophia saw the stricken look.

"What is't Lizzie?"

"It's for Uncle Bruce. Mary Jean says he should go to the hospital the now. Jamie had an accident."

* * * * *

"No visitors, only immediate family and clergy!" The stern-faced individual solidly blocking his path had a voice as crisply starched as her cap and apron thought Bruce, but he smiled as he answered, "I'm both, that's my great-granddaughter in there!"

"I'm sorry, but—"

"Yes, I'm sorry too!" Bruce merely kept on walking and miraculously the way cleared. Hannah, immediately behind him and echoing the word "Clergy", was inside the door marked "No admittance" before the startled nurse could catch her breath for the next objection.

"You can't go in there!" She followed them in and another nurse rose stiffly from her seat of vigilance beside the incubator, ready to add her protests to those of her colleague, she stepped hastily out of the way of the elderly man with the determination on his face. Belatedly she managed to say.

"You can't—" "Wheesht woman, that's my great-granddaughter in there and she needs me. Her own father isna' here to do this so then we'll just have to get on with it, will we no'?" Hannah took the top from the vial and held it out to Bruce. He cupped his hands to receive the oil as she poured it and then, having noted round openings on the sides of the contraption that held the tiny body, he correctly guessed their purpose and with no further hesitation he pushed his streaming hands through. Strangled noises issued from the two stunned nurses, but neither seemed able to move. Hannah was reminded of the Bible story where the onlookers had been in a trance-like state, unable to stop the miracle of God. Bruce prayed aloud.

"Father God, I anoint with oil your child and my great-granddaughter, little Mary Beth Boswell. I take the Name of Jesus and the Word of God as my authority and I pray that whatever is not right with these tiny lungs is now being put right. I do not understand this Lord, but You do and I do know that Your will for Mary is perfect wholeness. She is to do a work for You and for that she must be every whit whole. So, according to your instructions, I take this authority now, In Jesus Name I pray, Amen!" His oiled hands now moved from the tiny head, very gently but firmly traced over the indented chest cavity and all the way down to the miniscule toes. The baby was a miniature with black fuzzy hair and a tiny pug nose, all in perfect proportion, but so small, so pathetically small! When the message informing Bruce of the too early labour had reached him at the Lambert's house he had wasted no time on words. Hannah had followed him out and without direction had driven her runabout to the hospital. Bruce had clasped her hand before rushing off into the Emergency entrance.

"Praise God I have the oil and I'm right behind you!" While making her entrance into the world almost eight weeks before the expected date, the tiny child had drawn a breath so deep that her lungs collapsed, overloading her heart, it appeared to be only a matter of hours before that belaboured organ would give up. There was no sound as Bruce finished his prayer and all eyes concentrated on the tiny form, which had taken on a dusky hue. Suddenly the little body twitched and the four onlookers jerked in unison. Moments later the rosebud mouth opened as wee Mary Beth took hold on life and her yells, seen but not yet heard, proved it to be so. The four watchers moved, as if activated by the same button releasing them from their grim game of statues. Bruce laughed out loud as he began to shake Hannah's hand until she protested with a cry of pain. The nurse in charge resumed her authority and shooed them out of the nursery, all the while making futile remarks.

"Completely irregular" and "against all the rules!". Now that his Mary breathed safely, Bruce was ready to be his usual charming self and to submit to authority. He proceeded to placate the flustered lady with apologies and explanations.

"Can ye no' see how I had to go in? My great-grandchild needed me and I was bound to anoint her with the oil, lay on my hands and pray for her restoration. Ye saw the miracle did ye no'?"

"Well I've seen many things in this place but I will admit never anything like what happened in there just now!"

"Ye've been privileged to see the hand of God reaching down to men this day!" Bruce used his huge white handkerchief to wipe the excess oil from his hands as he s smiled again at the nurse who still appeared perplexed.

"I don't understand, why should God do this for you and your great-grandchild, when there are so many sick, in here and other places, who are not helped?" He had no chance to reply, a group of people, some of whom looked very officious, bore down on the nurse's desk, ready with questions about the happening already being talked about throughout the hospital corridors.

"Let us make good our escape!" Bruce whispered. Slipping out a side door conveniently marked "Emergency Only" the two conspirators made their way back to the car parked a short hour ago.

"We'll go to see Jamie later on, let the caffuffle die down a bit first!" "Good idea!" In complete agreement they smiled their satisfaction at each other as Hannah shifted the gears and the car rolled smoothly out of the hospital grounds and on to University Avenue, passing a long sleek motor car that John Robert would have recognized as a Willys Knight going the other way. Had Bruce not been so euphoric about his recent night's work he too might have recognized if not the make of car then the driver.

Henry Parker's voice betrayed his sarcasm as he addressed his passenger.

"There goes your Reverend relation by marriage Alice dear. Maybe we should have him pray for a miracle for you rather than have you go through these ridiculous tests again. One has about as

much chance to succeed as the other!" His wife turned her face
away. She had cried all her tears long ago. Today she would be dry-
eyed and close mouthed. She must not lose hope.

"The little Lord Jesus asleep on the hay", warbled the 'Cherub
Choir, quite an achievement, for most of the singers including
Debrah Ann Lambert, had not yet reached the age of four years.
Marta Semchuk heaved a sigh of relief along with her prayer of
thanksgiving, the cherubs were doing all right so far, and anyway,
whatever they did would be fine with such a receptive audience.
The Christmas concert was in full swing, the audience overflowing
the church hall tonight. Hannah too, from her vantagepoint off-
stage, sighed as she took a moment to relax and look at her youngest. Glancing then at the audience she noted Sophia's smile of
content, and no cat with a full saucer of cream ever oozed more
possessive pride than Willie at this moment. One could almost
hear him purr. No one in the family attempted to hide their delight as Debrah Ann piped her solo piece of the favourite old carol.
Hannah had suddenly become aware of the absence of the sinking
feelings, which usually plagued her whenever she heard this song.
    "Thank you Lord, my cup runneth over! Although I still don't
have complete peace about Lachie I am content at last to leave that
to You as well." Alone for a moment before she moved into place
behind the curtain to set up the table for the gift giving. Hannah's
mind had leaped back to that one terrible Christmas in the tenement, her mother had managed to scrape some pennies together,
enough to get a wee something for each of her children, a ha'penny
celluloid doll for Ellie, a real wooden pencil for Hannah and a pair
of shiny blue marbles for Lachie. She had also managed enough
extras for a bit of butter and sugar to make some shortie. Hannah
sighed as she recalled that taste. Even Mother Lambert's mouth-
watering shortbread didn't quite match the nectar of that taste.
Father had said nothing until he uncorked the whiskey bottle and
not one but three glasses had vanished in as many gulps before the

caroling outside the close began. Gavin's misplaced zeal for holy
things erupted in an unholy yell as he ran to the door and pulled
it open. "Get out of there the lot o' ye, blasphemin' the Word o'
God wi' yer screechin'."

The terrible sight of him brandishing his whiskey bottle had
shocked the carolers, but not understanding fully, their leader had
started them on another song, "Away in a Manger". Hurling more
abuse Gavin reached for the leader, he would have smashed him
over the head with the bottle only he did not want to waste the
contents. Instead he kicked the poor fellow to send him sprawling
in the gutter. Not waiting to see what happened after that he went
back into the house shouting over his shoulder.

"In John Knox's day ye would have been beheaded for your
blasphemy." He then proceeded to stomp on Ellie's wee doll smashing it to bits before reaching for Lachie's marbles. He threw them
into the fire but Hannah, knowing what would come next took up
her pencil and notebook and scrambled under the bed where he
couldn't reach.

Happier Christmases' throughout her young womanhood including her marriage and her travels across an ocean and a continent, had not erased the pain of those early memories until today.
At last she was free!

"I love that song, don't you?" Slowly Hannah brought her
attention back to the present time and place. The woman making
the statement did not expect an answer and therefore her surprise
was doubled when a radiant Hannah turned to her and replied
extravagantly.

"Oh indeed yes! I love it! I do, indeed I do. I love it! I truly
do!" Hannah laughed outright in sheer joy and delight. . . And I
do love it now she affirmed inwardly as she walked over to aid
Marta with the little ones coming down from the stage. On her
heels Alice Parker wondered what she must have said to bring on
all that enthusiasm. She had merely made the remark for something to say. "I know it was good but hardly good enough to deserve such rave notices. Oh well I should have listened to Henry

when he warned me not to come to the Sunday school concert, but like he says there's one born every minute!" Not sure if she meant herself or the radiant Hannah, Alice made her way back to join Mary Jean and James. Jamie and her Doctor husband were also in that row and Alice bit her lip again as Jamie turned in the seat to smile at her aunt thereby exposing for all to see her condition. Giving one of her false smiles in return Alice yearned for the moment to come when she could leave without offending anyone. Henry was right I should never have come.

Alice Douglass Parker and Hannah Lambert scarcely knew each other, in fact before Jamie's wedding they had never met. Alice, along with her husband Henry, left Edmonton every January and did not return to that frigid city until the frost and snow succumbed to the warming breezes of May or even June. Henry's temper, never too good, tended to grow worse as the year-end approached and his escape loomed. It was in order to get away from this that made Alice agree to Mary Jean's request to join the family at the concert. Not that she and Henry didn't attend church, although she knew her husband told her he believed none of it, and she herself had many doubts, their attendance was just that, attendance only. Sitting with the others now she applauded appropriately but the sight of Hannah's glowing face would not leave her. Suppressing the feelings inspired by that look she gazed about to find another focus but nothing happened, the vision refused to leave. Down inside Alice something stirred. A deep longing to possess whatever it could be that gave Hannah Lambert that clear shining glow. Habit died hard and she deliberately pushed aside the longing, answering Mary Jean and James, or anyone else who addressed her, in her usual cool manner. Neither she or Hannah could have dreamed then how the ripples, beginning from that small casual encounter, would reach out to form a lifelong friendship and into many other lives.

"Whatever that is Hannah Lambert has, I want it!" Hardly realizing she spoke aloud or that Henry could hear as he steered their huge Willys Knight Six through the crisp December evening.

After manipulating the clumsy vehicle out of the tiny lane behind the church Henry became fully engrossed in driving. "Do you think it's for sale?" She stole another glance at him. One never knew if he were serious or not these days. Taking her time she at last replied.

"It seems there are some things even you cannot buy Henry!" Their game of polite attack and counter attack resumed as he said.

"You're finding that out too m'love, finally?" The powerful automobile purred it's way through the streets leaving a wake of heavy gray exhaust. Trees appeared phantom-like through the gloom as bare branches took on the form of arms and legs gone awry, a pantomime of humanity decked in rigid crystal robes as the headlamps picked them out in silhouette. They approached the High Level Bridge, when suddenly the emptiness of it all hit upon Alice. Her eyes misted and she no longer saw or cared about the scenery. Her face crumpled and she buried it in her handkerchief in a futile attempt to hide the sobs proclaiming again her failure. His remark about purchasing joy reminded her of their latest attempt to 'buy' a child. She should have known from previous hopes, built up again and again, but it seemed she would never learn. It had all been arranged, when at the last minute, she had changed her mind and cried out a resounding 'NO'!" How much longer would Henry hold it against her. A fair-minded man in the realm of his business he reverted to cruelty at times like now. Realizing that his last remark had been uncalled for he reached over and patted her hand. Alice hiccuped a few times then settled to silence but not for long. She reopened the discussion nearest her heart at this moment.

"You know how the Reverend took the Lambert family under his wing when they all arrived here together on the train that time you—?"

"Yes! Yes! I remember, what about it?" His voice resumed its impatient tone but she continued. "Well Hannah, remember she's the woman who met young Gilbert in France, she glowed enough tonight to make the brightest Christmas tree envious when the Cherubs sang, so I just had to ask her why. She told me the strangest story about having her bad memories taken away. Henry it's real with her and with James too!"

"Shut up! Did you not promise me that if I allowed you to resume communication with your holy brother there would be none of this religious talk? Did we not have plenty of that prayer rot for Gilbert and yourself too during the Great War? For what may I ask? I will hear no more of it!" And indeed there the discussion ended. Alice knew him so well that when he used that tone to her she had better heed. The last thing she wished was to go back to the coldness of trying to ignore the existence of James and his family. . . 'I'll leave it for now.' She thought, 'But if there is the faintest possibility of a hope for me then I will find out somehow.' Soon the car was gliding into their own yard where the hired man waited to put the car away. Each one busy with their own thoughts they entered the spacious hallway of their home and as the maid helped them remove the heavy fur coats and boots no further words were spoken between them.

* * * * *

"We've had some cold winters here but this is the coldest yet. I didn't know your breath could freeze inside your nose!" Willie's Christmas gift to Hannah had been a muff made of the soft deep fur of the beaver and as she spoke she held the muff up to her face. The decision to walk back and allow the others to drive had been not so much for the exercise as for the chance to be alone together. Very few vehicles were abroad on Jasper Avenue as they quickened their already brisk pace. Willie pulled Hannah closer to his side as he whispered.

"I wonder if I could find you a nose muff somewhere?"

"Make sure it matches my other muff won't you?" They laughed happily as they turned into the home stretch between 116th and 117th Streets.

"It was good to see the Parkers at the concert tonight." Hannah mused.

"Make that one Parker m'love. I don't believe Henry honoured us with his presence. Hello Hannah, where did your mind go all of a sudden?"

"Oh Willie, I still feel awkward about mentioning how I met Gilbert in France. Actually I wasn't sure it was the same Parkers except that Gil had spoken of his Uncle Henry in Edmonton. The name is not that unusual but Henry cut me off so abruptly before I could say very much that I—"

"I'm sure there's more to that than we know or want to know for that matter as it is really none of our business."

"Just the same the message tonight as well as the children did seem to bless Alice. She could break your heart with all that money and luxury and yet she had such a lost look in her eyes. I felt sure that if she stopped talking for even a minute she would fall apart." Willie halted their progress as they reached the gate.

"Never mind the Parkers for a while sweetheart. Hurry up with the cocoa and then we can snuggle up in bed and be cozy." Obediently his wife hurried up the path but as they stood in the lobby removing coats and boots Hannah still had a further word on the subject.

"Still I do feel very strongly that we will see the Parkers again and many times. Sometimes I find it hard to believe that Henry was Gil's uncle, they have such different personalities. Sorry Willie, you are right we can forget them for the now."

"Hannah, it is Hannah Lambert, isn't it?" Not sure who called her name Hannah turned but before the elegantly clad woman could say more Hannah remembered, at the same time wishing she had dressed a bit more carefully this morning, instead of hurriedly donning this very plain wool dress for warmth and comfort more than style. Debrah Ann, to be five years old tomorrow, had not complained too loudly as her mother rushed out the door leaving her with her Aunt Maggie. That happened quite often these days and her aunt usually had some fun games for them to play.

Now, as Hannah stood at the wool counter in the Hudson's Bay Department store, trying to decide whether to shock Mother Lambert with a few skeins of yarn a brighter colour than the usual gray, she wondered anew what Alice Parker might want of her. Her eyes caught sight of the clock on the wall above the escalator and then she remembered Maggie's cheerful admonition.

"Don't rush, I'll cook an extra pot of mince and tatties and save your time. The "Bay" has some good after Christmas bargains on this week." Except for the wool Hannah had finished her other errands. She had Debrah Ann's birthday present, some paper hats and balloons for the party and. . .Here, facing Alice in all her finery Hannah felt very conscious of her own frumpish state and she had to ask her to repeat her remark.

"I just said how pleased I am that we ran into each other, you must allow me to take you to lunch, the food here is quite good and although it is almost one o'clock I'm sure they'll find us a table!" As Hannah still hesitated Alice's voice took on a note of pleading as she continued. "Please say yes, I've merely been putting in time this morning and I would love to talk to you." Suddenly Hannah began to discern the other woman's deep need, a look of hunger that had nothing to do with food. She nodded yes and truth to tell she would have found it difficult to speak as her companion rambled about a choice table, hopefully in a secluded booth, and what they still might be able to order as she led the way to the up escalator. Alice stopped speaking as they ascended but immediately upon reaching the third floor she resumed. No answer seemed necessary even as she regaled Hannah with question after question. "How's the family? How's the business? What is it like to have been in college and be a busy housewife and mother too?" Until finally, as a trimly uniformed waitress brought a menu to their corner booth, Hannah managed to check the flow with a question of her own.

"But really Alice, how are *you?*"

"Me? Why I'm just fine, nothing ever happens to change my circumstances, your life is much more interesting. Only last week I mentioned to Henry how—" Her voice trailed off as Hannah reached over to touch the beautifully manicured hands clutched so tightly together that the bones showed through the pale skin. She repeated her own question.

"No, I mean truly Alice. How is Alice Parker really?" A pair of brown eyes, reminding Hannah of Jamie, finally stopped their endless roaming about the room and came to rest on Hannah's face. The compassion she saw there was too much for the already overwrought lady and the held-in tears could no longer be blocked. A shocked waitress, returning for their order, hurried away to report excitedly to the other staff, most of them who knew Mrs. Henry Parker, renowned for her sharp tongue when annoyed and her overgenerous tips when in a different mood. The lady must have heard some bad news she was so upset. What passed between Alice Parker and Hannah Lambert that day would be shared dramatically with a select few at a later date but neither woman could foresee that on this day. However a healing work had begun and sometime later, as they left the booth, the expensive lunch so nonchalantly ordered barely touched, the same waitress overheard Mrs. Parker say to that dowdy, if pretty enough, person with her, something so strange it was worth repeating.

"Could this be one of those God coincidences the Reverend MacAlister talked about last Sunday", and then the laughing reply.

"Without a doubt Alice, without a doubt! Sorry, but I must rush, the family will be wondering if I went to Scotland for the wool. Will we see you again before you follow the sunshine to California?"

"Oh I will be in church on Sunday. We leave the following day." As Hannah disappeared toward the escalator and Alice called the waitress for a fresh pot of coffee. She was in no hurry home. Henry would not be there for hours yet and besides she had no desire to get into further arguments with him. Her thoughts flew to last week after the concert which had been bad enough. After dismissing the servants Alice had proceeded to make herself a pot

of tea and thinking she was alone she had begun her usual practice
of talking to herself.

"The Apostles Creed, how does it go again. '. . .To know Him,
to love Him and to serve Him in this world and to be with Him
forever in the next. . .' I wonder?" She jumped as Henry spoke
right behind her.

"What's that you're saying Alice?"

"Oh, just something the minister said tonight that reminded
me of a verse I learned as a child." Henry kept silent so she continued her soliloquy. "What if there really is a personal God like Bruce
MacAlister says, and what if He does know all things, and what
if—" Henry had heard enough.

"Don't be stupid Alice. I'm no Communist as you know but I
believe Lenin had something when he said that about religion
being an opiate of the people."

"I would trust James's father-in-law before I would believe anything Lenin said, and I am surprised at your source of information.
But I'm very tired and I am going up to bed. Goodnight Henry."

Alice sat on at the restaurant table still thinking about that
night. Although she would never tell him she had he noted Henry
where he had stood at the back of the hall, behind a pillar and out
of sight but not out of hearing. Maybe Bruce MacAlister's short
message at the end of the concert had affected Henry more than he
cared to admit. What if, as he sat on his chair in the study where
he often sat, before joining her upstairs. Would he, instead of going to the buffet for the whiskey bottle and a glass, rather give
some thought to her words about God, or had he been only too
serious about Davie the chauffeur driving her to church on Sundays from now on. Alice sighed and signaled for the bill. Today
was only Wednesday, who knew what Sunday might bring.

"But Davie only has the one free Sunday a month Henry, you
should know that." Henry paced the floor.

"Servants are supposed to be at our convenience not their own.
You're too soft with them Alice. Well in that case you'll just have
to stay home from your precious church service this morning."

"No I'll not stay home, I'll order a taxi." Henry reached for his coat.

"Oh all right I'll drive, anything to keep you from that sobbing we've had so much of lately. If you don't stop it soon I'll. . .anyway I'll wait outside the same as—" Alice's glance was questioning but she said not a word as they made their way to the garage but her husband kept muttering. "Next week we'll be away out of this damp weather. I hope you'll not be hankering after church services when we can be walking on the boardwalk or lying in the sun?" He still got no response so they proceeded in silence. Soon they arrived at the church and Alice walked inside while Henry decided that this time he would stay in the car. Why should he listen to all that again. He had heard enough of it. He had brought along his brief case and he opened it to check over once again the instructions he would leave for his staff at the office when they were at Palm Springs.

Time passed quickly and soon he was opening the door for his wife as she rejoined him. Alice smiled at him and he had the grace to smile back thankful that for once she was not crying. They still did not speak as the car approached the bridge. Henry's thoughts were somewhere between his office and the vacation so close now he could feel the sun, when it happened.

"Look out Henry!" Alice's voice rose to a scream as she felt the car slide away from under them and the tires hit a patch of invisible ice. Her scream seemed to last for ever as it echoed and reechoed while the big car slipped out of control and slid to the opposite guard rail. It did not stop there but plunged over in almost a slow motion while Alice continued to scream and Henry's voice joined hers in a seemingly endless.

"Oh no! Oh No! Oh No!"

Hannah and Willie had just reached their front porch and Hannah was gratefully anticipating their cozy kitchen where the prime rib would be putting forth its succulent aroma when they heard the siren. Being so close to the main thoroughfare made this not an unusual event and she continued with her plans for Sunday dinner. A few minutes to set the table and toss the salad and by then the rest of the family would be home via the Sunday school bus. At the thought of the bus the siren again cut rudely into her thoughts but she banished the awful suspicion at once. Bruce MacAlister had been her mentor and teacher for too long now and his teachings on the power of thoughts and the spoken word were very definite. The bus pulled into the curb at that moment and a trio of excited furry bundles erupted through the door in the form of Debrah Ann, John Robert and Lizzie. They were in the midst of a heated argument.

"It was so Parker's Willys Knight!" This from the all-knowledgeable John Robert with the arrogance only a ten-year-old with a set of cards with every car ever to take the road could have. Lizzie's response was equally as sure.

"But their motor is red and this one was black!" Debrah Ann was quick to add her piece.

"Their other car is red silly." She turned tear-filled eyes to her mother. "Oh Mummy, it was terrible. We were close behind and the Parker's car went silly, skidding across the street and right into the fence before it fell right down into the water. The bus driver wouldn't stop so we couldn't see what else happened—" Thank you Lord, and thank you Nik, was Hannah's grateful thought as she said aloud.

"Well now, one at a time. Calm down and let's stop guessing, if it is anyone we know then we'll find out soon enough. Wash up for dinner now and—" The telephone shrilled even as she spoke and as the three by now unwrapped bundles made for the hallway to answer it the head of the household took authority.

"I'll be answering that. . .Hello, oh yes, I will that, yes I understand and we'll be ready. Goodbye James." Willie slowly replaced the receiver and turned to face his now silent family. "It was the Parker's car right enough. We must not jump to any conclusions however but thank the Lord. The ice on the river is solid so we must pray and keep hoping for the best. Nick is on his way round again with the bus getting everyone to the Douglass's for prayer while we wait for news. The bus should be here about two o'clock and I said we would be ready. That gives us close to an hour. Time enough to eat this good food." Lizzie and Debrah Ann clung to each other and Lizzie sobbed quietly as she was wont to do in times of emotional stress. John Robert said.

"I'm not hungry!" A strange statement for him but he sat down in his place obediently. Hannah served the meal in silence but as she had suspected there were few takers. Her usual irrelevance began to work as she thought there would be plenty of roast beef for sandwiches and anyway we have that new refrigerator so everything will taste just as good tomorrow. The School Bus pulled up just as she put away the last clean plate.

* * * * *

"Mrs. Parker, you have had a narrow escape from serious injury, your husband too got off with only a broken collar bone, so I find no reason for you to be in this melancholy state." Receiving no answer the speaker glanced once more at the patient's chart. "In your delirium, when they admitted you, the nurse on duty made note of your words. They were and I quote: 'the baby! The baby! No hope for a baby now!' Mrs. Parker I have examined you thoroughly and I can find absolutely no reason why you cannot have another child!" At last the speaker was rewarded by a response. Faint at first but in fact when Alice turned her face from the wall and opened her eyes her apathy changed to amazement. A lady physician, who could just as easily have been mistaken for the maid, who cleaned the floors or removed the breakfast trays. However it was the woman's words that had made Alice gasp aloud. Alice sat up abruptly pulling the covers to her chin.

"Another child? What are you talking about, I have no child!" The expressive eyebrows lifted and the ensuing silence was tangible, thick with unspoken grief and something else, something that hovered there in the small private cubicle that housed Alice Parker. A week had passed since the accident, and although her

injuries had proved superficial and were healing, the medical staff
had been unable so far to lift her out of the deep depression. In
despair George had asked Dr. Scotstoun to wait on his aunt by
marriage. Dr. Scotstoun had a secret specialty, the little known
science of the mind. She recognized in Alice a prime patient for
her interest. For the moment though she decided to leave her alone.
Alice stirred to say one word.

"Please!"

"Worry not, your secret is safe with me. I'll be back later."
Alice reached for her dressing gown and slippers before crossing to
the chair by the window. She stared listlessly at the dismal scene.
Although a bright sunny day piles of frozen snow still lay in the
middle of the road, and the deep ruts made by the traffic overflowed with a sea of gray mud to form an impassable mass of what
was locally known as 'gumbo!', for obvious reasons. Alice gazed
blindly at the scene after Dr. Scotstoun left her alone. The woman's
parting statement still echoed through her mind when at last she
stirred. Slipping to her knees she began to pray.

"Oh Dear God, if You are real, and if You can hear me, please
show me what I must do now!" She heard her own prayer with a
shock of surprise as her voice seemed to echo through the otherwise silent room. At last Alice began to allow thoughts of the accident to invade her mind. Vague memories of others coming and
going round her bed, of gentle hands placed on her head. As memory
quickened she whispered her thoughts. "Something must have
happened because I surely died when the car hit the ice on the
river. Could my brother's prayers have brought me back from the
very brink? "Oh James, why did you not just let me go, then I
would not have to deal with these other painful memories or the
decision I must make soon, even today?" She shuddered as she
relived the spine-chilling moments when she realized the big car
was not going to stop at the barrier and in the split second before
oblivion she had cried out to God. "Please God, let it be quick and
not too messy!" The next memory was of the sound of her name
being called and of herself screaming. "No No! I do not want to go

back, let me stay beside this clear stream in this lovely meadow, such peace here, such delight beyond anything I have ever known!"

"Alice, Mrs. Parker!" "Alice, please answer!"

"My dear please open your eyes." Until finally Alice had allowed her thoughts to once more take in the reality of her surroundings. Upon seeing Henry and the doctor looming over her, one on either side of the bed, she quickly closed them again. She couldn't face Henry yet, but she was not to be excused so easily. Dr. Scotstoun had decided she was ready to assume life and face up to whatever had been the cause of her death wish.

The stage was set for her confession and at her own request, which she had immediately regretted, there would be no more evasion and no going back. The others in the room glanced at each other uneasily as Alice started to speak. Henry broke in.

"Alice my dear, do you really think—?"

"Please Henry, I know what I am doing and you must allow it." Her sigh echoed deeply through the silent room. The relief that followed her earlier decision to bare her heart to Hannah had been so great and she had only been waiting the right moment to tell all to Henry. The accident had hastened the whole matter and she had known that she must also include her brother and his wife in the disclosures. Her heart pounded so fast that the pulse in her throat was clearly visible and as she caught a glimpse of her image in the mirror across the room she noted the twin spots of color high on her cheeks and the irrelevant thought of that's what they mean by tiny flags of crimson. I do feel good and I believe I look almost pretty. She patted down her hair as Hannah spoke.

"You look wonderful Alice and we all thank God for answered prayer. We knew the Lord would answer but you were so far away for so long that we thought maybe He wanted to take you home to Himself." Alice smiled shyly.

"Yes, remind me to tell you of that too sometime but for the moment." Dr. Scotstoun hovered in the background, not wishing to intrude but ready with any emergency that might arise from all this excitement. Since this patient's admittance to the hospital the

doctor had witnessed many scenes of wildest delirium where the
patient's dark mutterings from her subconscious had caused even
the casehardened physician to gasp in amazement. In all her years
of practice since graduation as an M.D. in Minnesota in 1925, she
had not treated a case such as this where the patient subconsciously
but stubbornly refused to return to the reality of her present.
"Maybe I should have refused permission for this confrontation
seeing I know so much already but this woman is surrounded by
loving friends and family, even if her husband is a bit. . .well-"
Alice Parker had softly and purposely began her tale.

"After seeing young Gilbert off to the front, Henry's nephew
you know and he was very young, I was bound and determined to
get into the war myself! Henry couldn't go, we had no children
and not about to have any so, I felt free. Not merely as a volunteer
nurse or a hospital `gray lady` but into the same war as the men.
Women were not allowed to handle guns or other weapons during
the fighting but I had discovered a way. First I would volunteer as
an ambulance driver and that way get right up to the front lines.
Once there I would somehow get hold of a man's uniform, being
fairly tall and not too plump this should not be difficult. Actually
that part proved easy. As a Red Cross volunteer we had, among
other duties, to prepare the dead for burial parties. I just stole a
uniform from a cadaver who was close to my size, he wouldn't
need it any more and maybe I could kill a few Huns to make up
for it all. Before all this happened though I had to practice the
part. My girlfriend and I would try out on each other and by the
time we were on the troopship crossing the Atlantic we had become pretty good at it, or so we thought." She paused for breath
and to glance quickly at Henry who had moved uncomfortably in
his chair. He caught the glance.

"Alice are you sure. . .Doctor?" Ignoring him his wife continued
as she warmed to the tale.

"Yes, we had become over-confident and had placed ourselves
in extreme danger each time we sallied forth from our cabins in
disguise. Always at night of course as the ship was blacked out and

the salons very poorly lit inside too. Dorothy, my friend and reluctant co-conspirator, was older than I and had a knowledge of the
world and its ways far beyond my own. Many times since, as I
have looked back I realized she was really warning me, but I was
too naive or dense, and too headstrong and stubborn to heed her
warnings. One moonlight night on the ship she had cautioned me
that the light would give me away and I should not venture out,
but I was bent on proving that I could do anything a man could
do. Smoking, drinking, swearing, in all my sheltered life I had
never done any of these things, not even wine at Christmas, so you
see the drink knocked me for a loop." She paused again and this
time her eyes traveled round the circle of intent faces.

"Dear dear Henry, what a hard time I've been giving you lately,
and James, the most wonderful brother in the world. Mary Jean
the perfect wife for you and a wonderful sister to make up for the
one I never had. Why did it take me so long to appreciate you and
your father, Reverend Bruce, may you and God forgive me for my
irreverent treatment of you. I know now it was only fear of the
truth that shines from you. Hannah and Willie, when I get to
know God better I will thank him properly for such a family and
such friends. Back to the story—" Her audience now made no
effort to stop the flow. Hannah had closed her eyes as she clutched
Willie's hand and James made no pretence as he wrapped his arms
round his wife. Henry's face had taken on the look of granite as
Bruce sat in silent prayer.

"I was not used to strong drink as I said before, and so what
happened on that awful night on the ship was never too clear in
my memory, but the results of it came perilously close to ruining
my life and blighting my family for ever." Alice risked a glance at
her brother but just at that moment James had turned his attention to Henry who had uttered an anguished groan. She wrung
her saturated hanky without seeing it as she continued.

"So when I awoke the next morning I knew that our secret had
been discovered, the fact that we were women exposed, to my
shame literally. My head felt like one huge mass of pain and my

body, covered with bruises, joined in the unharmonious symphony of agony by throbbing to the beat of the ship's engines. I groaned my friend's name aloud and receiving no answer from the other bunk where I could see the outline of her body dimly under the gray army blanket, and hear the sound of her breathing, ominously heavy in the cramped space. Suddenly wide-awake I sat up screaming her name. 'Dorothy, Dorothy!', but even as I screamed memory stirred, ghastly memories, faint at first but then most cruelly clear.

"Quit your screeching, will you?" At that the bile rose in my throat once more and as it filled my mouth, I vomited on the blanket before falling back helpless on to the bunk. My next conscious thought was to wonder who could be tearing the skin off my face with a bit of sandpaper. This turned out to be only a piece of rough sacking of the kind we used for towels. My mouth tasted horrible and the rough cloth smelled worse. I struggled to a half sitting position.

"Who are you?" I croaked.

"No names no pack drill." A strange voice answered. Or was it not so strange as the memories started to roll again in a rush of pain and guilt more awful than anything I had ever experienced, and which I have never, until this moment been able to speak of, let alone put out of my thoughts, as for nightmares, well not even as I slept would they leave me." George and James made a simultaneous move toward the bed as George said.

"Say no more Alice, some other time you—" but she waved a hand at him.

"This is the time, please hear me out if I am to be healed. You see, a few days before, while exploring the ship Dorothy and I had chanced upon a crate of rum hidden in a lifeboat. Thinking it to be a great joke on whoever had placed it there, obviously illegally, we had started with one bottle, opening it and pouring the contents into the sea. The next day we repeated this and again the next until there were as many empty bottles as full ones in the crate. Then the day came when we, or rather Dorothy as it was her turn, anyway as she reached in for the bottle we heard a muffled oath and at the same moment her wrist was clasped tightly in a huge ham fist. She screamed but immediately her mouth was covered by another hand. Before I could run I was seized from behind and given the same treatment.

"God's Streuth 'tis a woman or maybe a tigress. Stop it ye bitch!" This last as I had bitten the hand and managed to free a hand to scratch. The voice continued in amazement. "Steal our rum would ye, well seein' ye're so fond of it let's see how much you can take in, in one go." My nose was grasped and I felt the bottle edge scrape my teeth. Forced to swallow the turgid yet fiery liquid, I was helpless and soon hung like a limp rag doll over the brawny arm of one of the assailants. "Not so cocky now are ye, wee bitch, bitin' and scratchin' when you're the one that did the stealin', well by God I'll teach ye a lesson now ye'll not forget in a hurry!" These words of prophecy would ring in my ears for many a long painful day but just then I was too drunk to notice as the rough hands began to rove over my body, ripping and tearing my clothes until I lay stripped naked. . .Dorothy helped me conceal the grim consequences of that terrible rape until, one night a few months later, while driving my ambulance close to the front lines I. . .it will be enough to say that poor little scrap of humanity never had a chance at life and I have been blaming myself—" A muffled sound came from the chair where Henry had been seated, unmoving and silent, for the last half hour. The eyes of the group swiveled toward him as he now rose from the chair.

"Enough, I say, that will be enough, we do not need to hear more!" Alice silently wept now and Hannah sobbed in unison from her place by the window. The doctors moved as one and Mary Jean stepped over to Hannah's side. Moments later only Henry and Alice remained in the room. Quickly he went to place his arms protectively round his wife.

"There now, as I said that's enough. Some day you can tell me the rest but for now, leave it. Don't ask me why but I'm feeling like a ton has been lifted off my shoulders too. Soon we can begin again but let it all go for the moment. I must insist." Alice hiccuped once and then with a sigh she subsided. Maybe this was only a dream. . .But Henry's arms were real enough and his voice, even if only a whisper was no dream as he said into her hair.

"I love you Alice Douglass Parker, now more than ever!"

* * * * *

Willie Lambert sang as he wielded the giant loofah to his back. Singing in the bathtub had become a habit since his healing much to the dismay of the other family members. He simply ignored the sarcastic jibes altogether or rebutted with such remarks as 'jealous eh?' which only invoked further criticism. As he sang on this day his thoughts circled round the fact that a fellow did not appreciate a good sit-in tub and a whole lot of other good things in life until he had to do without them for a while. Finished with his back he began to methodically scrub each foot slipping down the black enameled tub until only his head showed and his knees. The bath ensemble was the very latest in bathroom decor or so his wife had informed him at the time he had signed the cheque to pay the plumber. His grumbles had gone unheeded as the other occupants of their home knew very well that he was as justly proud of their modern house as they. The thought brought Hannah to mind and he exulted anew as he recalled her words of less than an hour ago.

"Mother Sophia will have to get her knitting needles out again, they've been idle too long!" It had taken him a minute or two to catch her meaning but when the full impact of her words hit him he let out a whoop to rouse the household and by the time the others joined them he had snatched her up to twirl her round the room to the accompaniment of King Charles's yipping and Hannah's half-hearted attempts to quiet him.

"Willie, put me down and stop shouting, do you want the whole of Edmonton to know?"

"Why not? I'd like the whole world to know." But sensing a quietness in her spirit he set her down gently before rushing about to fetch her a footstool and asking if she wished anything else, such as a cup of tea. . .

"Stop your nonsense, a cup of tea is the last thing I want." Slightly put out at this he sat down on the footstool and replaced her feet on his lap. Gazing up at her he had asked.

"You are happy about it Hannah aren't you?"

"Of course I'm pleased Willie, it's just that I don't know how the children will take the news, especially JR, after all he is nearly thirteen and he might be embarrassed."

"I think you're wrong Hannah, but if you like I will have a wee talk to him, man to man you know?"

"Oh would you dear, that might be better." But Willie could see that this only partly soothed his over sensitive wife as she extricated herself from his lap to move to the other side of the kitchen stove. Willie knew her well enough to allow her to take her own time to tell him what was on her mind. He did not have long to wait.

"Willie?" He laid aside all pretence at reading the paper and placed it on the table as he reached to take her hand. He gently unclenched the tightly squeezed fist, and still not speaking, he gazed at the lowered head until she was forced to meet his glance. Words began to pour out then.

"It's Alice, she is still so dreadfully disappointed that they have no children and of course the older she gets. . .Oh Willie, I pray it is not wicked to think this but I almost wish—" Before she could utter the wish Willie's hand came up to press gently against her mouth.

"Do not say it! It's not wicked but it is questioning God in ways that we have no right to question Him." She subsided and he took away his hand. After a moment she spoke again.

"It's so hard to understand. Both Dr. Scotstoun and George have assured Alice that. . .Oh bother that telephone." At the unusual tone of voice Willie raised his eyebrows as he went to answer the ring.

"Oh, 'tis yourself George, we were just speaking about you. Och no, nothing like that, come away on over then and I'm sure we'll manage a cup of tea or other like refreshment."

George was not alone when he arrived a half-hour later. Close on his heels came Henry Parker, looking even more strained than ever. Hannah unusually flustered for her brought out the obvious questions.

"Where are Alice and Jamie tonight? Would you like tea or coffee, or I could make a jug of cocoa, or—" A glance at George's face said more than words to stop the flow. They were not here for a social visit.

"Alice is at the University practicing for next week's concert and Jamie stayed home with our three for a change!" Hannah smiled uncertainly. The presence of Henry Parker in her living room un-nerved her no end. If they did not want refreshment then maybe she could slip out and leave the men. Another glance at George's face made her change her mind and as Henry began to speak she forgot all else.

"My wife still thinks she is being punished for her sins!" He began without preamble. " I have told her repeatedly that we must forget the whole matter. We've been reasonably happy all these years without, well anyway. . .I'm not sure what it all means and I want some explanations. If your God works that way then He is no better, or different, from men and why worship Him? Can any of you answer that eh?" Knowing she was the one expected to reply Hannah prayed fervently and for a long moment the only sound in the room came from King Charles as he moved in his sleep making tiny growling sounds.

"Henry!" Hannah spoke as her random thoughts began to take form. "You are a business man and you know that one of the rules or laws of business, especially in the area of food production, is the law of sowing and reaping?" Henry's brow creased with new questions.

"Yes, but what about it?"

"You also know it works because you have been reaping the benefits of wise investments, or seed sowing, for a long time, is that correct?"

"Yes, but I still don't see—"

"Did you, your own self, sow that seed?"

"Of course not and please Hannah, no prevarication, I'm serious."

"So am I Henry, very serious. The answer you are seeking is in this book and I can only refer to it as I try to help you. I too have been concerned about Alice and I have been asking some questions myself, but it has only been in the last few minutes that some answers are becoming clear." She paused for breath and the others waited, expectantly hushed. "Henry if you paid a man to sow wheat for you and he defied you without telling you and sowed something else, and then one day, as you passed by your wheat field, something strange catches your eye, something bright and colorful like flowers. Flowers in your wheat fields? It is too late now to sow more wheat for this year's harvest so what will you do with acres and acres of worthless flowers? But wait a moment are they worthless? A shrewd businessman like yourself Henry would not plough over the field, or even fire the seed sower, without some thought." Hannah stopped speaking to glance round the group of men. Willie would not meet her gaze and George too seemed embarrassed while Henry watched, politely enough but obviously without interest or credulity, Hannah plodded on regardless.

"All this is a parable I know but the Lord taught in parables when He walked the earth and He still uses them. There's a place in the Bible where St. Paul teaches that God is not mocked. [Gal 6: 7-10] I take that to mean that we, when we have been wronged, need not seek our own revenge, but that He will do it for us in His way and in His time. The same chapter goes on to say that a person's harvest in life depends entirely on what said person sows. Unlike the physical harvest though this spiritual harvest may not be so obvious. Alice sowed some foolish seeds and they produced crops in kind, but be sure that God knows about the adversary who took advantage of her youth and foolishness. He also knows that in her heart Alice desires to sow good seed and so the eventual harvest will produce fruit of that kind. She needs to know however that God is not punishing her but she is punishing herself and that must stop!"

Hannah paused sensing the cool appraisal from Henry as well as the puzzled reactions of George and Willie. Henry had begun to pace about puffing furiously on his cigar to fill the room with thick blue smoke that marbled in the rays of the dying sun as it streamed through the curtains. Heaviness descended on the company and Hannah sighed. She knew only too well that her words had made at best no impact on Henry and possibly even had an adverse effect. The silence grew heavier but at last Henry spoke.

"I cannot accept what you say Hannah and I'm sorry. I don't know exactly what I hoped for when I came in tonight. Maybe I want to experience that something extra I see in your life and the life of Reverend MacAlister, as well as the others in your families, but. . .well. . . I guess it's not for us. We should go George, we have to pick Alice up at the university." George nodded and with an apologetic glance in Hannah's direction he followed Henry out.

Hardly giving them time to close the door Willie was on his feet and beside Hannah. Sweeping her up into his arms he walked over to the old rocker his mother had brought from Scotland and where so many shawls and other useful baby items had been created. He sat down now and folded his wife across his knees and began to rock her back and forth as he spoke softly.

"My Love, I want you to think only of yourself and our little one for a wee while. You know in Isaiah where we are told to be very careful of those who are with young, and so now I propose to do just that. As head of this house I would request that you obey me in this regard!" Gratefully Hannah allowed him to soothe and comfort her for a while and soon she slept. Willie rose and being careful not to wake her he carried her to their bed.

King Charles, a grizzled and wise spectator to the many and varied happenings of the day, might have shaken his head in wonder at the strange sights and sounds made by his human family, but knowing no better he merely yawned widely before settling himself more comfortably on his blanket.

George and Henry soon reached the university and Henry said.

"No time to take you home first Geo, so we'll get Alice and than I'll drop you off."

"Will you come in for a while?" George asked quickly.

"No I don't think so, not tonight!"

"How did you happen to have George with you tonight Henry?" Alice posed the question as they drove away from his driveway.

"I called on him just after I left you at the university. I hoped he might give me some answers to those questions you and I have been arguing about so much lately." Alice waited breathlessly not daring to speak but her eyebrows had risen delicately. Henry resumed speaking.

"It was just as I suspected though. Neither he nor Hannah Lambert could tell me anything.." She let her breath escape in one long sigh.

"Tonight's practice was very good, I believe we might be able to conduct ourselves favourably at the concert." Receiving no response to that she wisely said no more for a time. She knew her man well enough to leave the next verbal move to him. The cool logic with which Henry Parker conducted his business life and most of his private life as well, emerged once again in his next words. They had reached their closed gates and the gatekeeper ran out to open them. Henry waited until they entered the circular driveway and the chauffeur had taken the car. Habit helped him to grasp his wife's arm as they climbed the steps. He stopped before they reached the door and he turned her to face him. She trembled but returned his frank gaze bravely.

"I have given your God a fair chance Alice and He miffed it eh? Now we will just forget about religion for a while and concentrate our energies and thoughts on something else. I have a business deal in Toronto soon. We will leave right after your concert and combine business with pleasure as we take a winter cruise in the South Seas. What do you say to that eh? We can bask in the sun and spend some time in a different clime, Sydney Australia maybe or—" The door swung open and the maid appeared. She had heard the car and wondered why they were still outside.

"Your supper tray is ready Madam, will you have it in the drawing room?" This last being the ritual when Alice was in rehearsal as she found herself unable to swallow food before leaving for the university. The maid disappeared as Alice nodded assent and nothing more was said until the maid had left after depositing the tray on a small table beside the window. Light still streamed in the long dormer windows but the Parkers noticed nothing. Very deliberately and also very quietly Alice spoke one word.

"No!" Taken up with pouring himself a drink at the sideboard Henry turned in amazement.

"What did you say?" She gulped but stood her ground.

"I said no Henry! No, I will not go with you, not now, not after the concert, not to Sydney, not on a cruise, just no! No! No!" Henry carefully placed his half-filled glass on the refreshment tray before slowly facing this stranger once again. Momentarily speechless he stared at her. She neither spoke again or moved. Finally he found his voice.

"You said no? Alice are you saying what I think you are?" But she had said it all and her throat and mouth dry with sobs she could not utter she just shook her head. A faint echo of her final "No" did emerge as she returned his look and mutely allowed her eyes to speak instead. What they said was more than Henry could bear and he strode from the room muttering an oath. Not until she had heard the outer door slam and the sound of a motor starting up did she relax her taut pose and allow her shoulders to droop.

"Oh Henry, I do love you but what should I do now and how can I make you understand when I don't understand myself?

Henry Parker did not believe in blind chance. As a successful businessman he had certainly taken many risks, and most of the time they had paid off, but a very few times he had lost. He could not allow himself to believe in a "Supreme Being", or a benign benevolence either, especially one who guided men's lives or cared about little people. Truth to tell, Henry felt that he was an excellent guide of his own life and therefore did not need help of this type. The first thirty years his life had been quite ordinary. Born in

1884, the only son of well-to-do parents, he had been reared uneventfully enough until he reached the age of 29. In that year his parents and his only sister had died in the terrible 'flu epidemic that swept through his home city of Toronto in 1913. Inheriting a flourishing business from his father and a mind that questioned everything before trying it from his mother, he merely carried on his life in much the same way as before the tragedy, spending only a few days in morose mourning before realizing the futility of energy wasted on something that could not be changed. That same logic and philosophy had served him well enough until he had met Alice Douglass at a benefit concert for the Red Cross. Introduced by her brother, the medical doctor James Douglass, Henry had known at once he wanted her for his wife, logic notwithstanding. Within weeks he had swept her off her feet and into a registry office. James and his own wife Mary Jean did not approve of this form of marriage, but Alice, bemused by his extravagant behaviour and meticulous manners, had ignored her family's disapproval. Declaring that so long as they had each other they needed no one else they kept to themselves for a time. It was not until after the visit to the station to bid farewell to his nephew, the only member of the Parker family in that generation when the dissatisfaction set in. Then Alice's rebellion with running off to the war, and later Gilbert's death, had all been factors in Henry's hardened attitude.

As he drove away from his home he struggled to bring his logical mind to the fore. Following Alice's confession and her return to what he called religious zeal he truly had tried to understand his wife but her obstinate no to his generous suggestion of going away puzzled him to the extent of blinding anger. He braked the car at an intersection and as the traffic was light he took time to study the highway signs. Without giving it too much thought he steered the car in the direction of the west bound sign. He spoke his thoughts aloud.

"Maybe I'll just keep driving, I haven't been to the mountains for a while. I can stop somewhere for the night and start fresh in the morning. Alice won't care obviously but I might get a message to her in the morning." The powerful motor purred as Henry pressed hard on the gasoline pedal.

Henry drove across the High Level Bridge before turning east and then south on to the Calgary Trail. He drove cautiously now, as he recalled the winter when he and Alice had the accident that almost took his wife's life. This brought up another question his logic could not answer, although he tried.

"Could it be that this is some sort of punishment, instead of dying and escaping the pain we have to live with it and suffer? No, I cannot accept that either. Well then, why is it, just when you should be able to relax and take life a bit easy, when you think you've reached the top, things start to go awry and you meet frustrations at every turn?" He smiled sheepishly as he caught a glimpse of himself in the driving mirror. To talk to yourself under your breath was one thing but if he was beginning to do it aloud! 'Oh Alice!' This came out more as a groan. "We have everything it seems, and yet we have not the one thing we want most. Maybe that's what it's all about, an ironic state where there is always something else beyond your reach. Hannah and Willie Lambert seem to have everything now but they could look back on some pretty rough times and even tonight there had been a strain in the atmosphere."

Henry did not for a moment attribute that strain to his own presence there as he continued his introspection. "As for any fairness or balance in the way things were meted out, you would think someone would figure out someway to make matters more equal. Oh I know it's been tried and with some improvement but it never seemed to work out so that people get what they deserve. When I've discussed this with Alice she has told me to be careful as I was getting dangerously close to playing God. That was funny as although for a while I came close to believing there could be a God, I quickly changed my mind. Not a just God anyway. If there is someone up there He is the one playing a cruel sadistic joke, almost like a roulette game with the poor little people. Well here is one poor little person who does not want to play!" The silence in the car grew tangible as Henry stepped gently on the brake to bring the vehicle to a stop by the side of the road. Pavement had long since disappeared and even as his headlights picked out a few scattered snowflakes they began to fall thicker and faster. Not content with speaking his thoughts aloud he had shouted the final sentence and it reverberated for a long time. At last some kind of rational thought took over and he wondered if he should turn back now before the snow got any thicker. Instead he put his head on the steering wheel and began to weep. Henry Parker never knew how long he sat thus before he became aware of his name being called.

"Henry!" He lifted his head quickly from the wheel.

"What? Who called me?" He wiped his wet cheeks on his sleeve as he spoke. Again the voice said his name and this time Henry knew this was no ordinary voice. Instantly Henry knew, as Paul knew on the road to Damascus, who called him. "Forgive me Lord, what would you have me do?" The gentle but firm voice replied.

"You do not have to do anything, you merely have to be. Learn of me and get to know me. Come to love me as I first loved you. What are your alternatives throughout Eternity?" Silence reigned in the car, a silence so deep it throbbed with the Presence. When at last Henry looked round he saw nothing and in that moment he thought he had been struck blind, however as his headlights gleamed on the snow he knew he could still see. Expertly he maneuvered the car out of the narrow space between the deep ditches and began the journey back to the city and home. Would he have a story to tell when he got back but even as the thought came he squashed it. 'I'll tell no one but Alice and even if she will say I fell asleep and dreamed it all, I know better. I still have a question though: Why me Lord?' This question, asked many times through the ages would take eternity to show the thousands of answered prayers, like the ones Hannah and others like her, had prayed for the Henrys. Evenso Henry continued to think aloud as he at last swung into his own driveway. 'I'm so glad I never need to doubt again. What indeed is the alternative? Thank You Lord!'

* * * * *

Alice became aware of the maid's hovering after the girl had picked up the tray and laid it back down numerous times. Suddenly she remembered this was the girl's night off.

"Jenny, shouldn't you be at home tonight?" The unexpected reaction, as she said the words, shocked her completely out of her recent self-absorption. A dam had burst and the floodwaters, held in check all day, erupted in a torrent. Engrossed in her own heartbreak Alice had failed to notice the maid's distress until this moment and even now she could make no sense of the words that spilled out. Finally a single phrase became intelligible, if most strange, and Alice could scarcely believe she heard aright.

". . .and so she can never go home again!" A fresh outburst of tears followed this statement, and as Alice gazed askance upon a Jenny who, until this moment, had always appeared coolly efficient, her own problems receded and she found herself leading the distraught girl to the sofa, picking up a napkin from the forgotten supper tray as she passed. Patting the red streaming face she now said.

"There there my dear, it's all right, calm yourself and then tell me all about it." As Jenny's story began to unfold Alice let out her breath in a deep sigh, not quite relief but more of an acknowledgement that this not uncommon tale could be, like most of our human problems, surmounted. She also discovered the truth of the fact of bearing another's burdens as her own diminished remarkably. She already knew some of the maid's family history as Henry made it a point of never hiring anyone unless they had been thoroughly investigated by his personnel department but that information had not included the character details Alice was learning here and now. Jenny was the oldest of five sisters and one brother. The modest home was ruled over by "Papa" as Jenny called their father and when Alice asked:

"What about your mother?" Jenny answered.

"Oh she is always sick and when there's any upset she just stays in bed." The significance of this flat statement escaped Alice for the moment to return later. The present upset soon came clear.

The sister next to Jenny was in "trouble"! She got herself that way when she defied her father and went to the "EX" with the delivery boy from Eatons. Alice found herself becoming more and more angry with Papa as the story unfolded.

"He picked her up and threw her out the door, right into the street!" Only too sure that she knew the answer Alice still asked.

"Where is she now?" Jenny hiccuped and wiped her face with the napkin before replying.

"She's upstairs in my room! Oh Mistress I didn't know what else to do. Rose somehow found her way here after wandering the streets half the night. Then she curled up on the doorstep and I found her there this morning when I went out to sweep. She was frozen cold and I put her to bed in my room." Alice shuddered to think of what her condition would be as the temperature last night had been reported as well below zero. Jenny talked on. "I'm sorry Mistress but I wanted to tell you but you were—"

"Who else knows?" Alice's mind worked double time.

"Nobody else yet. Cook might suspect something but I'm sure she doesn't know. She is a bit deaf you know?" Now that the full responsibility was hers no longer the maid was reverting to her usual competent self. "I could not leave my sister out there. Six hours in the freezing cold, wandering about the streets and then waiting here hoping that I would be the one to open the door and ready to hide in the bushes if—"

"How old is Rose, Jenny?" As Alice gazed down on the sleeping face of the young mother-to-be her heart melted.

"Seventeen, we're a year apart and I'm eighteen next month." Jenny's tears had miraculously vanished as she relinquished the fear and dread she had been living with all day. "Oh Mistress, if you could just help me, and tell me what to do now I'll always be grateful." Before following Jenny upstairs to her attic room Alice had stopped long enough to call George on the telephone. Completely forgotten were the circumstances in which she had said goodbye to him such a short time ago she had simply not given

him any details of the need now. He would ascertain the extent of
Rose's injuries and then he would tell them what to do next.

"She'll have to go into the hospital. The fingers of her right
hand might be okay but I doubt it and her feet look bad. Six hours
of exposure to 15 below in only her socks." George shook his head
as he spoke. "It's a lot to expect them to recover from. Her left
hand must have been tucked into her clothing as it seems to have
escaped and the long hair would save her face somewhat. She must
have had the sense to loosen it and spread it like a curtain—"
Alice's hoarse whisper interrupted this lengthy diagnosis and he
gave her a searching glance before answering.

"Oh the baby will be fine as far as I can gather without further
examination. Good hardy stock I'd say!" George turned his attention
now to Jenny who, relieved beyond measure, exclaimed.

"Yes, Mama is sick now but she was not always so. When we
were small she would tell us stories of her people, especially the
ones about when she was a royal princess with the Blackfoot tribe.
Her father, the chief, did not want her to marry Papa, a preacher
who had come to teach the natives about the bible but he also did
some trading of skins and stuff." At the mention of her father
Jenny's eyes clouded over again and quickly to avoid another torrent
Alice put her hand on the maid's shoulder as she said.

"Go and fix some coffee for us while we wait for the ambulance." Jenny left obediently and as she disappeared through the
door Alice turned back to George. "Well George, I wonder what
this is all about?" She whispered but a light in her eyes and the lilt
in her voice betrayed an excitement that her listener knew had
been missing in this woman's life for many a long day.

Jenny opened the back door of the Parker residence. This morning no furtive figure waited to claim her attention. Three quart
bottles of milk instead of the customary one, graced the top step
and Jenny smiled as she thought of the reason for the increase.
Spring had come to this northern city and the lilac bush, behind

the bare branches of which a terrified Rose had crouched, strained now to put forth its heady perfume in friendly contrast to the May blossoms on the other side of the path. Flowering Japanese cherry bushes, not to be outdone, also burst it would seem with joy, at the beautiful morning.

"Oh, you are all so gorgeous!" Sang Jenny, forgetting her dignity a little later as she swept the garden path and with one last loving glance closed the door.

The house began to stir as she placed the milk in the gleaming white refrigerator and she hummed happily as she worked thinking how well everything had turned out after all. Baby Jeremy was six weeks old today and the loveliest little boy. Oh, maybe a boy should not be called lovely but she could not think of a better word to describe him. Rose walked into the kitchen at that moment and the sisters greeted each other.

"I still think it a miracle that you can walk at all after what you've been through Rosie."

"One of a lot of miracles Jenny, and I'm so thankful for them all. Even if I lost a thumb and the tips of some fingers when I think of what might have been after that terrible night." She shuddered and Jenny placed her arms round her sister.

"Don't think of any of that, you've come a long way and you've a lot further to go when you go back to school in the Fall." Jenny placed the finishing touches to Mrs. Parker's breakfast tray just as the upstairs bell rang. "Oh dear, there's the bell, I have dillied about this morning."

The Parker's bedroom was a busy place at this hour. As Henry busied himself preparing to go to the office his wife had asked the nursemaid to bring Baby Jeremy to her. When the girl left Alice propped herself up the better to gaze at the boy while she ate her breakfast. Henry walked over to join her as he finished tying his cravat.

"The adoption papers should be finalized today then it will truly be official that Jeremy is ours. We must both be sure before we sign Alice!" She glanced at him in amazement.

"Of course we're sure Henry, you're not having second thoughts are you?" For answer Henry sat down on the bed and gently placed a hand on the baby's tiny one. At once the little fist grasped his finger and they both laughed.

"Someone else has no doubts it seems." They sat thus absorbed in the child until Henry caught sight of the time on the bedside clock. Still very gently he disengaged his finger, kissed his wife soundly and made for the door.

"Don't forget we're meeting the Lamberts for tea after we've seen the solicitor, Henry."

"Looking forward to it my dear." His words floated back to her as he raced down the stairs. Alice lay back on her pillows. If miracles were being counted in this household today surely she and Henry would have many to add, including the one where her husband had become a new creation overnight. A few minutes later she rang for the nursemaid to take the baby and Jenny arrived at the same moment for her tray. When she was at last alone Alice rose and knelt by her bedside to pray and thank the Lord for His many blessings.

Sensing a disturbing difference from the lovely warm feeling he had fallen asleep with, holding Hannah and exulting in the new life soon to be born, Willie sat up in bed. First he reached for her but her spot was empty. Next he struggled out of the cocoon of blankets and felt for his slippers and robe. Where was that wife of his? He quickly found her in the kitchen, a cup of cocoa in her hand and a blazing fire in the grate. She seemed not to notice him at first but he spoke very quietly and firmly.

"What are you doing Hannah, it's two o'clock in the morning? You're not in pain are you?" She laughed softly.

"No pains Willie, I didn't want to disturb you but I woke up with this feeling, nothing in particular, it's likely foolishness but I could not settle my mind so I decided to spend an hour in prayer. Then I got thirsty so I made some cocoa. Would you like some?"

"I'll get it myself. I don't suppose it will do any good to scold you so I may as well join you. Do you have anything more to pray about other than the usual?"

"No, that's the strange part, everything is so good at the moment. All our family is fine and so are our friends. I finished my studies at the college and my certificate is secure at last. The business is going well under its new name and board of directors. No, nothing comes to mind especially, but I've learned not to question just to pray. Finally too, I have peace in my heart about Lachie, when Mary Jean and James first told me that his ship was indeed lost at sea, I didn't want to believe it, thinking someone could have made a mistake, but now I have peace and I can let it go. The Lord knows what it's all about. Oh dear I hear someone at the side door. Mother Lambert, we didn't mean to disturb you, what is it?" The last as she caught sight of Sophia's expression. Her face held such a look of pain and bewilderment that Willie rushed to her side to assist his mother to a chair.

"What is it Mother, what's wrong, can you no' tell us?" Hannah stood up. I'm not waiting, I'm going to call George right now." Ignoring Sophia's frantic efforts to speak she rushed from the room.

"Why can God not make Gran better?" Debrah Ann was helping her mother with the dishes and Hannah, although anxious to finish the job before leaving for her daily visit to the hospital, stopped putting the plates away to concentrate on the child's question. The question was not entirely unexpected but it still came as a surprise just at that moment. During the meal the family had been discussing Debrah Ann's part in the school wind-up concert play that her class would present at that time. Leaving the dishes Hannah took her daughter's hand and led her to the sofa.

"I don't think it's because He can't Debrah Ann, because we believe that with God all things are possible. Indeed in our family we have experienced many great miracles of His healing and other things. I do not believe either that He won't because God's will for all His children is that they be 'every whit whole' like Jesus said. No! I must admit I am not sure of why, except, maybe God thinks it is time He took Gran home to Heaven." As she spoke Hannah's gaze left her daughter for a moment as she focussed her eyes on the caravan, Sophia and Lizzie's home. Much changed and improved from the vehicle they had purchased that memorable week of their arrival. How often had they tried to persuade Sophia to either move in with them or allow them to find her a house? Also in those early days she and Sophia had worked through some of the very questions the child was asking now. Days when they both needed answers regarding the early deaths of so many of their loved ones. No specific answers had come then, and none seemed to come now, but Hannah prayed for words of God's peace for Debrah Ann. Her reflections had taken her mind away from the little girl for a moment so the reaction took her by surprise.

"I don't want Gran to go to Heaven. It's terrible place and I don't think Jesus can be there and if He is I don't like Him!" She gasped this all out in one breath while she raced out of the kitchen tearing off her apron as she went. Hannah started to follow but decided against it as she heard the girl's door slam just as John Robert entered the kitchen, heading for the cookie jar.

"What's wrong with her? She rushed past me as though the place was on fire and when I asked what's up she snapped something about a boy would never understand. She's right, I don't understand. Gee Mum, your cookies are not bad, but Gran's are a lot better, I sure miss her." Thinking his mother was not listening or paying attention he helped himself to another handful of cookies and started to leave.

"For someone who doesn't like the cookies you certainly eat plenty of them, and did you not just have dinner with the rest of the family?"

"Oh well they're better than nothing you know and I need something to help me with my studies." The last as he returned to his room to do it. Hannah sighed as she sat back on the sofa, her thoughts chaotic. 'Willie will be at the hospital by now and if we

don't join him soon he will know something important has
happened and he won't be far wrong'. She resumed the task of
putting away the dishes. Lizzie, who always claimed that as her
job, was spending a few days with the LeTourneaus. Distracted,
Hannah missed the shelf and the pile of plates crashed to the
floor.

"Oh Lord, Oh Lord, help me. Have I been provoking my
children to wrath as Your Word admonishes not to? And if so I did
not mean to. What should I do now and what can I say to her?"
Her thoughts whirled as she tried to think of the reason for Debrah
Ann's outburst when she heard Willie's key in the lock. Since his
healing Willie Lambert rarely just walked, he strode. So now,
striding into the kitchen he called out as she hurried to greet
him.

"Why are you not at the hospital?" He delved into the cookie
jar as he spoke, with his mouth full he continued. " Hu! only
ginger snaps, I thought you were going to make shortbread today!"
To his utter amazement this innocent remark turned into the last
straw for his normally serene wife.

"I'm sorry that you, and your son, don't care for my cooking,
or that my daughter has suddenly taken a dislike to my company,
to say nothing of her dislike for Jesus, and I'm sorry—" Willie was
at her side in an instant.

"Now hold on there! Just a minute Hannah, what's this all
about? You're not making any sense." he pulled her into his arms
and she sank into his embrace to sob in a way she had not done
since his accident. "There, have a good cry then and I'll hear all
about it when you're ready to tell me." Two extremely subdued
and unusually quiet children now stood in the doorway, not sure
what to do. They had never seen their mother behave like this
before. Debrah Ann clutched an equally subdued spaniel dog to
her. Willie caught sight of the pathetic trio and signaled over his
wife's head for them to come into the room.

"Now will someone please tell me what is going on as I seem
to have missed something."

"At school today—" Debrah Ann screamed at the same moment as her brother and Hannah began their own versions. Willie held up his hand for silence.

"We will use the Divine order for this discussion if you please. Move the chairs and we will sit round the table. Isaiah says 'Come let us reason together', and that is exactly what we will do. Mother will you begin please?" As Hannah related the happenings of the evening she kept glancing at Debrah Ann, but that young lady refused to meet her eyes. When John Robert received permission to speak he told how he had heard his sister's voice in the hall and when he came out to investigate she had rudely yelled at him that he would never understand.

"Debrah Ann!" All attention turned to her and there was no escape, an explanation must be given and at once.

"We talked about heaven today at recess and Elizabeth, my best friend at school, says that in the movies when they talk about being in heaven they don't mean the same as I learned in Sunday school. How many heavens can there be? Will Gran be going to the one in the movies? Elizabeth says it's all about boys kissing girls and dates and sloppy stuff like that, and if she dies and goes there she won't be happy and. . .Oh Mother!" This last word ended in a wail and Debrah Ann became once again the little girl who needed to cry on her mother's shoulder. Hannah was ready as her truly heartbroken child poured out her woe in tears and sobs. The male members watched helplessly but Willie sighed in relief as his wife cradled the curly head. Now that they knew the problem they would search together for the right answer, and seeking they would find it. Hannah signaled with her eyes over Debrah Ann's shining head. Willie nodded and Hannah began to speak.

"Darling, Jesus tells us from His Word, not once but many times, about a heavenly home the Father has planned and made ready for the final dwelling place of the saints. You have learned that this includes us, all of us, Gran too of course. Let me tell you of a few of the ways Jesus describes it. In Matthew twenty He says: '. . .but lay up for yourselves treasures in Heaven, where neither moth nor dust doth corrupt, and where thieves do not break through and steal.' This tells us of a place so wonderful we cannot begin to imagine it. The very air we breathe here, and which contains the elements we need to keep our bodies alive, that same air and those same elements are the ones that cause rust to form. The place Jesus describes does not need this air it seems so there must be something so much better, something we cannot dream or imagine. The movie writers describe something else again, they use imagination but they also go by what they know and what the moviegoers demand. Sadly God's Word is seldom used." A hush descended on the room as Hannah spoke, John Robert and Willie listened intently. A faint sound came from the fire crackling in the grate and King Charles sighed contentedly in the security of it all as Hannah continued. "For instance, the Word says more about it in Matthew and other places: "Eye hath not seen nor ear heard, neither has in entered into the heart of man, what God has prepared for them that love Him.' Already we know that Gran is within both of these descriptions. That's not all my dear, read about it for yourself the many other places. Now I'm going to ask you a question and I want you to think very carefully before you answer and it is this. What do you think Gran would like best of all?"

"To be close to us."

"Yes, and she will always be that. What else?"

"To be able to do her knitting" An almost imperceptible giggle came from John Robert's corner. Hannah's smile was gentle as she said.

"Be sure that, as God has promised, anything we truly still desire He will give us. However it is my belief that everything will be so much better then. We are, at this point in our understanding, unable to comprehend what He has in store for us. Let me put it this way, 'will you still play with your baby toys when you reach High school? Certainly we can pray that God will let Gran stay with us a little longer and I am sure He would, but will that be best for her? What do you think now Debrah Ann?" The child ran to her father and climbed up on his knee.

"We want her here with us, but for her sake we will let her go. It will be like the time Uncle Bruce went to Australia for two months and stayed a whole year." The connection evaded Hannah but her relief kept her silent as her daughter turned to her once again. "Mum, tomorrow at school I'm going to tell Elizabeth what heaven is really like." Over her head the parents once again exchanged glances. Hannah's eyes danced with joy as she said.

"Praise the Lord! And now I think I still have time to visit the hospital." But even as she said the word a spasm of pain gripped her, a pain that she knew too well what it meant. She gasped aloud and Willie rushed to her side.

"Yes Willie, the hospital and for more than one reason. John Robert, you telephone your Aunt Maggie. Debrah Ann, you promise to be good and do as your brother and your aunt tells you. Willie, start the motor car and ooh, I better hurry."

"The Lord giveth and the Lord taketh away, but we do not usually see that happening so close together." James Douglass spoke to his son-in-law as they walked together through the hospital corridors. One had attended Hannah Lambert as she gave birth to a son, William Lachlan Lambert, the other had been with Sophia to close her eyes in her last sleep but not before she had touched the face of her latest grandson. The two doctors were on their way to Hannah's room with the news having left Willie and his sisters with their mother. For once Lizzie was not weeping, in fact she had been the one to comfort Maggie as she reminded her that their mother was with Jesus. Hannah took the news well as she too recalled her own words to Debrah Ann the night before. Sophia was at rest. After assuring themselves that the new mother was well and the baby in perfect form the doctors continued on their way, They had their own families to advise and that included Reverend Bruce MacAlister.

Sophia's instructions had left no room for doubt.

"Nae mournin' or keenin' dirges if ye please! Have as many flowers as ye want, but sing the songs I've come to love sae well! Is that no' whit it's all about, goin' to be wi' the Lord?" The words, in the rich Doric of her native Scotland, only slightly dimmed in the years since Sophia left it, echoed in Hannah's mind causing her to smile through her tears. Could it be only a week ago that the old lady sat beside them in this very pew, singing as hearty as any? Today she lay in state in her casket, as they called it here, the strong voice stilled.

I'm glad she didn't say no crying!" thought Hannah, fresh tears flowing unchecked down her face. "Mother Lambert was not a weeping woman, not like me, why even the first time we met at her husband's funeral, I saw no sign of tears. Through other ordeals we've weathered together as a family, she was always the pillar of strength, Maggie has that same kind of strength." Hannah glanced along the pew to where her sister-in-law sat on the other side of Willie, and Maggie, as if on a signal, turned to meet her glance.

"I wish I could cry like Hannah but I always wanted to be strong like my mother. Now, when I know it would be all right, I still cannot let go!" For the past hour, mentally asking the Reverend Bruce MacAlister, who was conducting the funeral as if it was a celebration, to forgive her inattention Maggie Lambert LeTourneau had allowed her thoughts to wander far away from here and now. To drift in fact to a time long ago when her mother was young and beautiful, a time when their Lizzie was just a wee thing hardly two years old, and their parents just about ready to admit, to each other at least, that baby Lizzie was not as quick as their other bairns.

A time when her brothers, Robert Junior, the terror of Eastkirk school playground, and Willie, quieter than Robert but every bit as determined to jelly the nose of anyone who dared say a word wrong about either of his sisters. A special day was coming to Maggie's mind now. It was one of their day trips to the seaside.

On the day she was thinking of now, the rituals had been taken care of, the delectable feast only a memory and Father, his red hair slicked back into place and his mustaches tidied up, had settled back with a contented sigh for a nap. Mother on the other deck chair, already had set her knitting needles flying and the boys paddled about noisily looking for such awful things as crabs and whelks in the shallows. Wee Lizzie was fast asleep on Father's lap. Maggie still recalled the poem she had memorized for Miss Paton, the teacher upon whose life Maggie had built her own plans. Glancing round quickly to make sure no one watched her now she began to recite under her breath.

"Winter's Gone. By Thomas Carew.

Now that winter's gone, the earth hath lost,

her snow white robes and now, no more the frost. . ." and that had been the moment when she had glimpsed a procession coming toward her. A funeral! Maggie's first close up of such a thing. A hand had touched her shoulder and suddenly her father was at her side with her mother close behind. She even recalled her father's remarks then. "You can put me away in style like that Sophia when my time comes! Eastkirk will turn out in full force to see the sight on that day!"

"Dinna talk sae daft Robert, wi' you still young and strong, tempting' the de'il you are!" Maggie shuddered. Recalling it all today, thirty years, an ocean and a continent later, she chokingly joined in singing her mother's favourite hymn, chosen long ago by Sophia for this very occasion.

Willie Lambert too was remembering other funerals as they sang.

"Mother always did have some kind of victory", he mused, and "Even on the day they buried my father it carried her through that dark time and for many days after." Those days when Willie's own life assumed the form of a nightmare. Overnight he had become the man of the house, with important decisions to make, and he knew he was unequal to the task. When called into a conference with Dr. Craig and Grandfather Cowan, he had been told that his father's body could not be made presentable. The coffin would remain closed. Sophia must not view the destruction the insensate locomotive had wrought in the man who had shared her life for the past twenty-five years. She amazed them all by agreeing.

"I will remember my man from this mornin' as he waved to me from the corner of Glebe Street. As for the funeral, he will have a horse-drawn carriage with all the trimmings. No smelly motor hearses for Robert Lambert." So it had been. The six glossy black horses, plumes held proudly above kingly heads aware of their important function in this human drama, led the procession down Eastkirk's main street. Robert had been right. The town did turn out in full force to see the spectacle. Gleaning black velvet draperies trimmed with the best silk tassles the undertakers from Glasgow could provide, had all contrasted strongly with today's simple ceremony. Willie rejoiced inwardly. This was how she wanted it. Usually his mother got what she wanted and what if her desires sometimes seemed strange to others. Even to the member of her own family.

Like the day of her birthday when she summoned the family for a conference after the tea party was cleared away. "I see no sense in makin' a will and you all waitin' 'til I die before you get what's for you. No! No! Hannah, dinna' try to stop me. I am of sound mind and I want to enjoy giving my children their inheritance while I am still here to see their pleasure."

"That explains why she insisted on Jake Semchuk being invited to the birthday tea this afternoon!" Hannah whispered to Willie. Jake a junior with the legal firm of "Semchuk, Gall, Semchuk and Davidson", had produced a folder from his case. Willie tried to protest but his mother had waved him away.

"No son, I want to do it this way!". The family exchanged glances as Maggie said to her husband Claire.

"When mother uses that tone we may as well give in gracefully!" Claire, thinking how similar mother and daughter were in that regard did wisely keep silent. More surprises came in the next hour as the listeners learned how, in addition to her assets in The Cowan Airplane Company", the family business, Sophia's wise

investment of her inheritance from Grandfather Cowan, had
produced excellent returns.

Apportioning the money to her satisfaction Sophia had sank
back into her rocking chair to enjoy the best part. The disposing of
the "Kist" and its contents. The beautiful chest of solid oak, formed
out of one piece and then so lovingly carved by her husband's own
hands during the long winter evenings those many years ago. would
be opened. A hush descended on the company and young Jake,
expecting at least a trumpet fanfare or a drum-roll, held his breath.
The design was exquisite. Each inch of intricate carving worked by
one who obviously loved the task. Robert Lambert, although speaking seldom his beliefs, had engraved them into this work of art.
Perfect in each detail the story of Exodus came alive around the
sides of the Kist, beginning with the finding of the baby Moses in
the rushes to the Tabernacle in the wilderness. the lid, a masterpiece by itself, showed Miriam leading the children of Israel in a
victory dance before the Lord, and fairly leaping from the wood.
Admiring it one could almost hear clashing cymbal and clamouring
tambourines as the scene unfolds. The hush had deepened as Sophia
moved her hands lovingly across the grooves and ridges, etching
them in her mind. At last she had spoken.

"The Kist is for you Willie. I know you'll take care of it!" She
had proceeded to assign the various other items. Carefully she had
emptied the list, each article perfectly suited to the recipient. The
sweet fragrance of lilac, Sophia's favorite flower, wafted about the room
as the cherished treasures were unwrapped and passed around. All
those present had recognized the honour being bestowed upon them.

The afternoon's guests had taken their gifts and departed leaving behind an exhausted yet triumphant Sophia. Willie was now
recalling the small clash of wills as his wife tried to get Sophia to
rest.

"I'll be fine now Hannah stop fussin'!" But Hannah, knowing
the signs, could be stubborn too. Bending over to retrieve the two
articles still in the box she had said firmly.

"Tea and then bed for you Mother Lambert. Doctor George will be after us if you overdo things again." Sophia ignored her. A plain tweed cap of the kind worn by working men everywhere had been clutched to her boson. Hannah waited suddenly quiet as Sophia had whispered.

"Aye! Here is ma man's cap. He was wearin' it thon day. They found it after in Jock Strang's hay field, you ken the one I mean Hannah?" Hannah, frantically signaling to Willie to intervene, had answered softly, she bent over to pick up the final item. "This picture Mother Lambert, do you remember the day we had it taken?"

"Indeed and I do that Hannah lass, We've a' come a long road since that day. Have we no'?"

"A long road indeed since that day." Hannah thought as she stood up with the rest of the mourners in the vast church listening attentively to her old friend as he pronounced the "Benediction". In a moment the family would be following Sophia Lambert's casket, borne by six strong men and true, the pallbearers for today. Sophia's son Willie of course sharing his place at the head of the procession with Sophia's joy and delight John Robert, as J.R. at 17, stood a head taller than his father Willie. Claire, George, Nik and James took their appointed places while Henry Parker, with a quick glance at his wife and son, left his pew to take his position as an honorary pall bearer. The great pipe organ began to peal forth the glorious triumphant anthem: "Mine eyes have seen the Glory".

At that precise moment Hannah realized afresh that God was real. These wonderful words true! They in this place, were seeing the Glory. They were being allowed to see the Lord, high and lifted up as His train filled the Temple. Just then Lizzie's voice came loud and clear in that domed and majestic cathedral.

"I can see Jesus and my daddy and our Robert and now Mammy is going there too. Ta ta the noo, Mammy!" Hannah's breath caught in her throat for a moment but then as she looked over at Willie she knew that it was all right. Everything was all right and how it should be. Stepping out into the street she gazed upwards into a glorious blue sky, turning to gold even as she watched.